Praise for the Martin Preuss Mystery Series

"There aren't too many mystery writers who can touch us so deeply [or] as beautifully as Levin does in this story."
    —Reader's Favorite, on *Cold Dark Lies*

"An engaging, emotional thriller that skillfully blends past and present. You'll be rooting for another Martin Preuss novel as soon as you finish!"
        —Elizabeth Heiter, award-winning author of The Profiler
        Series, on *The Forgotten Child*

"Great series! With this third Martin Preuss mystery, author Donald Levin has combined his gift for superb storytelling with a complex intertwining of shadowy war crimes ties to contemporary corruptions. . . . This may be both the brightest and darkest tale in this riveting series, where professional duty intersects with one's personal life."
        —Peter Chiaramonte, author of *No Journey's End*,
        on *Guilt in Hiding*

"A police procedural mystery characterized by well-developed characters each committed to his or her own agenda. It is an entertaining, even gripping, read . . . well worth the reading time for anyone who loves mysteries, police procedural investigations or who just loves reading about slimy crooks and the beleaguered detectives that chase them."
        —Clabe Polk, author of the Detective Mike Eiser series,
        on *Guilt in Hiding*

"Levin is a masterful storyteller and his character portrayals are so real it feels as if you can touch them. Highly recommended!"
 —Wendy Thomson, author of *The Third Order*, on *Guilt in Hiding*

"Riveting . . . enough mystery, suspense, drama, treachery, betrayal, and intriguing twists and turns [to keep] the reader guessing."
 —Jersey Girl Book Reviews, on *The Baker's Men*

"It's a gripping, exciting, smart, and ultimately moving crime thriller."
 —Andrew Lark, author of *Better Boxed and Forgotten*,
  on *Crimes of Love*

"Keeps you turning the pages . . . And it doesn't disappoint."
 —Detroit *Metro Times*, on *Crimes of Love*

"Delivers all the elements of a solid police procedural, including a missing child, a determined detective with a fractured heart, slimy suspects, and a surprising ending. I commend Don Levin for bringing realism to an outrageous story of love and violence."
 —Elizabeth Sims, prize-winning author of the Rita Farmer
  Mysteries, on *Crimes of Love*

COLD DARK LIES

Poison Toe Press
2019

ALSO BY DONALD LEVIN

THE MARTIN PREUSS SERIES

An Uncertain Accomplice
The Forgotten Child
Guilt in Hiding
The Baker's Men
Crimes of Love

POETRY

New Year's Tangerine
In Praise of Old Photographs

FICTION

The House of Grins

COLD DARK LIES

DONALD LEVIN

A MARTIN PREUSS MYSTERY

This is a work of fiction. All of the characters, establishments, events, locales, groups, and organizations portrayed in this novel are either products of the author's imagination or are used fictitiously and are not construed as real. Any similarity to real persons, living or dead, is coincidental and not intended by the author.

Inquiries should be addressed to
Poison Toe Press
PO Box 206
1221 Bowers
Birmingham, Michigan 48012

ISBN-13: 978-0-9972941-5-6
ISBN-10: 09972941-5-9

Cover by Publish Pros
www.publishpros.com

First edition published 2019
Printed in the United States of America

This book is dedicated to my readers,
with gratitude for your support

Wild nights - Wild nights!
—*Emily Dickinson*

Thursday, September 13, 2012

1

The hammering brought him back. Loud, insistent pounding on the door. And raised voices outside. And the door handle jiggling. Then more pounding.

He opened his eyes in darkness and rolled his head over the rug where he was sprawled. The smell was unpleasant: damp, sour, musty.

From where he lay, limbs outstretched, his eyes focused on the stumpy and scuffed legs of the bed, the tangle of clothes on the floor, the peeling caramel feet and brown cracked leather of the arm chair, turned on its side. The thick wall of the dresser.

The effort exhausted him. He closed his eyes. He was so tired. Why couldn't he just sink back into that void where he floated before the pounding on the door roused him?

The banging stopped. The voices receded.

Silence outside.

He listened. Silence in the room, too.

Was he alone?

He lifted his head. Intense pain shot through his neck and temple. As through every other part of his body, he now realized.

He didn't hurt before—he didn't feel much of anything—but now he was conscious of sharp aches in his head, ribs, face . . .

He licked his lips and tasted the thick, sweet tang of blood.

He raised his right arm and saw the sleeve of his white shirt rolled up to the elbow. The golden red hair that had furred his forearm ever since he turned fourteen. Around his wrist, the sleek black Fitbit, and, on the third finger of his hand, the ring his ex-wife had given him when he graduated Michigan State—the head of a Spartan warrior carved in intaglio carnelian in a gold setting, like a temple.

And flopping lazily from the crook of his elbow, a syringe still stuck into a vein, pulling at the skin.

Oozing a dribble of blood down to the threadbare, colorless weave of the carpet.

How did that get there?

He couldn't remember how.

Or why.

Or when.

He wanted to make sense of his situation, but thinking was too hard. His mind was too foggy.

He lowered his arm. In the silence of the room, blackness began to close back in on him, slowly, like a cloth fluttering down over his face.

He was relieved when his thoughts, too, began to close down. No more thinking. Not about what he was doing here, or anything else.

He closed his eyes. Gradually his pain eased, and he welcomed the release. There was only silence.

And finally there was nothing.

Tuesday, September 18, 2012

2

"He was a bad one," the woman said, and gave her head a sad shake, as though the memory itself hurt.

Martin Preuss waited for her to go on, but she said nothing more. She seemed lost in thought, gazing at the blank wall behind him. He sat with her in what she called the parlor, the front room in her large home in the Boston-Edison Historic District of Detroit. The place smelled of cat pee and old wood, the sweetish-sour odor that reminded Preuss of his childhood home.

All that was missing was the sound of his father raging upstairs while the rest of the family tiptoed around downstairs so they wouldn't disturb "Daddy's work."

Unlike his family's minimalist home, this one resembled a comfortable museum, with heavy wooden settees and huge armchairs from another age and lush Oriental rugs on the hardwood floors. In the other room, Preuss had noticed a massive Steinway grand piano when the woman, Sarah Posner, invited him in.

She lived here alone with her three cats, so their conversation was interrupted only by her memories. She had lived in this house for decades with her late husband and their three children, who were now grown and scattered across the country.

"You did know him, then," Preuss prompted, to bring her back from her remembrance.

"Oh, yes," she said. Her eyes returned from the past to land back on him with a bright intensity. She was small and hunched in the wingback chair where she sat. Her skin was the color and texture of old parchment, and the knuckles of her hands were swollen and stiff as she gripped the arms of her chair. Wisps of white hair peeked from the turban she wore.

"We all knew about him," she continued. "Izzie was already in prison by the time my Morrie and I were married. But Morrie know him when he was little. Izzie was Morrie's great-uncle, you see. I didn't meet Izzie until he got out of prison. He was an old man by then. Old and defeated. And, you know, Morrie's family used to talk about them. Izzie and his cousin Leon both. Morrie knew Leon, too, but Leon was killed in the thirties, so I never met him."

She thought for a few moments longer, then said, "They were all bad boys."

She drew her mouth together in a pinched frown of disapproval.

"They reflected so badly on us," she said. "It's one thing to say, all right, they were immigrants, they had to make a place for themselves, it was a bad time, they had no other skills. But it's another to look at what they did and how they did it. So cruel. And to know people would look at them and think they represented us all. People in this city already had enough reasons to hate us, between the poison they heard from Henry Ford and Father Coughlin."

She fell into silence as she reflected on her family.

Preuss sketched a fast diagram of the connections in his notebook. When he got back to his office, he would have to draw out a more detailed chart of the family relationships.

"You've never met my client?" he asked.

"No," she said. "Until you called, I'd never heard of her. But now I think I'd quite like to meet her."

"I'm sure she'd like to meet you, too."

"Maybe you could set something up," Sarah said. "She could come for tea."

"You can probably fill in a lot of family history for her. She seems hungry for it."

The woman nodded absently, and he wondered if she was off on another reverie.

He had asked her about her family's connections with members of the Purple Gang, the group of Jewish criminals around Detroit in the 1920s. They began as shakedown artists and petty thieves and wound up controlling the local bootleg liquor trade from Canada during Prohibition, subsequently hiring themselves out as hitmen and enforcers.

Preuss's client was a college student named Beverly Frankel. She hired Greene and Preuss, Investigations, to track down a rumor in her family that they were related to a few of the Purples. His search led him to this 95-year-old woman and the genteel poverty of her mansion.

According to Sarah Posner, the Frankel family's stories about their links to the gang were true.

But the family connections were to two cousins who were among the most savage of the crew, so Preuss didn't know how his client would react to the news. She struck him as someone looking more for colorful, romantic stories of outlaws to tell her friends, but Isadore Adler and Leon Glick's bombings, assassinations, and brutal enforcement methods weren't the stuff of romance.

Like many cases he had worked since joining Emmanuel Greene's detective firm after retiring from the Ferndale Police Department's Detective Bureau, the lesson here was, don't ask questions you might not want answered.

Before he could ask the woman any more about her relations, he felt his phone vibrating in his pocket.

"Sorry," he said.

"Do you have to get that?"

"Let me just check," he said. "It might be about my son."

He glanced at the screen. It wasn't about Toby; the call was from Rhonda Citron, the administrative manager of the detective agency.

"Excuse me," he said, "it's my office. I should take this."

She raised a wan hand in permission and took another sip of her tea. She stared into the air, as though she could see images floating there of the past they had been talking about.

He stood and walked to the parlor's bay window looking out on the broad, manicured lawns of Edison Boulevard. He connected the call. "Rhonda," he said.

"Are you still at your appointment in Detroit?"

"I am."

"For much longer?"

"I think we're almost done. What's up?"

"Manny has a one o'clock meeting with a new client and he just called," Rhonda said. "He's going to be late. He wanted to know if you could take it for him. He said he doesn't want the client sitting around waiting."

He held the phone away from his ear to check the time. Twelve-thirty.

"I can just make it," he said. "You might have to stall the appointment a little."

"Great. I'll let Manny know. Things okay there?"

"I found the link I was looking for. I just need to nail down the next steps. I'll wrap things up and see you soon."

He disconnected and returned to the parlor. "Unfortunately, I'm going to have to get back," he said. "Mrs. Posner, could we talk again?"

"Anytime," she said. "I don't know how much more I can tell you, but . . . next time, why don't you bring Miss—what was her name?"

"Frankel."

"Bring her when you come. I'd like to meet her."

"Excellent," said Preuss. "I'll set it up."

Sarah Posner said she would look forward to it.

3

By the time he returned to the agency offices in the low building at Telegraph and Twelve Mile in Southfield, the one o'clock appointment was waiting for him.

She shot to her feet from the couch where she was sitting. She was a woman in her mid-forties, small and compact. She had a rectangular, fine-boned face with a square jaw, but her most prominent features were her eyes behind black-rimmed frames—hypnotic blue, intense eyes that looked propped open and scarcely seemed to blink. She had thick honey-colored hair that hung in waves around her shoulders. She wore a dark blue tunic with a raised American Indian pattern texturing the material and mid-length sleeves. A leather satchel hung from her shoulder.

Rhonda Citron stood behind her desk. The firm's slender office manager wore a black turtleneck and black leggings. She wore her hair piled in its usual arrangement of impossible curlicues and waves bleached almost white. "Carrie Morrison," she said, "this is Martin Preuss."

The woman held out a hand and gave Preuss one vigorous shake. "Hello," she said.

"My pleasure," Preuss said. "Did you get any coffee?"

"Rhonda offered. I'm good, thanks."

"Great. Let's talk in here."

He led her into his office and closed the door behind her. He indicated the visitor's chair and she sat facing his desk.

Preuss said, "Rhonda told you Manny's tied up?"

"She did."

"He asked me if I'd meet with you to get things going."

"Good." She settled herself in her chair.

"What brings you in today?" Preuss asked.

"It's my brother," she said.

"Okay."

"He was," she began, then stopped. She stared at him with those blow-torch eyes without speaking; it was not an angry look, more the gaze of someone trying to size him up and make a decision.

"You know," she said at last, "don't take this personally, please, but I made my appointment with Mr. Greene. I think I'd rather wait to speak with him."

"Not a problem."

"It's just that my attorney told me Mr. Greene was the right person to take care of this."

"I'm his partner, but if you'd rather work with Manny, we can certainly set up another appointment."

"I was hoping to speak with him today. Rhonda said he was just being held up?"

"We'll have to check with her. She keeps his schedule."

He stood and opened the **door** to the outer office and said, "Rhonda, Ms. Morrison would rather wait for Manny. When will he be back?"

"He just called again. Turns out he's going to be out for the rest of the day. She won't be able to see him till tomorrow."

Preuss turned to the woman in his office. "Does that work for you?"

She considered it. "The thing is," she said, "this is sort of urgent. I'd rather not wait."

Preuss nodded to Rhonda and closed the office door.

"Why don't you let me know what the problem is, and we'll go from there?"

Carrie Morrison took a breath and seemed to resign herself to dealing with Preuss.

"My brother's in St. John's-Providence," she said.

The big hospital complex in Southfield. "Sorry to hear it," he said. "Was he in an accident?"

"No. At least, I don't think so. I just don't know."

Preuss pulled a pad of legal paper in front of him and said, "Let's start from the beginning, Ms. Morrison. You mentioned an attorney?"

She nodded. "His name is Brody."

"Maurice Brody?"

"You know him?"

"We've done work for him."

"He said Mr. Greene would help me."

Before Preuss joined the firm, Manny Greene worked for one local attorney, doing accident investigations. Once Greene Investigations became Greene and Preuss, the firm expanded its caseload, including a number of projects for Mo Brody.

At first, Preuss and Manny agreed they wouldn't take on any of the seamier domestic cases that formed the typical private investigator's workload. He hoped Brody hadn't promised this woman that Manny would take on a divorce or infidelity job.

"What's your brother's name?" Preuss asked.

"Greg. Well, Gregory."

"Last name same as yours?"

"No, his is Braiden." She spelled it for him.

"How'd he wind up in the hospital?"

"That," she said, and he got a glimpse of the nervous fright that possessed her, "is what I'm here about."

"Okay."

He put the pen down and waited for her to continue.

"Do you know anything about the Journey's End Motel?" she asked.

"In Ferndale?"

"Yes."

"Quite a bit, as it happens," Preuss said. "I used to be a Ferndale police detective. I can tell you, the Journey's End is well-known to the Ferndale PD."

"So you know what kind of place it is."

"I do."

"And what you find there. Prostitutes and drug users and every other kind of criminal."

"The City of Ferndale's had its problems with it."

"That's where my brother was found last week. Unconscious and completely strung out on drugs. The police told me he OD'd."

"On?"

"Heroin. They actually found him with a needle in his arm. Heroin! Can you believe that?"

"Opiate addiction is a huge problem."

"I know my brother. He's not an addict. He takes care of himself, he eats well, he works out . . . the Journey's End Motel is not the kind of place he'd want to be seen. Let alone *found*. You'll have to take my word for it."

"When was this?"

"Last Thursday."

"Who found him?"

"The police. The manager of the motel called them when somebody made a complaint about noise coming from this one room. When they checked it, they found Greg on the floor."

"How's he doing?"

"Not well. He's in a coma."

She began to tear up. She searched through her satchel, but Preuss took a box of tissues from the credenza behind him and placed it on the desk in front of her. She nodded gratefully and pulled one to wipe her nose and dab at her eyes.

"Sorry," she said. "They're saying he might not wake up. The police tried that drug on him—"

"Narcan?" The opiate antidote to help an overdosed drug user start breathing again.

"But they said he was too far gone by the time they got there. He was already in cardiac arrest. Now the doctors are saying he might have brain damage from lack of oxygen. If he even survives. I saw him in the hospital, and somebody beat him up, too. He looked so awful."

"I'm very sorry to hear that. How can we help?"

"I want to find out what happened. What was he doing at that place? How did my athletic, clean-living little brother wind up in the hospital with possible brain damage from an overdose of *heroin*? How did this nightmare happen? That's what I'd like you to find out."

"Those are questions we can do our best to answer," Preuss said, careful not to promise too much. "What else did the police say?"

"They said everything points to an accidental overdose, or a suicide attempt. But I don't believe either one for a second."

She paused, picking at the textured pattern on her dress. "My brother would never kill himself. As far as how he got there, the police don't seem interested in that at all."

"You spoke with the detective on the case?"

"Yes. Wait."

She removed a mini-tablet from her purse and opened a file on it. "His name was Bellamy."

Preuss nodded and made a note on his legal pad to cover his annoyance. Hank Bellamy would have been his first guess; nobody else over there would let this go without pursuing it.

"Do you know him?" she asked.

"I do," he said, but didn't say any more. Didn't talk about how in a force of good, competent cops, Hank Bellamy was, if not a bad apple, then at least a sour one. He could be a good cop when he wanted to, but he was lazy too much of the time.

"He said he thought my brother was at that motel, and I quote, 'Just getting his rocks off.'"

Even if it were true, he shouldn't have said that, Preuss thought. But that was Bellamy all over. Never say the right thing when the wrong thing will do instead.

"Is your brother married?" Preuss asked.

"Divorced. His ex's name is Heidi."

"Children?"

"A little girl. Kristin. She's eleven. He has her every weekend. She lives with her mother in Livonia."

"The mother's in the picture?"

"Yes. That's the thing: Greg loves Kristin to pieces. I can't imagine he would—"

She choked off the end of the sentence.

"Do Greg and Heidi get along?"

"Not really. They had an acrimonious divorce. They're still not on good terms."

"All right," he said, "Carrie, here's where we are. I can start moving forward on this now, with what you've told me, or we can get you set up with another appointment with Manny. I can bring him up to speed on what we just talked about, and he can take it from here. However you'd like to proceed."

"No," she said, "I don't want to wait. I want to get started. This is driving me crazy."

"Fine."

"So what's the first step?"

"I'll need to get more information from you—your brother's friends, any other family, his ex's contact information—and then you can talk with Rhonda about the financial details. I'll get in touch with my contact in the Ferndale police and find out where they are with this and we'll get moving."

"Sounds good." Her eyes burned through him, unblinking. "I don't know his friends, but I'll tell you as much as I can. I have a couple of pictures here if that would help."

From her satchel she withdrew two snapshots and handed them across the desk. One was a photo of a handsome, all-American guy sitting in a boat in the middle of a lake with his sunglasses up over the brim of his baseball cap. He looked to be in his late thirties, squinting slightly in the sun, a trim man in a green MSU tee shirt with the stylized Spartan head emblem. He had a calm, kind look, as though he were at peace with the world.

In the other photo, he was in a bar, holding aloft a half-filled tankard. He wore his ginger hair short and neatly parted on the right with a soft wave. He had an angular face and the bland good looks of a dozen interchangeable Hollywood actors. His head was slightly back, as though the camera caught him in the middle of a burst of laughter.

"Can I keep these to make copies from? I'll get them back to you."

"You can have them," she said. "I printed them off my computer. I can send you the files if you need them."

"Shouldn't be necessary, but I'll let you know."

He placed them on the desk and said, "I should warn you, you might have to prepare yourself for the questions we're going to be asking. Some of them you might rather not have answered."

"What are you saying? You won't take the case?"

"No, we'll take it, of course. I'm just saying, often these investigations take you places where you'd rather not go. You might learn things about your brother you didn't want to know. You need to get ready for what we might find."

She said, "I'm already in a place I never wanted to be. I'm not sure it could get much worse."

Oh, Martin Preuss thought, you might be very surprised.

4

Carrie Morrison left after signing the New Client Agreement form and charging the $1,500 retainer to her Visa. Preuss sat with Rhonda Citron for a few minutes and summarized his meeting, so she would know what was happening.

Her desk phone rang while they were talking. She glanced at the caller ID, said, "Manny," and hit the speaker button.

"Hey boss," she said. "Got you on speaker with Martin."

"Martin," Manny said. His voice on his car Bluetooth was hollow and echoing, but Preuss still heard the hoarseness that had troubled Manny for the last few weeks. At eighty-five, Manny was as natty and straight-backed as ever, but he seemed to have a problem with his throat. Preuss would have to remember to ask him about it.

Another one of those questions you might not want answered, he thought.

"Checking in," Manny said. "Anything going on?"

"Martin and I were just putting our heads together about that one o'clock he took for you," Rhonda said.

"Right," Manny said. "Thanks for that, Martin. How'd it work out?"

"She has a case she wants to hire us for."

"Anything interesting?"

"Her brother was picked up at the Journey's End Motel in Ferndale last week. Heroin OD. He's alive, but doing poorly. She wants us to look into it, see what he was doing there."

"Ferndale. Right up your alley."

"She started out wanting you to work it, but she's going to settle for me."

"Want me to give her a call, let her know she's in good hands?"

"I think she's okay with it."

"I'll leave it, then. How'd she find us?"

"Referral from Mo Brody."

"Rhonda, remind me to thank him."

"Will do," Rhonda said.

"I'll be in first thing in the morning."

"Everything all right?" she asked.

"Fine," he said, a bit too quickly, Preuss thought. "Call me if you need me."

They disconnected, and Preuss finished up with Rhonda and flew out the door. It was already quarter to three; he didn't want to be late for his son.

As a condition of joining Manny's agency, Martin Preuss made sure he had the flexibility to see his son Toby anytime he wanted. After he first retired from the Ferndale PD, he visited Toby every morning before the bus took the boy to his day program, and every afternoon when Toby returned. Because Preuss was working again, he couldn't spend his afternoons with Toby, as he used to do. But he tried to be there when Toby got off the bus a little after three, and always made a point of spending time with his son before returning to work.

And he stopped at Toby's group home in Berkley every evening to kiss his son goodnight.

By the time he got to Toby's, the boy was already in his room, relaxing on his bed. He was breathing softly with his eyes half-closed. Toby was small for his age—20 at his last birthday, the week before—and because of all his disabilities he was profoundly impaired and completely dependent on others for his care.

Despite everything—his cerebral palsy, cognitive delays, visual impairments, microcephaly, scoliosis—Toby was as cheerful and loving as anyone Preuss had ever known.

Preuss loomed into Toby's field of vision. "Hey," he said. "How's my boy?"

Toby purred softly in reply. He gave his father a twitchy smile. A rivulet of drool spilled down his cheek. Preuss blotted it with the bib Toby wore embroidered with, "Spit Happens."

Preuss took his son's hand, severely bent at the wrist from the CP contractures. "Did you have a good day at school?"

Toby made a small sound, a little grunt. He was non-verbal, but as familiar with his son's manners of communication as he was—Toby made his needs and moods known through facial expressions, body language, and vocal inflections—Preuss recognized the sound as part-affirmation and part-complaint.

"Too hot in there today?"

No response, except for Toby's gentle breathing. Toby turned his head slightly so he could see his father out of the corner of his eyes, which was where the vision therapist said his limited vision was strongest.

The temperature outside went only into the mid-60s today, seasonable for fall in Michigan, but the air conditioning in the classrooms at Toby's school had been on the fritz since the week before. It had been hotter and more summer-like then, and the heat still lingered in the classrooms. Preuss knew it would be hard on Toby even with fans in every room.

He looked for the notebook where Toby's teacher, Mrs. Rice, made her daily comments about how Toby was doing. It was in the tote bag that Toby's nurses sent in with him every day, containing several changes of clothes and extra diapers.

Mrs. Rice confirmed it was very hot inside the classrooms in Toby's program, but she said they spent most of the day outside and Toby enjoyed all the nature he saw and heard. The heat in his classroom aggravated his seizures, though. They hoped to get the air conditioning fixed by tomorrow.

"I bet you did enjoy the nature," Preuss said. "We've taken our share of nature walks, haven't we?"

Toby made another small grunt. On their outings, Preuss pushed his son's wheelchair around the area's nature trails and ponds, as well as around the neighborhood of the group home and Preuss's own home in Ferndale. Toby loved to be outside, with his father narrating the things they saw and heard and smelled.

Now, as Preuss stood in Toby's room watching his son, Toby's eyes fluttered, then closed all the way. His breathing evened out.

Sound asleep.

Preuss sat with him, watching the gentle rise and fall of Toby's chest. As he matured, Toby looked more and more like his mother, Jeanette . . . he had her thick, dark brown hair, her heart-shaped face, and, when he was awake, the same almond-shaped brown eyes. Preuss's older son, Jason, favored Preuss more than Jeanette. But Jason had Jeanette's ability to nurse a grudge forever, as well as her tinderbox temper—the temper that drove her to throw the boys in the car seven years ago and head up north to Traverse City, where her mother lived.

A collision with a drunk driver ensured she never made it. She died instantly in the crash, and Jason spent a month in the hospital with a closed head injury. The accident left Toby—cushioned by pillows in the back seat—with broken bones but no long-term injuries.

Jason blamed his father for the accident that claimed Jeanette's life because she was escaping a fight with Preuss when she was hit. As soon as he got out of the hospital, Jason left home and was now out of touch somewhere in America.

Preuss thought that's where he was, at any rate . . . the last he had heard through the police grapevine, Jason was serving a 30-day sentence for vagrancy in Portland, Oregon. But that was a few months ago. The boy could be anywhere now.

Where in the world is Jason Preuss, he thought.

An idea for a new kid's show on television.

Only instead of a vampy fugitive in a red fedora, it would star an angry, surly young man with—with what? Preuss hadn't seen his older boy in years, and wouldn't know what he looked like, or if he would even recognize him after all this time living rough on the road.

Preuss watched his remaining son for another few minutes. The thing was, in his heart Preuss knew Jason was right; he blamed himself for Jeanette's death, too. He walked around in a stupor for weeks after the accident, riven with guilt and sadness over what he felt he caused. His friends in the department—Janey Cahill, Reg Trombley, Tony Tullio, and John Singer, who died not long after Jeanette—got Preuss through it, as well as they could. Janey, in particular, was crucial, helping with arrangements for Jeanette's Ferndale memorial (Jeanette's mother insisted she be buried near Traverse City), as well as with the thousand incidental activities of daily life that Preuss was unable to perform in the aftermath of the accident.

He had to take time off from the department; he was simply unable to function. It was Toby—his dear Toby—who brought Preuss back. Toby was still living at home at that time, and it was Preuss's recognition that he still had to care for Toby and his multitude of needs that gave him the strength to manage his grief. People—Janey, mostly—reminded him that he had two sons he needed to be there for, but Jason took off almost immediately once he was released from the hospital so it was only Toby.

Toby wasn't able to manage any of his own physical needs, so by an enormous force of will, Preuss had to set aside his grief and make sure he cared for Toby. Toby needs you, he told himself day after day; he has his physical needs, but he also lost his mother and he's grieving, too; you have to be there for him.

So Toby brought him back from the brink—not of suicide, which Preuss never considered, but of the tortured vortex of guilt and sorrow within which the accident threatened to trap him.

If I'm walking around and even semi-functional today, he now thought, sitting watching his son, it was because of this guy. His best friend, his beautiful beloved child, who slept peacefully, his narrow chest rising and falling beneath the Ferndale PD tee shirt he wore.

When Toby stayed asleep, Preuss leaned over the bed and whispered, "Gotta go. See you later," into the boy's ear. "I love you so much."

He planted a gentle kiss on his son's forehead. Toby stirred but didn't rouse.

Preuss returned to his Explorer, where he called Reg Trombley's cell. The call went straight to voice mail.

"Reg," Preuss said, "it's Martin. I met with a client today who told me her brother OD'd last week at the Journey's End. She said Bellamy's the IO, but he thinks it looks like either accident or suicide. Give me a call when you get the chance, okay? Just want to go over a few things."

He disconnected and drove down to Woodward, where he headed south. Reg had been a junior officer in the Detective Bureau when Preuss was there. Now he was coming into his own as a fine investigator (thanks in large part to Preuss's mentoring, as Preuss knew and Reg would be the first to admit). Now that Preuss was retired, Trombley still came to him to bounce ideas around if a case was giving him particular trouble. And he was a good contact to maintain in the Bureau.

Even if they had to keep their connection quiet.

If his commanding officer found out Trombley was talking to Preuss, there would be hell to pay.

5

The Journey's End Motel was a long, two-story building on the corner of Woodward and Eight Mile Road, the border between Ferndale and Detroit. An outside group of rooms faced Eight, and an inside group faced the parking lot accessible from Woodward.

The plain lobby smelled strongly of bleach. From his days visiting here when he was in the Ferndale PD, Preuss knew what kinds of bodily fluids the bleach was meant to hide.

The registration desk sat behind a sheet of thick acrylic. The woman at the counter had dark, almost blue-black hair tied back with a red ribbon, and deep, haunted eyes. She placed a finger on a line of tiny print in the Bible she was reading and looked up at Preuss standing across the desk from her. She must have figured out at once he wasn't going to be a paying customer because suspicion fell across her face like a shade pulled down.

"Yes?" she said into the voice grill in the acrylic window.

"Is Adnan around?" he asked.

Without responding, she turned away and made a call on the cell phone at her elbow. She spoke rapidly into the phone, listened for a moment, and disconnected.

"You wait," she told Preuss. She raised a palm and made a downward gesture, rooting him to the spot.

In a few minutes, the outside door opened and Adnan Zakar entered the registration area. The manager of the Journey's End Motel was a big man with thinning hair and scars pitting the cheeks of his round face. He was rumored to be connected to the Chaldean mafia, centered in the large Chaldean community on Seven Mile and John R, a mile south of the motel. Chaldeans were a prominent ethnic group in the metropolitan Detroit area, Catholics from Iraq who had fled religious persecution by the tens of thousands since the beginning of the twentieth century and settled in and around Detroit, the vast majority peaceful and law-abiding and grateful for their new country. Zakar had never been charged with anything. But it was hard to imagine the drug activity and prostitution the motel harbored could thrive without the gang's permission.

The last time Preuss had seen him was several years before on one of his FPD cases, when a resident of the motel had been involved in a shooting at a Ferndale bakery. Now, as then, Zakar was sweating profusely and gave off an unpleasant body odor.

Zakar looked Preuss up and down.

Preuss said, "You remember me?"

Zakar gave a noncommittal shrug of his beefy shoulders.

"Martin Preuss." He handed Zakar a business card, which Zakar barely glanced at.

"The police found a guy unconscious in one of your rooms last Thursday. You remember *him?*"

Another shrug.

"I want to ask what you know about him."

"What for?"

"There's a question about what he was doing here," Preuss said. "I'm trying to find out for his family."

Zakar shook his head. "I got nothing to say. Get lost."

Without waiting for a reply, Zakar turned away and the woman buzzed him into the registration office, where he disappeared through a door into the back.

The woman behind the desk threw Preuss a last suspicious look, then returned her attention to her Bible.

Preuss went back to his Explorer, where he sat, fuming, until his phone rang.

The return call from Reg Trombley.

Who told him they needed to meet.

6

"Not the best news you heard all day, I suppose," Trombley said.

"No, but no surprise," Preuss said. "As soon as she told me one of the detectives was putting her off, I knew who it was."

"The one and only."

The two men sat in the Starbucks on Main in Royal Oak. Martin Preuss was persona non grata with both the chief of police and the chief of detectives in the Ferndale Police Department, and he knew it wouldn't be a good idea for anyone from the FPD to see him and Reg Trombley together in public (even though everyone knew Preuss and Trombley were long-time friends).

"I can tell you what I know about the investigation," Trombley said, "from our update meetings. There's another one tomorrow morning. But I'm not going to be able to get my hands on the case file."

Preuss understood. The case files were supposed to be available to anyone who had the password to the Bureau's intranet site, but Bellamy was famous for not using the server. He still wrote out his notes in longhand and gave them to the Bureau's administrative assistant to enter them after the case was closed. That meant he kept control over all the information he was collecting about Greg Braiden.

"Bellamy said he thinks it's an accidental overdose. I'll find out what else I can," Trombley promised. "And I'll get as much as I can from Hank."

"Don't mention my name," Preuss cautioned.

"Don't even have to remind me."

At one point, toward the end of Preuss's career with the FPD, Hank Bellamy decided he would undermine Preuss however he could—so Trombley knew to keep Preuss's name out of it.

Trombley knew, too, never to utter Preuss's name anywhere in the corridors of the Eugene Shanahan Law Enforcement Complex. Everyone—from the patrol officers to the former police chief—knew Preuss had been an outstanding detective, the best in the Bureau. But the current chief, Nick Russo, was the father of Preuss's late wife Jeanette, and he—like Preuss's own son Jason—blamed Preuss for Jeanette's death. And like Jason, Russo was a grudge-holder.

Russo's hand-picked chief of detectives, Stanley Chrysler, continued Russo's campaign against Preuss without even knowing much about him.

"So we could have talked about this on the phone," Preuss said. "What did you want to meet for?"

Trombley's face, the color of caramel and model-handsome with high, sleek cheekbones, turned grim. He leaned forward against the commotion of the coffee shop. "Got more bad news, my brother. Wanted to tell you in person. It's about Tony."

A chill went down Preuss's spine.

"I talked to Adele this morning," Trombley continued. Tony Tullio's daughter, in Livonia. "Last night he had another heart attack. A big one."

"Nuts."

"Yeah."

"How's he doing?"

"Adele said he's in bad shape, but he's hanging in. They got him on life support. Too soon to tell what the future holds."

"He's a fighter," Preuss said, knowing that might not be enough.

"I had to bet, I'd put my money on him pulling through. Adele didn't have anybody else's number," Trombley said, "so she called me. I told her I'd spread the word."

"She's going to keep you posted?"

"She said she would. I hear from her, I'll let you know."

"Thanks."

"You have her number?"

Trombley told him and Preuss entered Tony's daughter's cell number into his phone's contact list.

"Poor Tony," Preuss said.

"Adele asked us to keep him in our prayers."

Yeah right, Preuss thought. That'll definitely work.

Trombley left and Preuss sat finishing his coffee, remembering Manny's coffee-snob opinion of Starbucks: bitter and overpriced. He thought about Tony. Tony Tullio had been the senior detective in the Bureau until a health crisis forced him to retire a few years ago. He and his wife moved to Florida. Preuss saw him the year before, when Tony and his wife came back to Michigan for the funeral of the wife of another of their colleagues. They had promised to keep in touch, but as life goes, they hadn't.

Tony had been to Preuss what Preuss was to Reg Trombley: Mentor, teacher, guru, and friend. As well as a shield against Russo's wrath.

He sat for a while longer, typing out notes on his laptop about his day's meetings. When he was finished, he stood, ready to go, and his cell phone rang.

He looked at the caller ID on the screen and punched the connect button.

"Hey," he said.

"Hey," Janey Cahill said. "Where are you?"

"Royal Oak. About to head home. What's up?"

"Got plans for tonight?"

7

She opened the door as soon as he rang the bell. She stepped aside and he entered. The house was unusually quiet.

"Where's the gang?" he asked.

"All out," she said. "Come in. Got news. Want a coffee?"

"Thanks, no. I've been drinking coffee all day."

"I can do tea?"

"Do you have honey?"

"Since when do you take honey?"

"I'm evolving," he said.

She screwed up her mouth, said, "Charles Darwin, over here. I think I have a jar somewhere."

She led him through the house into her kitchen, where she searched through the cupboards and came up with a plastic bear-shaped container. The contents were crystalized and dark brown.

"This is all I have. I'll stick it in the microwave, be good as new. Go in the sunroom. I'll be right there."

He stepped down into the sunroom, formerly a three-season screened-in porch that her husband Tommy had remodeled during one of his extended layoffs as a union carpenter over the past few years.

Shortly, Janey brought in a tray with two mugs, a teapot, and pitchers for sugar and milk. And his honey bear with the honey now golden and liquified.

"We'll let the tea steep," she said, and sat in a chair beside his. "Doing okay?"

"Sure," he said. "So tell me this news."

"It's about Tony Tullio. It's not good."

"I know, Reg just told me."

"You talked to Reg?"

"We had coffee right before you called. Unless there's something new?"

"Not since this morning," she said. "He told me at the station when he found out. I was slammed all day and didn't have time to call you."

"Don't worry about it," he said, though this was another reminder of how distant he now was from Janey and Reg; neither one thought to make time to call him when they heard the news about their mutual friend and former co-worker.

"Poor Tony," she said.

"Yeah. Been thinking about him ever since Reg told me."

"Evidently he's on life support. Doesn't mean he can't come back from it, but still."

"When was the last time you talked to him?" he asked.

"Not since Debby Blair's funeral"

"Same here. I told him I'd keep in touch, and then didn't."

They sipped their tea in the silence of regret.

Then she said, "The other thing I wanted to tell you is, Tommy's moving out."

"Really," was all he could make himself say.

"Yup."

"When?"

"This coming Saturday."

"I thought he couldn't afford it?"

"He's moving in with a buddy. Turns out this guy has a spare room, and he's only going to charge Tommy rent as long as he's working. This is still his busy season, so he's got money coming in. If and when he gets laid off again, the rent'll stop and Tommy'll live there rent-free. He just has to buy his own food and kick in a bit for utilities. He'll still be able to give us money from his union unemployment bennies."

"What brought this on?"

"Oh," she said, "we sort of had it out last week. I told him this wasn't working for me."

"How's he feel about it?"

"He's not happy. But I told him, I said, Tommy, it's the right thing to do. It's been the right thing ever since we decided to separate."

"With him living in the basement, it hasn't been much of a separation."

"That's what I told him. I said I thought if we were going to move on with our lives, we needed to do it already. I'll be mother," Janey said. She poured the steaming tea into their mugs. Preuss squeezed honey into his and stirred.

"Anyway, he said okay," Janey went on. "That's where the boys are. They're painting his room."

"Where is it?"

"Clawson. Just off Main Street, north of Fourteen."

Clawson was a few suburbs up from Ferndale, on the other side of Royal Oak. Close enough for the kids to visit, far enough from the basement.

"Well," he said, raising the tea mug in a toast, "here's to your new life."

She raised her mug in return, sipped from it, and replaced it on the table.

They sat in silence for a few moments. He was certain she was doing the same thing he was: considering what this meant for the two of them.

She broke the silence. "How've you been? We haven't talked much."

How had he been? That was an interesting question. He wasn't sure he knew.

"Same as always," he decided. Whatever that meant.

"Toby?"

"Toby's good."

"That's good."

"Yeah."

"Work okay?"

"Yeah," he said, "Manny's great, he really is."

"Doing a lot of peeking through keyholes at cheating husbands, are you?"

"He doesn't take on those jobs. And I won't."

"Uh-huh."

"It's true."

"We'll see. What kind of cases do you have? Anything good?"

He told her about Greg Braiden.

"Oh, right," she said. "That's Bellamy's, I think."

"That's what Reg said. I asked him to find out what he can without mentioning my name."

"Smart move."

A silence fell again. We used to have a lot more to talk about, Preuss thought. And it was a lot less awkward before we started tiptoeing around seeing each other as more than friends.

"Have you heard from that girl again?" she asked.

"What girl?"

"That reporter."

"I wouldn't call her a girl. She's in her thirties."

"Yeah, early thirties. Young enough to be your daughter."

He took a long drink of tea to give himself time to think about how to play this.

Earlier in the summer, Shelley Larkin, a reporter on staff with the local alternative newspaper, the *Metro Voice*, had been in contact with him about a case she thought he'd be interested in. A few years ago, they met when a little girl went missing in Ferndale, and she was trying to weave the disappearance into a larger story about how society treated its children. They had connected in a way that Preuss thought might lead to something between them, but it never happened. And likely never would.

"Are you going to start seeing her again?" Janie asked.

"You know, there never was anything between us. It turned out she was seeing another woman."

"Maybe she's changed her mind."

"And her entire sexual orientation?"

"You don't know. She might be bi. So? Are you going to see her again?"

"She was part of the Douglas case last summer. I hadn't heard from her for months before that, I haven't seen her since, and I have no plans to see her again. All right?"

Janey whirled the tea in her mug and examined the patterns in the liquid.

"And you're interested in this because—?" he asked.

When she didn't answer, he said, "Is this really why you wanted to talk to me? You want to know if I'm seeing her?"

"No. Yes. Maybe."

"That pretty much covers the options."

"I also wanted to tell you about Tommy. And Tony."

"No, you're jealous."

"Don't be silly."

"No, admit it. You're jealous of Shelley Larkin."

"Martin, I just wanted to know where you stand with her. I think she's a manipulator. I know she hurt you before, and I don't want to see you go through that again. That's all. Simple."

Before he could respond, the front door burst open and her two boys spilled into the house with Tommy behind them. Janey rose and met them in the front hall. She gathered the boys with all their puppyish energy into her arms.

"So?" she said. "How's it look?"

"It's great, mom," TJ, the eldest boy, said. "There's a pool in the backyard!" It's so cool!"

"I know where you're going to be spending next summer," she said. "Will I ever see you guys again?"

Both boys started talking at once and she raised her hands over their heads to quiet them. "All right! It's late. I think you two should go upstairs and get ready for bed."

They made feeble and futile complaints, then turned their attention toward racing each other up the stairs. Janey gave Preuss an apologetic look and followed her sons.

"Hey Martin," Tommy said. "How's it going?" He held up a hand to Preuss, who was standing in the doorway of the all-season porch. Preuss held up his own.

"Going good. I hear you're in a new crib."

"Yeah. Guess it was time. According to the boss, anyway." He pointed his head upstairs.

"The boys seem to like it," Preuss said.

"Dunno how much time they'll spend there. We'll see."

"Best of luck."

"Thanks, pal. Hey, I'm going to say goodnight. Been a long day."

Tommy went into the kitchen and disappeared through the door to the basement, where his living quarters had been for the past year.

Preuss walked into the living room and stood by the staircase leading to the second floor. He felt awkward and unnecessary as this household chugged along without him.

Soon Janey came down, running her fingers through her electrified curly blonde hair.

She paused at the foot of the stairs. "You're not leaving?"

"Yeah. I'm fading fast. And you have your troops back."

"You didn't finish your tea."

"No. Or our conversation. We'll finish another time."

She followed him to the front door. He paused, half in and half out of the doorway. They shared a long look and not for the first time he had the urge to lean forward and kiss her . . . just for a second, but full on the lips, which they had never done before. They had kissed each other's cheek, but this would be the first full-on lip kiss.

No, he thought. Not the right time. Not yet.

Instead they hugged. He drew back and she patted him on the shoulder, and he turned and trotted down the front steps into the cool of the evening.

Toby was in bed, ready for sleep, rosy and fragrant from his bath. Preuss kissed the boy on the side of his warm face and sat in the chair beside his son's bed and chatted with him about the events of the day, as he loved to do. Toby couldn't articulate words, but he turned his head toward his father with a blissful post-bath smile and attended to everything Preuss said about Carrie Morrison.

Judy Collins, Toby's usual music to fall asleep by, sang softly in the background on Toby's CD player. She wondered who knew where the time went.

Don't ask me, Preuss thought.

Toby nodded off, and Preuss sat watching his son for another half hour, then rose and kissed the boy gently on the forehead and said goodnight to the group home staff.

At home, inspired by Judy Collins's version of "Who Knows Where the Time Goes," he sorted through his CD collection and found the disk with the track by the song's author, Sandy Denny, recorded with her band at the time, the Strawbs. Denny's version seemed more meditative, with a rawer emotional power in the faint Scottish inflection in her voice.

He took a glass of milk out onto his back deck and leaned against the railing overlooking his small back yard. He could smell the unmistakable scent of autumn rising from the soil in the darkness. The oak trees had just started losing their leaves; in another month, he would be hip-deep in them.

Preuss was not, in general, an optimistic man, so he was cautious about speculating what Janey Cahill's new situation might mean for them. The year before, they decided to back off from each other. She was still married to Tommy, and the separation they maintained was mainly theoretical, since Tommy lived in their basement because they couldn't afford to get a divorce. She had said it felt too strange to let her long friendship with Preuss grow into something more—something that they both admitted wanting—under those circumstances.

In the year since they put things on pause, he had often wondered what he might want from a closer relationship with her. They spoke every week or so and saw each other occasionally for coffee or lunch. The last time he saw her was the evening last month when Reg Trombley had them both over to his house for dinner with Sandy, his wife, and their two girls. Preuss and Janey knew the meal was Reg's thinly-disguised attempt to bring them together, and both knew they didn't need the excuse of a dinner at the Trombleys for that, but they went along with the ruse. It gave them a sort of secret to share between them.

But what now? The obstacle to their getting together—Tommy's continued presence in the home—seemed to be disappearing. So what would happen?

More to the point, what did he *want* to happen?

Maybe, he thought, they had had their chance, and their time had passed. Just like with Shelley Larkin. Was that possible, or was that just Preuss finding another excuse for not letting someone get close to him?

Especially someone whose standard operating procedure had been to reel him in and then push him away. Like tonight, he thought . . . Why couldn't she just admit that yes, she was a bit jealous at the thought of Shelley Larkin ("that young girl") coming back into his life. Hadn't Janey encouraged him to pursue her, back when he and Shelley seemed on the verge?

But now she wouldn't even admit she was jealous, because that might lead him to believe she had feelings for him. And we couldn't have that, oh no, never that. So she came up with a line about not wanting to see Shelley hurt him again (which had not even happened; he had been disappointed by her, but not hurt).

He took another drink from his glass of milk, then poured the rest of it into the hostas beside the deck. Even milk was too gritty in his throat tonight.

Time for bed.

He started up the stairs, but the beams from a pair of head-lights stopped him. They raked through the living room as a vehicle pulled in his driveway.

He heard a car door slam and footsteps trotting up to the front porch.

Then the pounding on his front door.

.

8

The man on the porch peered straight into the viewing window in the door. In the porch light, Preuss saw he had an angular, dark-complected face, full lips, and carefully razored short black beard. His head was shaved to stubble except for a little pad of short curly black hair on his crown.

His eyes bored into Preuss's looking back at him through the viewing glass.

"Mr. Pree-us?" the man said.

"Preuss," he corrected. "Rhymes with juice."

The man's eyes glowed with ironic merriment, as though it didn't matter to him what the pronunciation was, and he was amused it mattered to Preuss.

"Somebody wants to see you. Come with me. I'll take you to him."

Preuss stared at him, then swung the front door open so he was facing the man through the screen door.

The guy was dressed in gangster chic: black shirt, open collar, grey sharkskin suit that was tight on his fit body.

"Who would that be?" Preuss asked.

"Mr. Aklawi," the guy said. "Jake Aklawi. Big Jake. You never heard of him?"

"I know him," Preuss said. Jawslip—Big Jake—Aklawi was reputed to be the head of the area's Chaldean mafia. Preuss had never met him personally, but when he had been on the Ferndale PD he would hear local Chaldean party store owners say the name with a combination of reverence and dread. "What's he want with me? At this time of night?"

The man on the porch shrugged. "I do what I'm told, guy. He tells me he wants you, I come get you." He reached out to jiggle the screen door handle, which was locked. "How about opening up? C'mon. Let's go. Don't want to keep him waiting."

He jiggled the handle again to hurry Preuss along. "You coming or what?"

"Thanks, I'll pass," Preuss said, and began to close the door.

The man on the porch produced a utility knife from his pants pocket. He flipped the blade up and stabbed the top of the screen and with one long stroke sliced the mesh all the way down. He stepped through the opening and kicked the front door open.

Preuss backed up, ready for a fight.

"I hate to damage property, guy," the man said, holding up the knife. "But Mr. Aklawi, he don't like to be kept waiting."

Preuss sat in the front seat of the Camaro as the man sped through the empty streets. They didn't speak at all until they pulled into the lot of a party store at East Twelve Mile and Hoover in Warren. The Hoover Party Store was a nondescript local convenience store, a small, stand-alone brick building with bars behind windows that advertised fresh subs and cans of Bud and Bud Light (3 for $5) and Newports. One window was taken up with the season's schedule for the Detroit Red Wings, courtesy of Bud Light.

The driver turned the car off. "Out," he said, his first word since he persuaded Preuss into his car with his knife.

Preuss stepped out of the vehicle and the driver nudged him toward the building. They entered and the clerk behind the counter looked up from behind thick acrylic security windows. He nodded to the driver behind Preuss, gave Preuss a quizzical look, and waited till Preuss and the driver went up to a door that led into the back of the store. Then the clerk pressed a button, and the door buzzed and the driver urged Preuss though it.

The clerk finished ringing out a customer who was buying a gallon of milk, a pack of diapers, and a case of Labatt's Blue.

Once they were through the door, the driver laid a hand on Preuss's shoulder and steered him through a small storeroom and another door, this one leading down a flight of steps into a larger storeroom. The driver pushed Preuss around metal shelving loaded with boxes of Better Made chips and candy, as well as cases of vodka, whiskey, rum, and cheap versions of gin.

They rounded another corner and came to a desk surrounded by cases of Coke. Sitting at the desk was the man Preuss recognized as Jawslip Aklawi. In his mid-60s, he was a heavy man with a bald pate fringed with white and a bushy salt-and-pepper mustache. He wore suit trousers and a white shirt open at the collar showing curling white chest hairs. He sat with a cell phone at one ear and a landline receiver at the other.

He looked Preuss up and down in complete disinterest and indicated a chair by pointing his head toward it.

The driver standing behind him gave Preuss a shove toward the chair.

Preuss sat.

Aklawi hung up the landline and mumbled into the cell, disconnected, and set it on the desk in front of him.

He gave Preuss a distasteful look for a few seconds. Then he said, "You're the private detective?"

"I'm *a* private detective," Preuss said

"A comedian, too."

"He's the one you wanted, Mr. Aklawi," the driver said. He stood between Preuss and the exit.

Aklawi regarded Preuss for another moment. "Give you any trouble?" he asked the driver.

The man shrugged.

To Preuss, Aklawi said, "Victor treat you okay?"

Preuss looked at Victor, who glared defiantly back at him, as though daring him to say something.

When Preuss didn't respond immediately, Aklawi said, "What?" He looked from one man to the other. "He lay hands on you?" Aklawi demanded of Preuss.

"He was a perfect gentleman," Preuss said. "But he killed my screen door."

"What happened?"

"He sliced it with a boxcutter. It's ruined," Preuss said.

Aklawi looked at Victor. "You do this?"

"I asked him to come nicely," Victor said. "Like you said. He wasn't moving, so I gave him a little encouragement."

"By cutting his screen door? I tell you to do that?"

"I thought he needed persuading," Victor said.

"So you damage his *home?*"

Victor put his hands in his pockets and glared at Preuss, then lowered his head and looked at his own shoes.

Aklawi shook his head in disappointment at Victor.

Good help is so hard to find, Preuss thought.

"I apologize for Victor," Aklawi told Preuss. "I gave him instructions not to hurt you, but I didn't think I'd need to ask him to respect your property."

"Don't worry about it."

"No, I'll make sure he takes care of it."

Aklawi unfolded his heavy body from the chair. He was a taller man than Preuss thought, standing another three or four inches over Preuss's height. With his thick body, he was a substantial presence. He was thought to be in charge of a large portion of the metropolitan area's illegal gambling and extortion rackets, as well as a piece of the heroin trade. He had fled Iraq in the 1960s, and his accent was still as heavy as his belly.

He walked up to Victor. For a moment, Preuss thought Aklawi was going to deck him, but instead he gave Victor a rough pat on the cheek and said, "You got a lot to learn."

"Sorry, Mr. Aklawi. He—"

"Shut up. Go get me a Diet Coke."

Victor turned at once and went back through the maze of storage shelves. "Cold, but no ice!" Aklawi called after him.

He turned back to Preuss. "I'll make sure he fixes the door."

"It's fine. I'll take care of it."

"No. He's gotta learn."

Aklawi reached out to shake Preuss's hand. Aklawi's hand was large and rough as steel wool, the hand of a working man. "My word on it."

Aklawi returned to his seat and indicated a folding chair for Preuss to sit. Aklawi pulled his chair close, so their knees were almost touching.

"You went by the Journey's End today," Aklawi said.

"I did."

"Zakar called me. Said you asked about the trouble there last week."

"He told me to get lost."

Aklawi gave an apologetic shrug. "He thinks he's taking care of the business. It's what I pay him to do."

"Do you know anything about it?"

"No. But you want to go back and talk to him?'

"I do. I'd also like to see the room where it happened."

Aklawi said, "How about we make a deal? I'll tell him to help you, and you do a favor for me."

"What kind of favor?"

"There's a guy who sometimes stays in that room."

"The room I want to get into?"

"Yeah. Young guy. He's trouble. Runs girls, sells drugs."

"At the motel?"

"Yeah."

I'm shocked, Preuss thought.

"I don't want him there no more," Aklawi said.

"Why not have Zakar tell him to leave?" Preuss asked. "Or let Victor persuade him."

"Zakar told him. Makes no difference. I got Victor looking for him. Victor's good for certain things. Not this. This kid, he's disappeared. I just want to talk to him, let him know he's not welcome, convince him to go somewhere else. He's a troublemaker."

Preuss wondered what kind of trouble he could make that would be worse than what happens at the Journey's End on a typical Saturday night. Or a typical Monday night, for that matter.

"Is he mixed up in what happened last week?" Preuss asked.

"Could be."

"What do you want from me?"

"Just find him and let me know where he is. I just want to talk to him, convince him he wants to stay gone. You agree, I'll call up Zakar right now, tell him to give you all the help you need with this other thing. Deal?"

"What's this guy's name?"

"I don't know names. You find what you want to find out at the motel, you'll run into this guy. Guaranteed."

"And what are you going to do with him if I find him?"

"I just want to talk to him. Word of honor."

"So you get Zakar to talk to me, I do what I can about finding your guy. That's the deal?"

"That's it. Easy."

Before Preuss could say yes or no, Aklawi slapped a hand on the arm of his chair. "Done." The conversation was over.

"When Victor comes back with my Diet Coke, I'll have him drive you home. Then I'll call Zakar. He'll do what I say."

Aklawi held up a finger, bounced it in the air a few times. "I'm a man of my word. Find that kid, and let me know where he is, I'll consider it a personal favor."

He extended his rough hand to Preuss. "I can be good to my friends. And terrible to my enemies. My advice to you? Decide which you want to be."

Wednesday, September 19, 2012

9

In the morning, Toby's brown eyes were still heavy with sleep. He turned his head to gaze at his father. He heaved a great sigh and said, "Num, num, num," as he smacked his lips.

Martin Preuss folded the boy in a hug. Toby's breath was yeasty; he never ate anything by mouth, so there was never any sour odor. Preuss kissed the boy's cheek and smelled ammonia on his skin, the clue he needed his pants changed.

"Did he wake up at all last night?"

"No," Melissa, Toby's aide, said. She scurried around the room laying out Toby's clothes, a Bob Marley "No Woman, No Cry" tee shirt and a pair of denim shorts. "He stayed asleep all night long."

"Must have had nice dreams, then," Preuss said. Toby hummed softly. "Did you have good dreams? That why you don't want to wake up?"

Toby smiled his dreamy, crooked smile.

Melissa went into the adjoining bathroom and filled up a plastic tub with soapy water. Preuss helped Toby out of his nightshirt, carefully bending the boy's stiff arms, and opened the sticky flaps on Toby's diaper to let him air out until Melissa returned with the wash basin filled with soapy water and a washcloth and towel folded over her arm.

Preuss stepped aside and let her clean up his son and get him ready for the bus that would take him to his day program.

"Gonna be another gorgeous day," she said. "Supposed to be sunny and warm."

"I hope they fixed the AC in your school, Toby. Otherwise I don't know how you're going to stand it."

"His teacher said they should be done by today."

"I hope so," Preuss said. "Otherwise I'd rather keep him home."

He laid a hand on his son's arm and Toby looked at him out of the corner of his eye. "Honey," he said, "I'm going to say bye for now. Have a wonderful day at school, okay? I'll see you this afternoon when you get home. And stay cool!"

He leaned across Melissa and planted a juicy kiss on the side of his son's face, damp and sweet from the soapy washcloth.

"I love you," Preuss said.

Toby hummed a sleepy reply.

"This way," Adnan Zakar told Preuss.

Jake Aklawi was as good as his word. When Preuss showed up at the Journey's End, Zakar didn't mention the day before, simply led Preuss outside the office and up a metal stairway to the second floor, then down the outside walkway to 203.

Huffing from the exertion, Zakar removed a keyring from his pocket and rapidly thumbed through the keys. When he found the one he was looking for, he unlocked the door and held it open for Preuss to step inside. No police tape blocked the door; Bellamy obviously didn't consider this a crime scene.

"This was where he was found?" Preuss asked.

From the doorway, Zakar said, "Yes."

Now he's going to tell me he's not responsible, Preuss thought. That was always his default whenever Preuss talked to him in years past.

As though Zakar had read his mind, he said, "I am not responsible for what happens in these rooms."

"Right," Preuss said. He loved it when people acted like themselves.

The room smelled damp and held cheap veneered furniture spotted with cigarette burns despite the no-smoking policy. Rumpled sheets drooped lazily off the bed. The bedside lamp was smashed on the floor and the single armchair had been overturned. The mirror over the dresser had a crazy star crack in the center of the glass, as though from someone's head.

Women's clothing hung in the closet, and women's underclothes filled the drawers. The bathroom was filthy and stank of urine. Bottles and tubes of women's cosmetics covered the narrow counter.

"Has anybody been in here since last Thursday?"

"No," Zakar said. "The cops told me don't let anyone touch it until they said okay."

"I don't see any sign of drug works. Did you clean that up?"

"The cops took it."

"Who found him?"

"Cops."

"How?"

"There was a complaint about noise coming from the room. The cops got called, and when I let them in, he was there, on the floor."

Zakar pointed to a spot beside the bed.

"What kind of noise?"

"People fighting."

"'People'? Men? Women?"

Zakar shrugged. "A fight."

"Physical or verbal?"

"They just said fight."

"Who called?"

"A guy staying next door."

"Left side, right side?"

"Left."

Zakar put a big fist on the crook of his arm. "The guy on the floor, he still had the needle sticking out. Like this."

Preuss remembered Carrie Morrison had said her brother was badly beaten. Could this have been a drug deal gone wrong?

"Anybody else in the room with him?" he asked.

"No."

"What time was this?"

"Nine-thirty. Little after, maybe," Zakar said.

"So," Preuss said, "somebody called the cops. Then what happened?"

"They came. Two, three. They did CPR until the ambulance came, and I couldn't see after that. I was on the walkway."

"Whose room is this?"

Zakar pulled out his cell phone. He punched in a number and after a rapid-fire exchange in his language, he told Preuss, "Wait, I tell you. She's checking."

Zakar listened and disconnected. He pocketed his phone.

"The room is registered to the guy."

"The guy who was found? Greg Braiden?"

"Yeah. He pays by cash."

"What do you mean, 'he pays'?"

"He's been paying for the room for six months."

"Six months? Starting when?"

"April."

"Was he staying here?"

"No idea."

"I see women's clothes here, and cosmetics," Preuss said. "But no men's clothes. Is there a man who stays here or not?"

Zakar shook his head.

"No, or you don't know?"

"I don't know."

"You don't know who's staying at your motel?"

"I got better things to do than keep tabs on what happens in these rooms."

"Isn't that the definition of manager?"

"I manage. I don't watch. Believe me, what goes on here, you don't wanna know."

"So you don't have any idea who was staying in this room?"

"People rent their room, what they do in it is their business."

"Yeah, right," Preuss said. "You are not responsible."

Zakar nodded, as though pleased his slow student finally got something right.

Zakar locked the room and lumbered back down to the office, leaving Preuss alone on the second-floor walkway. He knocked on the door to the left of Braiden's room, where the initial complaint came from, but there was no answer.

He knocked at the door of the room on the right side of 203. He heard a slow scraping behind the door and knocked again with his cop's knock.

An emaciated woman with puffy eyes and ashy skin cracked opened the door. When she saw Preuss, she thrust her jaw out and said, "There a problem?" Her voice was raw and raspy. Behind her, inside the room, Preuss heard the dry, sarcastic drawl of Judge Joe Brown haranguing a defendant on television.

He handed her a business card. "My name's Martin Preuss. I'm a private investigator. Do you know who stays next door?" He indicated Braiden's room.

She turned her head slowly and looked toward the door to the next room. "What if I do?"

"I'd like to ask you a few questions about him."

"*Him*? Ain't no *him* stay next door."

"No? Who is it?"

She looked at his card. "You not po-lice?"

"No," he said.

She leaned against the door and looked more closely at him. "You sure? Kinda look like po-lice to me."

"Used to be. Not anymore."

"Yeah," she said finally, and gave him the faintest slash of a smile that was missing a few teeth. "I remember you. You busted me one time."

"Very possible."

"You not po-lice no more?"

"No ma'am."

"You don't remember me?"

He searched through all the names and faces he had come into contact with over the years. "Yeah," he said at last, "I think I do. You're Angela, right?"

She flashed him a broad smile now. She was right—he had busted her, and not just once, for soliciting. Not at the Journey's End, though. It was at another motel around the corner on Eight Mile, just as skeevy as the Journey's End. She used to work out of there.

But this was years ago. She looked the worse for wear these days. He hoped she was retired from the life; she looked sick.

"Okay," she said, nodding, pleased. "You do remember me."

"I work private now," he said. "I'm looking for anything you can tell me about whoever stayed in the room next door."

"Well, wasn't no guy, I'll tell you that for free. Was a young lady."

"Know her name?"

Another sly, flirtatious smile. "Why I should tell you?"

"Because I'm asking nicely?"

"What's gonna happen, you stop axing nicely?"

"Angela," he said, "I only ever ask nicely."

She guffawed.

"Seriously," he said, "you live next door, you must've seen her sometime."

"She in trouble?"

"She may be. She may also be in danger."

Angela thought about that for a few moments, then said, "Yeah, funny thing, you know, my memory don't work so good nowadays. Especially in the morning."

He took out his wallet and handed her a twenty. "I hear this helps."

She pocketed the bill and said, "Call herself Michelle. Time to time she have a man in, but she steady stay there alone."

"Same guy all the time, or different?"

"Different. But only one guy ever spend the night."

He showed her the photo of Greg Braiden in the bar that he got from Carrie. "This guy?"

She shook her head. "Seen lots of different white mens come around. Never saw him stay."

"The guy who stays overnight with her have a name?"

"Probably. Never told me."

"How often does he stay with her?"

Angela raised a skinny shoulder. "Time to time."

"You've seen him? What's he look like?"

"Big. Could be white, could be Spanish. Could be a light-skinned brother, but I don't think so."

"Michelle have a last name?"

"Lee."

"Spelled L-E-E?"

She shrugged. "Never saw it written down."

"When was the last time you saw her?"

"End of last week."

"When the police were here about the guy who OD'd next door?"

"Uh-huh."

"That'd be Thursday. But not since then?"

She shook her head.

"Was she here when the guy OD'd?"

"Can't say. Didn't see."

"Okay. Anything else you can tell me?"

She thought for a moment, then said, "This girl, Michelle, she a party girl, know what I'm saying? But I look in her eyes, and I can tell."

"Tell what?"

"I look at her and think, 'This girl too lost. Too alone.' We all fugitives here, but this girl, she running from something. Can't tell what, but it's something."

She looked into her room behind her, then said, "Now you don't mind, I got my programs I'm missing."

10

"Can you do something for me?"

"Sure thing," Rhonda Citron said. "Whatcha got?"

She stood at the coffee maker in the supply closet, filling it with Manny's special Ethiopian beans. He claimed they were the best in the world, available only online. Considering Manny's mania for coffee, Preuss believed it. The machine was spaceship-sleek, all black enamel with chrome nozzles and switches and probably costing as much as Preuss's Explorer.

"I'm looking for anything you can find on a woman named Michelle Lee," Preuss said. "Not sure of the spelling of either name. The works. DMV history, criminal record, anything you can find on her. Current address might be the Journey's End in Ferndale. She might have priors for soliciting."

"When do you need it?"

"Soon as you can."

"I'm working up the final financials for one of Manny's cases. I'll get to this after that. Should be after lunch. That okay?"

"Perfect, thanks."

She fired up the coffee machine, and while it was grinding and hissing, she went back to her desk. Preuss dawdled at the coffee-maker until it ran through its program, then filled up his mug and took it into his office and closed the door. He pulled up the Braiden file on his laptop and read through the notes he had typed up at Star-buck's the day before. He added to them here and there, filled in to-day's activity, and wrote up the full record of his visit with Jake Ak-lawi the night before.

On the way home, Victor the driver had been surly and silent until Preuss was about to step out of the Camaro in Ferndale. Then

Victor grabbed his arm and said, "You didn't have to tell him about your door. I would of fixed it for you."

Preuss pulled out of Victor's grasp. "You didn't have to destroy it."

In the overhead light in the car, Victor's black eyes burned into Preuss's. "I won't forget this, guy."

Preuss made sure to add that to his report. He would also mention it to Aklawi the next time they spoke.

He finished off his coffee and opened his door and told Rhonda, "I'm off to do interviews. Back later."

"Okay," she said. "I'll have your info by then."

"You're a gem."

Heidi Huber, Greg Braiden's ex, worked as an accountant in the business office of St. Mary Mercy Hospital in Livonia. She was not pleased to see Preuss, and even less pleased to discover what he wanted to talk about.

"Taking a smoke break," she told the young woman on the desk in the outer office of the business suite. She led Preuss through the busy hospital corridors out to a patio around the back where a clutch of nurses in blue scrubs sat smoking. Preuss followed her to an empty bench and sat beside her. She immediately knocked a cigarette from the pack in her purse and lit up.

Greg Braiden's ex-wife was a tall, slim, haughty woman with dark brown hair worn in a flip that framed a long face with sharp features and bright blue eyes. Her complexion was perfectly smooth, without a pore, and between her blue eyes and freshly scrubbed look, she might have just come in from practice with the Olympic ski team. She wore a sleeveless top that emphasized the prominent bones of her shoulders and her toned arms.

She was not, however, smiling. "I feel like you're ambushing me," she said.

"Sorry," Preuss said. "I just want to talk about your ex-husband for a few minutes. You're not in any trouble."

"Damn right I'm not." She took a quick toke on the cigarette and blew out an angry cloud of smoke.

"When was the last time you saw him?" he asked.

"What's this about?"

"Do you know what's happened to him?"

"To Greg?" She shook her head, staring hard at him.

"Your sister-in-law hasn't been in touch?"

"I never talk to my sister-in-law. And the only time I see my ex is when he picks up our kid for their visits."

"In that case, I'm sorry to let you know your ex-husband is in St. John-Providence Hospital."

She gave no perceptible reaction. He wondered if she heard him, until she said, "What happened?"

"He was found at the Journey's End Motel in Ferndale last Thursday with an apparent overdose."

"An overdose!" She opened her mouth in surprise; her teeth were white and perfectly shaped. "Of what?"

"Heroin, evidently."

She was silent as she processed that.

"Your ex-sister-in-law hired me to find out what he was doing there. I'm trying to get background on him. If you have any insight into what might have happened, I'd appreciate hearing it."

When she didn't say anything, he asked again, "When did you last see him?"

"Weekend before last. He has visitation rights with our daughter on the weekends. He was supposed to pick her up last Friday, but he didn't show and he didn't call. Kristin was pretty upset. I tried to get in touch with him but I only got his voicemail."

"Did he ever do drugs when you were married?"

"No. Greg was as straight-arrow as they come. An *overdose*?"

"Yes ma'am," Preuss said.

"That wasn't the Greg I knew. The guy I was married to was a total fitness geek. He wouldn't even let me smoke in my own house."

"How long have you been divorced?"

"A little over a year."

"So drug use wasn't a factor in the divorce?"

"Of course not. The factor was, he was an asshole and I couldn't stand living with him any longer."

"In what way was he an asshole?"

She stood and took two paces toward the parking lot, then turned. "Not sure how that's any of your business," she said.

"I'm just trying to get a fuller picture of him."

"I divorced him because I was tired of being criticized constantly, if you must know. It didn't have anything to do with any drug habit, because I never saw anything like that."

"Did his personality change at any point?"

"No, he was always a controlling asshole. I just got to the point in my life where I didn't want to be subject to him anymore. And I didn't want my little girl to grow up in the same house with that kind of father."

"Was he violent?"

"Never physically. Not with me or Kristin. No, his abuse was psychological. Have you ever lived with somebody who tried to control your every move?"

He thought about his father the alcoholic college professor, and his mother the enabling college professor, and how she insisted Preuss and his brother tiptoe around the house when their father was "working," the family euphemism for an alcoholic rage in his office in their home.

And he thought about his brother, who dealt with the painful family dysfunction by retreating into his own world of morphine addiction.

And he thought of the triad formed by his father and mother and brother, and how they effectively squeezed him out of the family unit. Which saved him from the Preuss family insanity, but harmed him nonetheless.

"Yeah," Preuss said. "I have."

"Then you know what it's like."

He changed the subject. "What about his friends?"

"What about them?"

"Does he have any?"

"A few close ones. Mostly people he grew up with."

"Where was that?"

"Bloomfield Hills. I know: poor baby, right? We met in college. Michigan State. I was an accounting major and Greg was a double major in business and computer information systems, so we had a few classes together. We got married right after school. His parents died while he was still in high school, and they left him and his sister quite a bit of money. When we graduated, he took a couple of jobs he wasn't happy in before he landed where he is now."

"He likes what he does?"

She shrugged. "Used to. Used to say he wanted to work there till they hauled him out feet first."

Which might be sooner rather than later, Preuss thought.

"As for now," she continued, "I don't know. Or care. His friends might know more."

"Do you know them?"

"Two or three. Assuming he's still friends with them."

He opened his pad. "Can you give me names?"

She gave him three men's names. "Those are the ones he used to hang with. He grew up with two of them. But like I say, I don't know if there are others."

"How about women? Anybody he was seeing?"

She snorted. "I'm sure I'd be the last to know. I can't imagine any woman with a sense of self-worth wanting to spend two minutes with him. But hey, that's just me. I divorced the guy."

After you married him, Preuss thought, but declined to point out.

"Does the name Michelle Lee mean anything to you?"

"Isn't she an actress?"

"Different person."

"Only Michelle Lee I know is that actress."

"But you saw him the weekend before last?"

"When he brought Kristin home on Sunday night. That was the last time I saw him."

"How'd he seem?"

She shrugged. "Same as ever. Full of himself and basically intolerable."

"Didn't seem depressed or upset?"

"Not as far as I could tell."

"Did he ever talk about killing himself?"

She scoffed. "He had too high an opinion of himself to deny the world the pleasure of his company."

"Did you talk to him after that night?"

She shook her head. "But we're usually not in contact, unless it's about Kristin. This happened last Thursday, you said?"

"He's been in a coma since then."

"That explains why he never picked up his daughter. Or called. Or texted. I thought it was just Greg being Greg."

"Any idea where he might have been during the day on Thursday?"

"If it was a normal day, he would have been at work."

He checked his notes from Carrie Morrison. "Jameson Training?"

"Yeah. In Troy. He works in IT."

Preuss examined the list of names she gave him. "Any of these guys work there?"

"One. Ryan Bennett, he also works at Jameson. Ryan's about as good a friend as Greg has. Or had. Like I say, I don't know the ins and outs of his life anymore. You said he was found in a motel in Ferndale?"

"Correct."

"What kind of place is it?"

"Not a very wholesome one."

"Boy," she said. "You think you know the person you're married to."

She took a final drag on her smoke, then plunged it into a bucket of sand beside her. "I gotta get back."

She stood. "I don't mean to come across as hard-hearted, Mr. Preuss. And I'm sorry to hear about Greg, I really am. I'll have to tell Kristin why he never showed. Sorry I can't be more helpful, but our marriage was over a long time before we got divorced. I just don't know much about his life anymore."

He handed her a business card. "If you think of anything else, would you give me a call?"

She stuffed the card in her purse and headed back into the building.

At his office, he searched for phone numbers for the names of Greg Braiden's friends that Heidi Huber gave him. Of the three names, he found a phone number for only one; he tried it and left a message. The other numbers were unlisted cell phones.

He asked Rhonda to use her contacts to find the numbers of the other men, then closed up his office and went out to Troy.

11

Jameson Training was a sales and technical training corporation that served the automotive industry. A towering glass and sandstone building housed the main offices; the building had receding tiers like a ziggurat set back from Big Beaver near the Somerset Collection mall in Troy.

Preuss stopped at the "Concierge's Desk," which is how a sign over the circular pod near the entrance doors described the reception area. The concierge was a glossy young woman in a cranberry blazer with the company's logo, a square made up of three smaller squares and a triangle set in the bottom right corner.

He asked to speak with Greg Braiden's work supervisor.

"May I ask for what purpose?" she said.

"I'm representing Mr. Braiden in a personal matter."

"Are you an attorney?"

"I'm a private investigator."

She held up a perfectly manicured fingernail and made a call. When she disconnected, she said, "Mr. Jolliffe will see you. He's on the fifth floor."

He stepped off the elevator into a workspace that was entirely beige, the only sounds the whirring of refrigerator-sized computer processors tended to by human minions. He stopped the first minion he saw and asked for Mr. Jolliffe.

"Through there," she said. She indicated a zig-zag path around a line of machines.

He found himself in a clearing in a corner where a glass-walled cubicle bore the nameplate "Bob Jolliffe."

There was no door so he knocked on the doorframe.

"Come!"

Inside the cubicle, a small, bullet-headed man in shirtsleeves sat behind a desk, a spreadsheet in front of him.

"Mr. Jolliffe?"

"Bob, please," the man said. He rose and extended a hand. "You the private eye?" Jolliffe flashed a toothy grin that screwed up his eyes.

"I'm the private eye." Preuss handed Jolliffe a card and Jolliffe studied it.

"Never met a real private eye before. Thought you guys were only on TV and in the movies."

"We're real," Preuss assured him.

"Take a seat. Wanda said you're here about Greg?"

"I am."

Preuss sat in the visitor's chair across the desk from Jolliffe. "Are you aware of what's happened to him?"

Jolliffe leaned back in his chair and folded his hands across his belly. "His sister called me last Friday. Told me he's in the hospital. Said he'd had an accident."

Deciding not to go into more detail about Braiden's circumstances, Preuss nodded.

"How's he doing?" Jolliffe asked.

"Not well, unfortunately."

"Sorry to hear that. If you see him, would you tell him I'm praying for him?"

Preuss didn't respond. Thoughts and prayers: the first (and too often last) impulse from people who had no intention of actually doing anything.

"How can I help?" Jolliffe asked.

"I'm tracing his movements for last Thursday. I understand he was working here all day?"

"He was. We had a meeting in the afternoon and he was there."

"Did you notice anything unusual?"

Jolliffe considered that. "Nothing I can put my finger on."

"He wasn't acting strangely, maybe saying different kinds of things than he might have said before?"

Jolliffe looked at Preuss's business card and tapped the edge of it three times on his desk. "Say," he said, eyes narrowed, "who are you working for? Are you working for Greg? Or for an insurance company?"

"I've been retained on Greg's behalf," Preuss said. "No insurance company is involved, and no claim involving this organization. I'm trying to find out what happened to him. Has his work changed lately?"

"In what way?"

"Has he been missing work? Not following through on projects? Has he seemed distracted, anything like that?"

"Not that I've noticed."

"How close are you?"

"Well," Jolliffe said, "we have a working relationship. I'm his direct report, so if anything had been wrong, I'd have known about it, either from him or from one of his co-workers."

"Do you know much about his personal life?"

"Don't know, don't care. Long as he gets his work done, we're good."

"What does he do here?"

"He's a database systems manager." Preuss said nothing and Jolliffe said, "Want me to explain that in English?"

"If you wouldn't mind."

The little man grinned and said, "Nobody ever knows what that means. In plain English, he designs software systems for managing the marketing data our clients generate—creating it, retrieving it, updating it, and so on. Greg works on the GM see two account."

"'See two'?"

"Oh, sorry, Custom Communications. 'C2.'" He made air quotes with his fingers. "It's one of our proprietary GM projects. It targets our clients' customers with personalized right-time communications. As part of that, there's a program called AO1—stands for

Audience of One—that directs specific communications at key individuals. Need more than that?"

"No," Preuss said, "I think that'll do it. What kind of hours does he keep?'

"Normal business hours, for the most part. If we're under a deadline, he'll put in extra time. Just like we all do. But by and large, he keeps a regular schedule."

"Do you know what time he left last Thursday?"

"Didn't see him go. Sorry. I assume it was his normal time, around six."

"Anything else you can tell me about how he's been?"

"Nothing I can think of. He's the perfect employee. Gets his work done on time, works late when we need him to, doesn't give me a hard time, isn't a prima donna . . . What's not to like?"

"I won't keep you, then," Preuss said. "Before I go, I understand he's friends with a co-worker, Ryan Bennett?"

"Right. Ryan's one of the video producers for C2. One of the creative guys."

"Where can I find him?"

"Usually he's at our downtown Detroit office. That's where the production facilities are, to be close to GM in the RenCen. As luck would have it, he's out here today for meetings. Want to talk with him?"

"I do."

Jolliffe stood. "It's probably easier if I just took you where he is."

12

"Let's sit over there."

Ryan Bennett stopped to load up his coffee with sugar from the Starbucks stand on the first floor of the Jameson building, then led the way to an empty table away from knots of his coworkers congregating in the employee canteen. Bob Jolliffe had guided Preuss through a maze of corridors to a video production studio where a new car stood on a whitewashed floor, its features hyperreal under the video lights, detailed and specific as an insect under an electron microscope. As soon as Preuss told him he wanted to talk about Braiden, Bennett suggested they go for coffee.

He was a tall man, slender with dark Irish good looks, like a young George Clooney. He wore levis and a black denim shirt, no doubt relying on his status as a "creative guy" for his casual dress in the thoroughly corporate environment of Jameson.

"I just want to get away from prying eyes and ears," he told Preuss.

"Sure."

They settled themselves at a table and Bennett said, "So what can I tell you?"

"I understand you and Greg Braiden are friends."

"We are."

"Do you know what's going on with him?"

"Just that he had an accident. Don't ask me how I know. This company's like a small town. It doesn't take gossip long to make its way around here. Is that what this is about?"

"It is."

"So he's in the hospital?" Bennett asked.

"He is. When was the last time you saw him?"

Bennett took a sip of his coffee. "We had lunch last Thursday."

"How'd he seem?"

"Same as usual." Bennett shrugged. "I didn't notice anything odd about him."

"Did he say anything about his plans after work?"

"No."

"Did he ever mention a place called the Journey's End Motel?"

Bennett thought for a few moments, then shook his head. "Never said anything to me about it. Wait, is that the one on Woodward and Eight Mile?"

"That's it. Ever been there?"

"Certainly not. What's that place have to do with him?"

"Just covering some bases. So you've known him for a while?"

"We both started here the same time. I didn't know him before then. We met at orientation. He was a data entry guy, and I'm a video producer. We went through the ranks in our departments, and we got friendly over the years. I'm probably his best friend—not just at work, but in general."

"What's he like?"

"He's a great guy. Smart. Likes his fun. Loves sports. We play in a volleyball league every Tuesday night."

"Was he there last Tuesday?"

"Yeah. Seemed like his usual self. Every so often we'll play a little golf together, though I'm not very good. He's way better than I am. Everything he tries, he's great at. Pool, bowling, hockey, you name it. The consummate jock."

"Is he in a relationship with anyone? I'm asking to see who else I need to speak with."

"Not that I know of."

"You'd know if he was?"

"Sure."

Bennett looked across the atrium where they were sitting. A giant replica of the Jameson logo hung on the far wall.

"When Heidi filed for divorce," Bennett said, "he was devastated. Pretty sure he's still not over her. For a while he was hoping she'd come back to him, but I think he's made peace with the fact it won't happen. He sees his daughter all the time . . . he's a great father."

"Does the name Michelle Lee mean anything to you?"

Bennett thought for a moment, then shook his head.

"To your knowledge, is Greg involved with drugs?"

"No," Bennett said quickly. "I do know that. Greg's as straight as they come. He likes a drink now and then, but drugs? No way."

"He never talked about getting high on the weekends, that type of thing?"

"Absolutely not. If Greg's taking drugs, I'd know. And I don't indulge, either," he added, answering a question Preuss didn't ask. "Except I do enjoy a joint now and then. But that doesn't count, right?" He gave a vulpine smile.

Preuss ignored it. "Is he close to anybody else here?"

"He has work buddies," Bennett said. "For lunch and whatnot. But I think he tends to keep to himself."

"You see him outside work? Besides volleyball?"

"Sure. We used to socialize, me and Greg and Heidi, when they were still married. I'm divorced, so I don't have a partner. But yeah, we spend time together. We stop for a drink after work when things around here get intense. And we go to ball games together, hockey games, things like that. Sometimes we just hang out."

"Can you think of anyone else I should talk with?"

"Here?"

"Here or outside."

"He's got a few other friends."

Preuss showed him the list of names Braiden's ex-wife had given him. "These guys?"

Bennett ran through the names. "Yeah. These are the ones I know about."

"Meaning there could be others?"

"Could be. He's an outgoing guy, but he's hard to get to know. It's like he keeps a guard up all the time. I suppose he might have a whole other set of friends he never talks about."

Bennett was silent, then asked, "What kind of accident did he have? Was it a car accident?"

Without actually answering, Preuss said, "He's in bad shape."

"That woman you mentioned?"

"Michelle Lee?"

"Yeah. She have anything to do with it?"

"She might," Preuss said, not wanting to go too far into it with Bennett. He might be Braiden's best friend, but Preuss didn't want the information spreading all around the small town of Jameson Training.

"The Journey's End. Sounds like Greg might have a bit of a secret life," Bennett said, with admiration.

Preuss gulped down the rest of the coffee. "Thanks for your time. If you think of anything else, will you call me?"

"Absolutely."

Preuss left him to ruminate about the man who was his friend and the secrets he kept.

Preuss heard Rhonda in Manny's office. As he passed Manny's open doorway, he waved to them both.

"Martin," Rhonda called.

Preuss backed up.

"I emailed you that information you asked for on that woman. Still waiting on those phone numbers."

"Great. Thanks."

"I found a lot of Michelle Lees, nobody with an AOR at the Journey's End. I took a chance and narrowed it down by arrest records and didn't get many hits at first by spelling 'Michelle' the normal way, so I tried different spellings. Turns out the one you're probably looking for spells her name 'M-e-e-s-h-e-l-l.'"

"Great work, thanks."

"Martin," said Manny, "everything okay?"

"Never better."

Manny gave him a thumbs-up, and Preuss continued to his office. He opened the attachment to Rhonda's email. She had gotten hold of Meeshell Lee's expired driver's license. Her photo showed a young woman with an oval face and warm reddish-brown skin. Her eyes were large and hard and unhappy.

Rhonda had found out little about Meeshell Lee beyond a few arrests for prostitution. Her residence of record was listed as an address in Detroit.

Nothing new here, Preuss thought, no background at all, not even a Social Security number. Considering all Rhonda's contacts, and how much information was available about everyone these days, it was surprising there wasn't more. He wondered if Meeshell Lee was the woman's real name. With a record for prostitution, she might well have wanted to reinvent herself.

If this was even the right Meeshell Lee.

He needed to find her.

13

The address on Meeshell Lee's license was on Appoline, a street south of Schoolcraft near the Jeffries Freeway, inside the Detroit city limits. Where once a neighborhood thrived with streets lined with one- and two-story bungalows, now widely scattered homes were surrounded by empty fields where other houses used to be before they were abandoned, burnt, and torn down. Here and there, plots had been turned into urban gardens.

The downtown of the city might be coming back, Preuss thought, but renewal hadn't spread to the neighborhoods yet.

The windows of the house he was looking for were boarded up with plywood sheets, and the high grass in the front lawn had gone to seed. The place looked like it had been deserted for a while.

He knocked on the front door, tried it and found it locked, and went around to the back. The rear entry was boarded up and spray-painted with gang graffiti, hastily scrawled tags and tridents with six-pointed stars with the number 6 in the center.

From the back of the house, Preuss saw a fire had partially destroyed the rear roof. Against the cloudy afternoon sky, he could see scorched ragged rafters. The plywood on the back windows had been bashed in and the metal security grates had been pried off.

He shone the light from his iPhone inside and stuck his head into a window opening, but the putrid smell of dampness and dead animals forced him back.

He returned to the Explorer and sat watching the house. No one had stayed here for a while; how did Meeshell Lee come to use this as her address? Had she ever lived here? When did she move out?

He called Rhonda Citron at the office.

"Rhonda," he said when she answered, "can you find out who owns that property on Appoline?"

"Meeshell Lee's address? Piece of cake."

"Text me the particulars when you get them, okay?"

She said she would, and they disconnected.

Immediately his cell phone rang. He didn't recognize the number, which had a 248 area code. Oakland County.

"Uh, yeah," said a hoarse woman's voice. "Who's this?"

"Martin Preuss. Who are you?"

"You know me," the voice rasped. He heard the roar of traffic in the background.

"I do?"

"Yeah. You know who this is. You remembered me, right?"

And he did—he recognized the rasp. Angela, from the Journey's End, in the room next to the one where Greg Braiden was found.

"All right," he said. "What's up?"

"Somebody in Meeshell room."

"Right now?"

"Uh-huh."

"Did you see who? Is it Meeshell?"

"Couldn't see who. Could be Meeshell. I can hear noises coming through the wall, somebody moving around. First time anybody been in that room since last week. Thought you'd wanna know."

Before he could thank her, she hung up.

He parked the SUV in the rear of the motel lot.

There was no activity outside the motel room, nor on either the upper or lower walkway. From his previous dealings with the Journey's End, he knew there wouldn't be much action until later in the afternoon, when the residents would begin to stir. The men and women who called the motel home would appear out of their rooms, stretch, blink at the sunlight, and begin to drift from room to room and down into the office as the day got busier for them.

Things wouldn't really pick up until the late afternoon turned to evening, and the evening turned to night and the nocturnal residents of the motel came fully alive: cars coming and going, johns entering rooms, taking care of business, and leaving. Business on this balmy weekday would be brisk.

By night, the parking lot would be full and loud music would pour out of the rooms, along with the heavy, sweetish-sour odor of marijuana. It would be an unusual night if the Ferndale cops weren't called at least once.

It also wouldn't be unheard of, Preuss supposed, for the upright Greg Braiden to stop here at the end of a stressful workday for a walk on the wild side. He wouldn't be the first to do that. It was, after all, the raison d'être for the Journey's End.

And maybe as part of his evenings, he thought, remembering that Braiden had been paying for this room for six months, Greg started dipping into drugs. And more: Developed a taste for them, developed the pernicious need of addiction . . . He wouldn't be the first straight arrow who did. And maybe he went overboard last Thursday and Meeshell, who had been with him, got shook and took off.

Maybe it was as simple as that.

If it walks like a duck, and so on . . .

As he watched room 203, the door to Angela's room opened and Angela peeked out.

What was she doing?

She left her room and tapped on the door of 203. Curiosity must have gotten the better of her.

The door flew open so fast it surprised her and forced her backwards.

She spoke with the occupant of the room, whom Preuss couldn't see.

As Preuss watched, a man burst out of the room. He was a hulking guy in his thirties with a Tigers cap worn sideways. He had on a spotless white baggy tee shirt with a gold chain and light grey sweat pants. White, as Angela had said, or possibly Spanish.

A wannabe banger.

He struck out at Angela with a push to her shoulder. He knocked her backward, almost over the railing behind her. Then he shouted something into her face that Preuss couldn't make out, and disappeared back inside 203.

Holding her shoulder, Angela retreated to her room.

What the hell?

Preuss left the Explorer and sprinted up the stairs to the second floor. He exited the stairwell just as the door to 203 opened again and the man stepped out of the room. He slammed the door behind him and started toward Preuss.

When he caught sight of Preuss coming toward him, the guy made a quick U-turn and trotted in the other direction, his heavy footfalls pounding on the shuddering concrete walkway. He moved toward the stairwell on the other side of the building.

Preuss yelled, "Hey! I want to talk to you," and took off after him.

The door to Angela's room opened again and Angela stepped out at the exact moment Preuss was passing. He knocked into her and the collision sent him sprawling onto the walkway. Angela cried out and fell back into her room.

Preuss scrambled to his hands and knees in time to see the man disappear down the steps. He heard the clanging of the man's feet as he jumped down the steel stairs, then the slapping of his running shoes as he crossed the parking lot and jumped into an old Monte Carlo.

Preuss watched through the railing as it squealed out of the lot and disappeared into Woodward Avenue traffic.

He turned his attention to Angela.

She lay on her side in her room, half in and half out of the doorway. He bent down and extended a hand to help her up, but she slapped it away.

"Lemme alone!"

"Are you okay?"

"I look okay?"

"Let me help you."

She slapped his hand out of the way again, but when he extended it a third time she relented and let him help her to her feet. She was shaking and woozy, and he got her to sit on her bed and put her head between her knees.

"Are you hurt? Did you hit your head?"

She didn't answer. He brought her a cup of water from the bathroom, and in another minute she caught her breath.

"Better now?" he asked.

She nodded.

"Was that the guy you've seen before here?"

Another nod.

"Why'd you try to talk to him just now?"

"I waited for you to get here," she said. "When you didn't, I thought I'd see if it was Meeshell."

"That's when he slugged you?"

"Told me to mind my own business, so I came back to my room. When I heard all the commotion, I looked out to see what was going on."

She rubbed a hand across her face. Her skin was remarkably smooth for a woman of her age and history.

"And ran smack into yo' stanky ass," she said.

14

After making certain Angela was okay, Preuss stopped at the Tim Horton's on Woodward for a bowl of chili, a coffee, and a maple donut. He had missed both his lunch and his chance to get Toby off the bus. He opened his email on his phone while he ate and found a message from Rhonda with the numbers of Greg Braiden's friends whom he couldn't reach before.

He got through to one of them, who told Preuss he'd help in any way he could. There was no answer for the other, so he left a message.

Both men lived in Grosse Pointe Park, the furthest west of the Grosse Pointes, directly bordering Detroit.

He drove there and parked on a street in front of a center-entrance Colonial with a long driveway and a massive front yard. A woman with long grey-blonde hair came to the door. He explained who he was, and she invited him inside and called, "Adam!"

A man with hair the color and length of his wife's mane came through the archway from the living room. He was big, taller and huskier than Preuss, with soft brown eyes and a full brown beard shot through with grey.

Preuss told him his name, and Adam Sandford said, "Sure, come on in."

He led Preuss through the living room—"Excuse the mess," Adam said, though there was no visible mess in the neat room, just walls covered with watercolors—into the kitchen, which was a genuine mess. The large aluminum sink was filled with the remnants of carrots and turnips and leafy vegetables. A pot of soup bubbled on the stove and filled the room with a rich fragrance.

"Coffee?" Adam asked, and Preuss said sure.

It was already made, so Adam poured it from a coffee maker and said, "How do you take it?"

"Black is good."

Adam set the mug in front of Preuss and poured another for himself. They sat on stools at an island in a kitchen that looked as if it had not been updated since the 1950s. "So you want to talk about Greg?" Adam said.

"I do."

"Yeah, we've known each other for years, since elementary school. We grew up together and went all through school together. Until he went off to MSU and I went to Toledo."

"University of Toledo?"

"No, Toledo Museum of Art. I went to art school. When I moved back here, we reconnected."

"Are those your paintings in the living room?"

"Everything in the house is mine."

"They're very good."

Adam ducked his head in embarrassed thanks.

"When I quit art school, I thought, 'Ah, I don't have any talent, I may as well find something else to do with my life.' But I always came back to painting, so I figured, well, maybe this is what I'm supposed to do after all."

"Good for you."

From the back of the house came a terrible shriek, then a high ululation.

"No problem, I got it," came Adam's wife's voice.

"Everything okay?" Preuss asked.

"Yeah. That's my son. He's autistic. Every once in a while, he has to let loose like that. Helps him let off steam."

"How old?"

"Twelve."

Adam listened, but there were no more screams.

"Well," Preuss said, "let me ask you about Greg Braiden and I'll get out of your hair."

"Sure," Adam said.

"You heard what's happened to him?"

"Ryan called me this afternoon. Said he's in the hospital. Said you talked to him?"

"Earlier today. When was the last time you saw Greg?"

"Couple weeks ago. Usually I see him at volleyball, but I missed last week. My boy was sick, so I stayed home."

"Did you ever hear him talk about the Journey's End Motel? It's in Ferndale."

"Never."

"How about a woman named Meeshell Lee?"

"Nope. Sorry."

"To your knowledge, was he ever involved with drugs?"

Adam hesitated. "There was a time," he said, "when we were in high school. But everybody tries it in high school, right? Otherwise, Greg was always like, 'I'm not gonna pollute my precious bodily fluids, man.' He was always a straight arrow. To the point of boredom." Adam grinned.

A straight arrow. The same term his ex-wife used.

"How'd he seem the last time you saw him?" Preuss asked.

Adam thought for a moment, then shrugged. "Same as always."

"Nothing was bothering him?"

"He didn't say anything if there was."

"One of the theories is that he gave himself an overdose in a suicide attempt. Does that sound like him to you?"

"Not really. But you know, we've been friends for years, and it's still hard to know what he's thinking. So who knows?"

Adam blew across his steaming mug and seemed to be formulating his thoughts carefully.

"Greg," he said, "he keeps people at arm's length, like he doesn't want to let them get too close. Even me. Sometimes I look at him and think, 'Dude, who *are* you?' It was different when we were young, we were really close. But it's like something happened when he hit puberty. He changed completely. Might have something to do with his parents dying, I don't know."

"You don't know who he is because he does things you don't expect, or what?"

"Because he seems . . . I dunno, opaque. It's like he deliberately keeps himself that way so you won't be able to see what he's really like. I mean, he's a great guy and everything. But there's a part of him that's always like hidden."

Preuss considered that, until they both heard another blood-curdling scream from upstairs.

"I think that's my cue," Adam said. "I better go up and give her a hand. Anything else I can tell you?"

"Not right now," Preuss said. "You've been helpful. If you think of anything else, can you give me a call?"

"Sure thing. And hey—if you see Greg, give him my best, okay? Tell him I'm pulling for him."

When Preuss got to the home of Braiden's other friend, Roger Garland, he discovered the man was not around.

A woman stood in the doorway to their home, a Tudor on the better side of the city. "Sorry. He's not here," she said.

"Do you know when he'll be home?"

"His class lasts till ten. He usually rolls in around ten-thirty."

"Is he a professor?"

"No, he's a psychologist. But he teaches a class on Wednesday nights."

"I'll catch him another time, then," Preuss said.

He started to turn away, then caught himself. "Do you know Greg Braiden, by any chance?" he asked.

"Greg? Sure."

"Can I talk to you for a few minutes?"

"About Greg?"

"Yes."

"I don't know what I can tell you about him—Roger knows him a lot better than I do. But yeah, if you want."

"Can I come in?"

She stepped aside and let him enter a cavernous living room with minimal furnishings—a sofa, two chairs, and a massive coffee table made of a slice of tree. "Have a seat," she said.

He sat on the sofa, which was surprisingly uncomfortable.

"Can I get you anything? By the way, I'm CeeCee."

"Martin Preuss."

They shook hands.

"I won't take up much of your time," Preuss said. He explained where Greg Braiden was. She had not heard, and expressed the same kind of shock everyone else had.

"How long have you known him?"

"Roger and I are married nine years, so I've known Greg a little longer than that. I used to see more of him when he was married to Heidi. We used to go out together, the four of us. Sometimes the six of us, including Adam and Jeannie."

"The Sandfords?"

She nodded. "But since Greg and Heidi split up, Roger mostly sees him by himself."

"What can you tell me about him?" Rather than ask a specific question, Preuss wanted to give her room to answer in whatever way she wanted.

She considered that, and shook her head. "Honestly, he's not that easy to know. I mean, guys in general tend to hide their emotions. And it's hard to know what they're thinking. I'd have to say Greg is worse than most."

"Have you noticed any changes in him? Especially recently? The last year or so?"

"Not that I can put my finger on. Like I say, I don't see him that much anymore, just occasionally with Roger."

"And you haven't noticed anything different about him?"

"Maybe he's a little more depressed than he used to be. But he and Heidi had a terrible breakup, so there's that."

"If he's so hard to know, what makes you think he's more depressed?"

"He's even quieter than usual when I do see him. Maybe it has to do with me being in the room, I don't know. But he'll go a whole night without saying a word. I just assumed if he was depressed, it was because of his marriage."

"Did you ever know him to be involved with drugs?"

She waved it away like so much smoke. "Absolutely not. I can't even conceive of it."

"A real straight arrow," Preuss said.

"For real. He always says he's high on life."

15

By the time he got to Toby's, his son was asleep for the night. Preuss sat in the chair beside the bed and held Toby's crooked hand as he watched his son sleeping, Toby purring.

The presence of his son calmed him. As always.

Preuss sat for a while, watching the boy sleep and replaying the day in his head. He was getting a consistent picture of Greg Braiden. He wasn't actually learning much about the man, but at least the people he had talked to that day presented the image of somebody who enjoyed his life on the one hand, but who seemed to keep the world at bay on the other, and was therefore difficult to get inside.

He sat for another half an hour, then rose and bent over the sleeping boy's form and kissed him lightly on the forehead so he wouldn't wake him.

He took himself home.

He didn't notice the screen door until he was approaching his front porch. The entire door, including the ragged screen, had been torn off its hinges and thrown into the bushes. The light over the door had been smashed.

He climbed the front stoop and heard the quick scrape of soft shoes on the concrete behind him. He felt rather than saw something long and ugly coming down at him fast.

He spun away from its arc, stumbling backward against the front of his house and scraping both elbows and forearms on the brickwork and porch.

His attacker came at him again, this time taking a low swing with what Preuss now saw was a baseball bat with its barrel studded with nails. He rolled out of the way and the bat took out a chunk of brick. He heard the crack of the wooden bat splitting.

On his back, Preuss waited till the attacker made another run at him, then kicked out at the guy's knee. He didn't recognize the man in the darkness of his porch.

His kick pushed in the other man's knee and hyperextended it. The man yelped in pain and lost his balance. He tumbled off the front steps to sprawl on his back on the front lawn.

Preuss clambered to his feet and jumped down the steps and swept up the bat before the other man could get to it. He swung it to wallop the guy, but the man scuttled backwards crab-like over the grass, dragging his hurt leg. On the sidewalk, the guy got his feet under him clumsily and, hopping on his good leg, dove headfirst into the Camaro that screeched to a stop in front of Preuss's house.

Before the car sped away, Preuss saw the sudden interior light illumine the sides of the driver's head—shaven except for the little pad of tight black curls on his crown.

Preuss watched the tail lights of the car disappear around the corner, then took the bat inside his house. He rested it against the wall in the front hall and went upstairs to clean the scrapes on his palms and elbows.

He was toweling off when he heard the doorbell.

Downstairs he grabbed the bat and peered through the window in the door. When he saw who it was, he stuffed the bat in the hall closet and opened the door to Ferndale PD Patrolman Paul Vollmer standing on the porch. The flashing lights of his blue-and-white strobed the houses on the street.

Preuss opened the door.

"Detective," Vollmer said.

"It's just Martin anymore," Preuss said.

"Yeah, I know. Hard habit to break."

"Come in."

Preuss stepped aside and Vollmer entered. The two shook hands.

"What's up?" Preuss asked.

"We just got a call about an altercation," Vollmer said. "Involving you."

"Yeah," Preuss said. "I just had a little scuffle. One of the neighbors must have called it in."

"Everything all right?" Vollmer nodded at Preuss's abrasions. "Looks like you did have a little trouble, there."

"It's nothing. Misunderstanding, that's all."

"Yeah? The call-in said it looked pretty vicious."

"Wasn't as bad as it looked," Preuss said. "You know how these things go. They flare up and they're over in five seconds. A guy with too much testosterone doesn't know what to do with it. Thanks for checking, though."

"Okay," Vollmer said, unconvinced. He stood in Preuss's hall for another few moments, like he was trying to decide how to play this.

"So you don't want to file a complaint?" he finally asked.

"Not necessary."

"Got to write it up anyway."

"Not a problem, Paul. Seriously. Do what you have to. Far as I'm concerned, whatever it was, it's finished."

Knowing, of course, that the trouble with Jake Aklawi's thug was most likely just beginning.

Thursday, September 20, 2012

16

Toby was dressed and wide awake and vocalizing loudly in bed in the morning. When he heard his father's voice, Toby yelled even louder.

"Hey you, noisy guy," Preuss said. He leaned over and gave his son a juicy kiss on the cheek and Toby's happy foghorn scream rose into a falsetto. He beamed and squealed in happiness. Alone of anyone else in his life, Toby made his father smile.

After his aide Melissa got Toby dressed, Preuss sat on the side of the bed and pulled his son upright so they were sitting together. Preuss held Toby against him with an arm around the boy's shoulders because Toby couldn't sit up by himself. His son nuzzled and snuffled into Preuss's chest.

"I love you so much," Preuss said into the boy's hair.

More rubbing and snuffling.

"Hey," Preuss said, "how'd you like to hear some live music?"

Toby hummed.

"I'll take that as a yes."

"Are you playing?" Melissa asked.

"No. A friend of mine has a blues band. Toby's met him before and heard him play. He's doing a gig around town in a couple of weeks. I told him I'd bring Toby to see him."

"Oh boy, Toby," Melissa said. "That sounds like fun."

Toby took a deep gulp of a breath, collected himself, and shrieked in agreement.

Rhonda Citron gave Preuss a handful of phone message slips as soon as he entered the offices of Greene and Preuss, Investigations. "These came for you, you popular guy."

He thanked her and settled himself in his office with the door closed. For all Rhonda's technical savvy, Manny insisted she take his phone messages the old-fashioned way, on these salmon-colored "While You Were Out" message pads, so he'd have hard copy records of his calls. She did the same for Preuss.

He flexed his arms, which were sore from the tussle the night before, and quickly sorted through the slips. Two were from Carrie Morrison from earlier in the morning, wondering what progress he had made on her case. One was from Beverly Frankel, his Purple Gang client.

First he called Beverly Frankel, who told him she wasn't going to be able to make their appointment in the afternoon. They decided to reschedule for the next day.

Then he called Carrie Morrison.

"How are things going?" she asked.

"Making progress. I've been to the motel, talked to a few people at your brother's work and a couple of his friends, and I've gotten good information."

"I guess I was hoping you'd be further ahead by now."

By now? he thought. It's been all of two days since she hired him.

Unwilling to sound defensive, he let the comment pass. Instead he asked, "Does the name Meeshell Lee mean anything?"

She considered that. "Never heard of her. Who is she?"

"She lives at the motel. Apparently she stays in the room where your brother was found."

She was quiet as she processed that.

"So was something going on between them?" she asked. "I'm not sure I understand."

"She's gone missing, so it's not clear what her involvement is. I'm trying to track her down."

"What is she, one of the whores who hangs around there?"

Tony Tullio used to say, "When all else fails, try honesty." Preuss decided the best way forward was to be honest with her.

"I'm not certain how she fits in. Carrie," he said, "what's becoming clear is that your brother had secrets, and these kinds of secrets don't reveal themselves easily. I'm trying to find people who spend their lives not wanting to be found. As soon as I have something solid to share with you, I'll let you know."

There was a pause at the other end of the line. "Maybe I should have waited for Mr. Greene after all," she said.

Okay, Preuss thought. You want to play it that way.

He had still not made the transition all the way from public safety officer to private contractor, and wasn't used to people talking to him like this, especially when he was trying to help them. He and Manny had talked about it, and Manny assured him that he had no obligation to put up with people's shit. "If they're unhappy with the work the agency is doing," he once told Preuss, "they're free to take their custom elsewhere."

This was different from dealing with victims as a police detective, he had realized over the past year he had worked with Manny. Clients were paying for their investigator's services, just like dry cleaning, and like all consumers they complained when they felt they weren't getting their money's worth.

On the other hand, he thought, the flip side of providing a paid private service is that he could tell the client to go to hell in a way that he never could do as a public servant.

On the third hand, he knew he had to take a slightly less hostile stance with the people upon whom the business depended.

Having given himself a few moments to calm down, he said, "I'm sorry you feel that way."

"So am I."

"If—"

She disconnected without saying goodbye.

He watched the light on her line on the telephone console blink out.

He gave her five minutes so *she* could calm down, during which he told himself she was under a lot of stress, told himself she was lashing out at him because she didn't have anyone else to lash out at right now. Told himself to rein in his own temper.

He called her back. She picked up on the first ring.

"I'm sorry," she said. "I didn't mean to snap at you."

"It's not a problem."

"This is a very hard time for me. It's very stressful."

"I understand."

"I don't usually talk to people this way."

"How about we meet again and you can fill in some gaps about Greg for me? I can share what I've found in more detail, and you can give me a better sense of him."

"Sure."

"How's today?"

"Hang on."

He heard her paging through what must be her calendar. "The only time I have is over lunch. I have meetings in downtown Detroit all day. Can you meet me down there?"

"That works," he said. "Where and when?"

"First off," she said, "I wanted to apologize again. I'm sorry I spoke to you like that. I know you're doing all you can."

"It's forgotten," Preuss said.

"If you knew me, you'd know I'm not like that at all."

He waved it away. "So I've spoken with Heidi, and two of Greg's friends. I also visited his workplace."

"You spoke to the ice queen? Was she as warm as always?"

"She couldn't tell me much."

"Couldn't or wouldn't?"

"I thought she was being honest. She said she doesn't have much to do with your brother anymore, except when it comes to their daughter."

"Did she tell you why she and Greg broke up?"

"No."

"Oh, she didn't tell you about her affair? That was convenient."

She dug her fork into her chicken shawarma salad as though it and not Heidi had betrayed her brother. They sat in a Lebanese restaurant on Cass Avenue in what was now called "Midtown." It was formerly known as the Cass Corridor, part of Detroit's old skid row.

Though Midtown and downtown were starting to come back from their burnt-out, deserted days in the seventies and eighties, the homogenized upscale bars and retail shops popping up everywhere were making it look more and more like a suburban shopping district than a historic urban area. Which was probably the point.

"Yeah, she was seeing a guy while they were married," Carrie continued. "That's why they got divorced. Greg wanted to try to save the marriage. But she wanted out."

"They've been divorced for a year?"

Carrie nodded. "Evidently, Heidi's affair had been going on for a long time before that. I don't know who it was with. Greg wouldn't tell me. I'm not even sure he knew."

"She never told him who she was having an affair with?"

"She just broke it to him one day. Said she'd been seeing someone from her work, and didn't want to be married to him anymore."

"Is it still going on?"

"Couldn't tell you. Don't care."

They ate in silence for a few moments. He tried to fit this new information into his timeline: Heidi had been having an affair for a while; then they've been divorced for a year; and Greg had been paying for a room at the Journey's End for six months.

Newly divorced, probably depressed, cut off from the security of his previous life, Greg Braiden may well have lost his moorings in the whirlwind of temptation at the Journey's End.

"I'm getting a picture of your brother as a very private person," Preuss said. "He even keeps himself aloof from his friends. Is that your sense of him?"

"Is that what people have been saying about him?"

"It is. They say he's a great guy, but seems to maintain an armor around himself."

Not unlike me, Preuss realized. How many people would say that about me?

"He really likes to socialize," she went on. "If he's among people he knows, he can be very outgoing. But it's true, he can seem a bit stand-offish. Moody, almost. Once you get to know him, and he gets to know you . . ."

Her voice trailed off. He waited for her to continue. When she didn't go on, he said, "Heidi gave me the names of a few of his friends. I spoke with two, Ryan Bennett and Adam Sandford. I tried to see Roger Garland, but he wasn't home. I talked to Garland's wife, and she could tell me a few things but not much."

"Greg's known Adam and Roger since grade school. Ryan's a friend from work."

"Is there anyone else who's close to him besides these guys? He wasn't seeing anyone?"

"Seeing as in romantically? I think my brother was taking a well-deserved time-out from women."

Or maybe not, Preuss thought, depending on what role Mee-shell Lee had in all this.

"If he has other friends, I don't know them," she said.

"Okay. Anything else you can tell me about him?"

She chewed her salad thoughtfully for a few moments. "He's a good man. He was a good husband until, well, you know. He's a great father. Loves his kid to pieces. He's very regular in his habits. He wakes up at the same time every day, goes to sleep at the same time, we go out together for dinner every Monday. Greg makes Kristin's after-school sports events and always takes her when it's his time to see her.

"When he was married, they'd go on vacation at the same time every year, to the same place, a camp in Pictured Rocks National Lakeshore, up north. He takes good care of himself, he jogs, he works out, he eats right, he's not on any medication . . . He's a social drinker, no drugs at all, despite how they found him."

She paused to reflect on what she just said. "He's very like our father. Except old Charlie, he was always the life of the party. Any party. The original Good-Time Charlie."

Preuss picked up the sour note of resentment in her tone.

"I understand your parents died when you were in high school."

"Greg was in high school. I had already started college. There're four years between us."

"How'd they die?"

"One-car accident. They were driving out west and my father lost control and went over a cliff. My mother was with him. They were both killed instantly."

"Must have been tough on you."

"It hit us both hard, believe me. Greg went a little crazy for a while. We moved in with our grandparents, except I had pretty much left home by then anyway."

He remembered Heidi Huber saying the children were left with money. "What did your parents do for a living?" he asked.

"Our father was a theatrical producer. He produced national touring companies of Broadway plays and musicals. Mom was an attorney. She was also an heir to the Fortunato real estate development money. Do you know about them?"

"I've seen the name around."

"They got the contract to build Northland and the other three malls for J.L. Hudson's in the inner-ring suburbs around Detroit in the fifties. At that time, Northland was the biggest mall in the world. They went on to get contracts for a lot of the building that took place as the suburbs spread out from Detroit in the sixties. Anyway, that was the source of our inheritance. It went into a trust for us until we turned twenty-five. It wasn't a fortune, by any stretch of the imagination—there were four other Fortunato siblings besides my mother, and a ton of cousins. But we were both still well-off."

"How did you both use the money?"

"I used it to open my art gallery in Birmingham. And I could paint without having to go through the starving artist drama. Greg bought himself all the usual expensive toys. But even with the inheritance, we both still have to work for a living."

This might explain where her brother got the money to pay for Meeshell Lee's room at the Journey's End, Preuss thought.

"Have you noticed any odd behavior in your brother?" he asked.

"Like from drugs?"

"Or anything else."

"Not at all. Honestly, I don't know what you're looking for. The man I've known all his life wouldn't be caught dead in a place like the Journey's End Motel."

And yet, Preuss thought, that was almost what happened.

"I just can't even imagine him in a place like that," she said. "Is it possible he wasn't there of his own volition?"

"Anything's possible."

"What I mean is," she said, "is it possible somebody—maybe that woman you asked about—lured him there, or forced him there? And then forced those drugs on him?"

"Could be. But the fact is, Carrie, your brother's been paying for a room at that motel for the past six months. It's not like somebody just kidnapped him and dragged him there one night."

She stared at him, uncomprehending.

"I don't understand. He's been *paying* for a room?"

"Yes. The room he was found in."

"How do you know this?"

"I spoke with the motel manager."

"Is it possible he made a mistake?"

"There's no doubt."

She tried to process that information. "And this Meeshell Lee you asked me about?"

"She's the one who lives in that room. I won't know who she is or what their relationship is until I find her."

She stabbed disconsolately at her salad. "That must be one of those secrets you mentioned on the phone."

"You had no idea he was doing this?" Preuss asked.

"None. Sometimes when I wanted to see him, he'd tell me he was working late, or having drinks with his buddies. But he never said anything about keeping a room at that place. And I used to ask him point blank if he was seeing anyone, and he'd tell me no. He must have been lying to me. About everything."

When he said nothing, she went on. "Let me know what you find."

Her brother wasn't the guy she thought he was, Preuss reflected, and the knowledge seemed to have deflated her.

"I will, of course," he said. "Is there anything else you can tell me?"

She put her fork down and stared at it for a long moment.

"Just—I can't believe we're talking about my little brother. Though I have to say, you warned me, didn't you? You warned me about what we might find."

"That doesn't make it any easier," he said. "But we have to go where the evidence takes us."

She nodded dully, and picked again at her salad before laying down her fork and pushing the plate away.

17

Preuss took a cup of Manny's coffee into his office and closed his door. Victims of crime and their families were often displeased with the progress of police investigations and were loath to believe the facts of the case, especially when the facts clashed dramatically with their own sense of the realities of their lives.

He heard two sharp raps. Rhonda's knock. "It's open."

"Got this for you," she said. She laid a sheet of paper on his desk alongside the coffee cup.

"It's info on the woman who owns that house on Appoline in Detroit," Rhonda said. "The one you asked me to check out. Got the name, address, and phone number of the owner."

"Antoinette Lee," he read. "What do you bet she's related to Meeshell Lee?"

"My Magic Eight Ball says the odds are good."

Antoinette Lee turned out to be the vice president for human resources at the gleaming new campus of Beaumont Hospital in Troy. She was also Meeshell Lee's mother.

Her secretary made him wait for twenty minutes while her boss took an unscheduled conference call in her office. Sitting in the reception area, Preuss heard a steady murmur behind the closed door.

When the murmur ended, Antoinette Lee stepped out and beckoned him inside.

She was a tall black woman in a blue business pantsuit with long processed salt-and-pepper hair. They shook hands and she indicated the sofa at the side of her office. Preuss took a seat and she sat in a chair facing him.

"So," she said. She clasped her hands in her lap. "You want to talk about Meeshell."

"Yes ma'am." He had explained who he was and what he wanted on the phone when he made the appointment with her.

"What kind of trouble is she in now?"

"I'm looking into the situation of a man named Greg Braiden. Meeshell seems to be connected to him. Do you know the name?"

She repeated it as if tasting it on her tongue, then shook her head. "What's he to Meeshell?"

"Hard to say at this point. Lately, she's been living in a room at the Journey's End Motel in Ferndale."

"I do know that."

"Since April, it's been paid for by this Greg Braiden."

She dropped her chin to her chest and rubbed her forehead. "Do I want to know what's happened to him?"

"Last week he was found overdosed in Meeshell's room. He's in a coma."

"And you think Meeshell's responsible?"

"I'm not sure how she's involved. That's what I'm trying to find out. She may be a witness to whatever happened to this man. Or she might be connected in some other way."

"Oh, sweet Jesus."

She shook her head with sadness at this latest turn in her daughter's life.

"As you can probably guess," she said, "Meeshell's been a problem for a long time. She's *had* problems for a long time."

"She seems to have dropped out of sight over the past couple of days. Would you know where I can find her?"

"The only address I have for her is that motel."

"So she's not staying with you at the moment?"

She gave a short, bitter laugh. "I don't allow her to stay with me anymore."

"When was the last time you heard from her?"

"It's been four or five months. She's usually only in touch when she needs something. Primarily money."

"I know what you're going through."

"You have your own Meeshell?"

"I do."

"Then you know there's nothing you can do about them, Mr. Preuss. They're adults. It doesn't mean you ever stop worrying, but you can't make their lives better, no matter what you do."

"It's true," Preuss said. "I found your name through your house on Appoline. Was Meeshell staying there?"

"At one time. I own it and used to rent it out. A couple of years ago, I told her she could have it. I thought if she had a stable place to live—other than with me, that is—she might be able to turn things around for herself. And she did stay there for a while. But she decided she didn't want it, so she just walked away from it. But not before trashing it. Just like everything else I've tried to do for her. I don't think she's lived there since last year."

"No," he said, "I saw it. It's deserted."

"You said she's missing? Since when?"

"Nobody's seen her since the night Greg Braiden was found, which was last Thursday. Apparently, he wasn't staying in the room with her, but another man might have been. Would you know if there was a man in her life?"

She scoffed. "I'm sure there are *many* men in her life."

"But anyone steady?"

"I'd be the last to know. Though considering who she always seems to wind up with, I've probably met his type before."

"What type would that be?"

"A predator," she said. "A man who lives off her. Who leads her deeper into trouble. Not that she needs a guide. She got into that lifestyle on her own just fine. And whenever she gets in trouble, I'm the one she calls to bail her out. Every time, I tell her it's the last time, but when it's your own child . . ." She let the sentence trail off.

He waited.

"The last time I let her stay with me," Antoinette Lee continued, "she stole all my sterling silver. Every piece—all my flatware, a tea seat, bowls, trays, serving utensils—all of it. Been in my family for generations. All gone. I sure don't know where she learned her bad habits, Mr. Preuss. Drugs, prostitution, crime. She certainly never learned them from me. She was so promising when she was a girl . . . she was normal, you know. More than normal: exceptional. I brought her up right. We were well-off, I gave her all the advantages. She used to say she wanted to be a writer when she grew up. She was a good girl, Mr. Preuss. A girl I could be *proud* of."

"Does she have a cell phone?"

"If she does, she never gave me the number. And I'm not sure I'd want it. As for where she might be?"

She looked around her office, thinking about that for a few moments.

"I wouldn't know any of her friends, of course. And she's burned her bridges with most of the family. The only one I know who might be in touch with her is a cousin up in Pontiac. She has her head on straight these days, but once upon a time they ran together. It's possible she might know where Meeshell is."

She opened her cell phone and searched till she found what she was looking for. She reached over to grab a pad off her desk and with quick strokes wrote out a name and two numbers. "First one's her cell, second one's her home number," she said.

She handed them across to Preuss. He read *Ramonda Hudgens* and two numbers with 248 area codes.

"I'll ask you one favor, please," the woman said.

"Of course."

"When you find her—if you find her—please tell her not to get in touch with me."

She sat back in her chair.

"I'm sorry if this sounds harsh, Mr. Preuss. But I don't want to see her. I truly don't."

18

Ramonda Hudgens was a pretty, thirtyish woman with large eyes and dark, almost blue-black skin. Her jet-black hair was pulled back into a tight bun.

Preuss introduced himself and said, "I'm an investigator trying to get ahold of Meeshell Lee. Meeshell's mother gave me your name. I understand you and Meeshell are cousins?"

Concern clouded Ramonda's expression. "Okay."

"You were once close?"

"What's she done now?"

"I just need to ask her questions about a case I'm working on. When was the last time you spoke with her?"

She closed her laptop lid and leaned forward across her desk at Catholic Charities of Southeast Michigan in Pontiac. "First you need to tell me how much trouble she's in."

"Honestly, I'm not sure. She might be in a lot of trouble. She might also just be a witness to somebody else's trouble. Does that make a difference when you last saw her?"

"No, but it makes a difference how much I tell you. The last thing I want to do is cause her even more problems."

"She's been staying in a room in a Ferndale motel where a man had a drug overdose last week. I'm trying to find out what she knows about it."

"You think she's responsible?"

"I won't know till I speak with her."

Ramonda studied his face, then looked at his business card again.

"The best thing you can do to help her is tell me where she is, if you know," Preuss said. "She has the answers to a lot of questions."

"I don't know where she is now," Ramonda said at last. "But I did speak with her last week."

"When?"

She pulled out her smartphone and clicked to her calendar. "It was right after I made a nighttime home visit, so it was Thursday. I'm a social worker," she explained. "I make a lot of home visits at night, when the families are there."

Thursday night. The same night Greg Braiden was found.

"About what time was this?"

"Ten forty-six."

"She called you?"

"Yes."

Adnan Zakar at the Journey's End said Braiden was found at 9:30. So Meeshell called her cousin after that.

"What did she want?" he asked.

"She wanted to know if she could stay with me."

"Did she say why?"

"She told me she had to disappear for a couple days."

"But she didn't say why?"

"No. And I didn't ask because I didn't want to know. I wasn't going to let her, anyway. She sounded pretty frantic, though. This guy who OD'd—when did that happen?"

"That same night," Preuss said. "An hour before she called you."

"So they're probably connected?"

"It's likely. Do you talk with her often?"

"Not very. Couple times a year, at most. Usually she asks for money, and this time once I told her she couldn't stay with me, she asked me for a loan again. By now, I know her loans are really gifts. I never see that money again. And I told her I'm through enabling her."

"I take it she's gone through this with you before?"

"Oh, many times. When she isn't outright asking for money, she's running a scam she wants me to help her with. Like last year. She decided she wanted to get out of the life, go straight. Said she wanted to take classes, make something of herself. Thought that was gonna help her change her life."

"And you helped her?"

"I did. I laid out money for tuition. She sounded so sincere. She thanked me and said she'd pay me back as soon as she could. And I know from personal experience education can change your life. It's how I changed mine. So I couldn't say no. But you think I ever saw that money again? You think she ever finished a course?"

"What did she do when you told her she couldn't stay with you this time?"

"She tried to wheedle me into changing my mind, but I stood my ground. The last time she stayed with me, half my jewelry went missing."

The same story Meeshell's mother told.

"Do you know if she found someplace else to stay?"

"When I said she couldn't stay with me, she started yelling at me, cursing me, calling me every name under the sun. I had to hang up on her."

"Do you still have the number she called from?"

"It's in my phone."

"It might be a way to reach her."

"Be my guest."

She found the number and handed the phone across to him. He took a photo of the screen with his own phone.

"Just so I'm clear," he said, "you don't have any idea where she might be?"

"Meeshell has a bunch of new friends she's made since she's been in the life she's leading. I'm sure any one of them might give her shelter. I only know of one person from our old days together who's still in touch with her. Besides me, that is. Nikki's the only one I know who can still put up with her long enough to give her a place to stay."

"Nikki?"

"Nikki Bardellini. She's an old friend of ours. Want me to find her contact for you?"

"Please."

She searched through her phone contacts. "In the meantime," she said, "I can try to get in touch with Meeshell. Tell her you want to talk with her."

"I'd appreciate it. Could you try now?"

She hit redial on the number. She listened for a moment, then shook her head. "Not in service."

"Probably a burner she's already ditched. If you hear from her again, you might let her know I want to help her. I don't want to jam her up."

Back at the agency office, he called the number for Nikki Bardellini. He left a message on her voicemail, asking her to call him back about an important matter.

Rhonda appeared in his doorway. "Got a minute for Manny?"

"Sure."

Manny was reclining in his desk chair, scrolling through his phone.

"Martin—come in."

Manny pointed him to his visitor's chair and sat up. He smoothed the crease of his pants legs. He was an elegant man, with a full head of silver hair combed straight back and a dress shirt made of plush cotton.

"Got time for a funny story?" Manny asked.

"I could use one."

"Sid called me with a suspected fraud case," Manny said. Sid Geershon was the attorney specializing in accidents and social security denials whom Manny did most of his work for. "Guy was in a car accident and claimed to be totally disabled, but his insurance company denied his claim. Their investigator discovered he had a part-time job as a limo driver. The guy hired Sid to get the insurance company's decision overturned, and Sid hired me to prove the guy really is disabled. So I hired Freddy to stake out his apartment."

Freddy Rousseaux, a cop from Birmingham Manny hired for jobs when he was off-duty.

"Freddy parked in the lot of this guy's apartment building in Madison Heights, and his neighbor came out, nice little old lady. She was watching Freddy, and she came over to the car and asked him what he was doing. Freddy tells her, 'Madam, I'm waiting for your neighbor, Mr. So-and-so.' And she says, 'Oh, you won't find him here now.'

"'Why not?' Freddy says.

"'Because,' she says, 'he's invisible.'

"'Invisible!' Freddy says.

"'Yes,' she says, like this happens every day. 'He has a machine that makes him invisible.'

"'And how does he do that?' Freddy asks her. You know, plays along. Thinks the old girl's pulling his leg.

"'Do you know how?' she says. 'Because he's a *space alien.*' Just as matter of fact as if she was telling him the guy was from Cleveland."

Manny threw his head back and laughed so hard tears came to his eyes. "A *space alien*! I just now got off the phone with Freddy. A *space alien*! Did you ever hear anything like that?"

Preuss agreed that he hadn't, and Manny laughed until he started coughing. Then he took off his glasses and wiped his eyes, still coughing and chuckling to himself.

When his mirth subsided, Manny said, "You really have to love this job."

"It's true," Preuss said.

"How are things with you?"

"Good. Making progress on the Braiden case."

"Glad that's working out."

Preuss leaned forward. "Can I ask you a question?"

"Fire away."

"Are you feeling okay?"

"Why wouldn't I be?"

"You sound a little . . . off."

"Off as in crazy?"

"No, off as in not yourself. You seem too hoarse lately for too long."

"Just a cold," Manny said. "Having trouble shaking it, that's all."

"You're sure?"

"I appreciate your interest. But Martin, don't worry about me. Please."

Convinced Manny wasn't telling him the truth, but unwilling to push him further, Preuss nodded and went into his office after exchanging a worried glance with Rhonda standing in Manny's doorway.

As though waiting until he sat down, his cell phone rang.

"Mr. Preuss?" said a woman's voice on the other end of the line.

"Yes."

"It's Ramonda Hudgens."

"Hello again."

"I think I might know where you can find Meeshell."

19

Ramonda got in touch Nikki Bardellini after he left. Nikki said she had talked with Meeshell the week before, and Meeshell stayed with her for two nights, Thursday and Friday. Then she left, and Nikki thought Meeshell was staying with her boyfriend at a house in Detroit.

"She didn't mention the name of this boyfriend, did she?"

"Yes," Ramonda said. "Well, she didn't, but I asked her if she knew. She said his name is Ray Tomatoes."

"Ray Tomatoes?"

"That's what she said. Do you know him?"

"No. But I may have heard about him." He remembered what Jake Aklawi had said about the man who stayed with Meeshell. That might be Ray Tomatoes, Preuss thought. The man Angela heard inside Meeshell's room at the Journey's End.

When they ended their call, Preuss stared at the address he wrote in his notebook. Ramonda said the house belonged to a friend of Ray's. It was on Tuxedo Street off Second Avenue in Highland Park, a small city completely surrounded by Detroit. Once a solid residential area that had steadily gone to seed over the years, it was now beginning to come back along with Detroit itself as people were buying up homes and renovating them.

He parked in front of a red-brick Arts and Crafts bungalow from the 1920s, the kind that dotted Highland Park in better days. The houses up and down the street were newer, neat and well-maintained, but this one was an original bungalow, and it cried out for work. Paint peeled off the wooden piers that held up a sagging hipped roof over the front porch, the wooden front steps were split and rotted, and cedar shingles were missing on the second-floor exterior.

The house had an empty driveway made of broken concrete pieces, and a gate hung askew from the grey hurricane fence around the weedy back yard. Broken bricks and construction rubble were piled against the side of the house.

Preuss carefully climbed the damaged front steps and briefly thought about knocking on the door. Where the doorbell used to be was an empty socket.

Deciding it would be a bad idea to warn whoever might be inside, he tried the doorknob. It turned in his hand and he pushed it open.

He took a step inside the house. No furniture in the front room, just a fireplace at the far end with an inglenook with broken benches on either side. The room reeked of damp old wood and various human bodily excretions. The oak floor was almost black with old shellac and littered with the remains of fast food meals: Arby's wrappers, giant McDonald's cups tipped on their sides, pizza boxes open with congealed cheese.

Moving slowly over the wooden floors to keep the creaking to a minimum, he went through the rooms on the first floor. The stairway to the second floor was, oddly, in the kitchen, and as he carefully went up the steps he smelled the sweet, skunky odor of marijuana.

He hugged the wall as he approached the room where the smell was coming from. He peeked around the door and saw a slender black woman sitting cross-legged on the floor facing him.

He stood in the doorway and said, "Meeshell."

She gave an exaggerated flinch and jumped to her feet, the blunt hanging from her lips. She wore a black silk do-rag and her eyes were wide with surprise. She had on Levis torn at the knees and a red, green, and orange tunic.

She threw a look beside him as if judging whether she could squeeze by him.

He held his hands up. "Easy. I just want to talk."

"Who are you?"

"Martin Preuss. I'm a private investigator."

"What are you doing here?"

"I want to ask you some questions about Greg Braiden."

At the mention of his name, she backed away, toward the window behind her. The room faced on Tuxedo. For a moment, he thought she was going to turn and jump through the window.

"Meeshell, don't jump out and try to slide down the roof, okay? Please. Just don't do that."

"What kind of questions?"

"Were you with him when he OD'd last week?"

"No," she said, too fast. He knew she was lying. And he could tell that she knew he knew.

"Meeshell," he said, "his family's worried about him. They just want to know what happened."

A shout came from the back of the house outside, a male voice, loud and angry. Preuss turned his head at the sound, and in an instant she sprang toward him, knocking him off balance and leaping past him down the stairway.

He was up after her at once, but she was faster. She raced out the back door and slammed it shut at the back of the house. He heard a racket of cans and bottles and boxes as she burst through the back-yard.

He pushed through the back door into a mountain of trash in time to see Meeshell scrambling over the hurricane fence at the rear of the yard. The metal collapsed under her and she stumbled but kept going. She disappeared down the alley behind the house.

He followed. The alley was a forest of leggy weeds and mulberry trees. He saw her sprinting with a long stride toward Third Avenue. He chased her down the overgrown alley but when he got to the cross street she was gone.

He walked another block each way around the neighborhood, but he had lost her.

Meeshell and Ray Tomatoes had both outrun him. I must be losing my edge, Preuss thought.

Or maybe just getting too old for this anymore.

He returned to Tuxedo. He moved the Explorer two streets over and walked back to the house.

He checked out the rest of the building, basement to attic, and went back upstairs to the room where he found her. A makeshift sleeping pallet was on the floor, a folded blanket for a mattress, and clothes doubled up for a pillow. She had fled the house so quickly she left a tote bag filled with clothes and scattered identification cards— an expired driver's license in the name of Meeshell Lee, a State of Michigan Bridge Card in the same name allowing her access to social services, a battered Social Security card, and receipts for the White Castle in Ferndale and other fast food restaurants. The tote also held a textbook and a wire-bound notebook.

He also found $432 in cash, and a supply of capsules and a glassine envelope filled with powder.

He looked out the room window. No cars on Tuxedo.

He went back downstairs. Hoping she wouldn't abandon all the money and drugs, he waited for her to return.

And waited.

At five o'clock, he heard the front steps creaking. He slipped into the closet off the living room and peered out through a crack in the door. From his vantage point he couldn't see the front door, but he heard it ease open, and then tentative footsteps entered the house.

The form of a woman crossed his sightline as she walked slowly through the living room and into the dining room.

When he stepped from the closet, the woman cried out and whipped around with a small pistol pointed straight at him.

"Whoa," he said, and threw up his hands. "Don't shoot."

After a tense moment, the woman recognized him and lowered her weapon. "I almost blew your head off," Ramonda Hudgens said.

"Could you please put the gun away?"

She stowed it in her purse and he relaxed.

"Thank you," he said.

"Sorry," she said. "I make home visits in some unsavory places, so I have a CCW. Never shot anyone, but it helps to know it's there if I need it. Did you find Meeshell?"

"She was upstairs when I got here. I talked to her for a second, but she got by me and took off. I chased after her, but I lost her."

"Is Ray here?"

"I haven't seen him. Meeshell's stuff is upstairs, but it doesn't look like there's anybody else living here."

"I wonder where he is."

"Must have found another hidey-hole."

"I was sure they'd be together," she said.

"I was hoping she'd come back. There's a lot of money upstairs, and some drugs. I wouldn't think she'd walk away from all that."

"We can't leave it here," she said. "Kids break into these empty houses all the time."

She went upstairs and in a few minutes came back down with the tote bag. "All in here," she said.

She pulled her cell phone out of her purse and punched in a phone number.

"Nikki?" she said at last. "It's Ramonda. Yeah. Yeah. I'm at the house. Listen, she's not here. Have you seen her since we talked? I got her things."

She listened for a few moments, glancing at Preuss, then said, "Okay then. Okay. Tell her to stay put, will you? I'm coming over. Okay. Thanks, honey."

She disconnected and dropped the phone back into her purse. "She's at Nikki Bardellini's."

"Which is where?"

"Southfield."

"How'd she get there?"

"She drove. She's got this old beater of a car."

"I didn't see one in the driveway. She must have parked it away from the house."

"She got there a little while ago," Ramonda said. "And you might be interested in this: She said Meeshell's waiting for Ray Tomatoes to come and get her."

"You're right. I am."

"Are you going there?"

"Fast as I can," he said.

"Do you mind if I follow you?"

20

Nikki Bardellini lived in a Colonial on Templar Circle, the center of a series of concentric streets in the northern suburb of Southfield. The home had no visible activity . . . no cars in the driveway, no people out front, no sounds from the open windows.

Preuss knocked on the front door just as Ramonda pulled up behind his Explorer in her Focus.

She joined him on the front stoop and when no one answered his knock, he knocked again. Ramonda took out her cell and punched in numbers. A phone rang inside the house.

"Nikki," Ramonda said when the line was answered. "I'm out front. Where are you?"

The front door opened, and a woman stood there with a cell phone to her ear. She disconnected and stepped outside. She and Ramonda hugged. Preuss could see a slender man sitting in a wheelchair inside the dim house. He was not the same man Preuss saw at the Journey's End.

"Sweetie," Ramonda said to Nikki, "how you doing?"

"Same as ever."

"This is Martin Preuss. We both want to find Meeshell."

Nikki Bardellini gave him an unfriendly look. She was a short, heavy-set, pasty-faced woman whose black hair drawn back into a tight ponytail was badly thinning on top.

"Is she here?" Ramonda said.

"You just missed her," Nikki said. "She was waiting for Ray, but when he didn't show, she took off by herself. Told me to tell him she'd catch up with him at the usual place."

The usual place . . . where was that? Preuss didn't think they'd risk going back to the motel. So where was the usual place?

"What did she mean by that?" he asked.

Nikki Bardellini ignored him.

"She was antsy to get away," she continued, speaking only to Ramonda. "I asked her to stay and let me make her a bite to eat—I don't think she's eaten for a couple of days, she looks awful. But she didn't want to wait that long."

"Did she have any money?" Ramonda asked.

"She didn't ask me for any. But I saw her take a few checks from my checkbook. She won't get very far on that."

Ramonda shook her head. "That poor girl. Just getting in deeper and deeper."

Preuss said nothing more, since Nikki was ignoring him, but nodded to Ramonda and stepped off the porch and returned to his car.

"Call me if you hear from them, okay?" Ramonda said.

"Are you gonna tell *him*?" Preuss heard Nikki ask.

"Just call me, okay?"

"Sorry," Ramonda said. "Wild goose chase."

"No," Preuss said, "it's fine. I appreciate your help." He stood with his arms folded beside the Explorer, examining the Bardellini house for signs of movement.

"So I guess you're back to looking for her again?"

"You really think she's gone?" he asked.

"Why? You think she's in there?"

"I get a funny vibe from Nikki. Like she wouldn't be so quick to tell me the truth."

"I've known her for a long time," Ramonda said. "I don't think she'd lie to me."

"Maybe. Think I'll keep an eye on the house for a while, see if anything happens."

"I guess you know best."

He nodded. "I'll find her. Matter of time."

"If I hear anything else, I'll let you know."

"Thanks. Appreciate your help."

"Sorry about Nikki's attitude," she said.

"Not a problem."

"Probably thought you were a cop."

"Yeah," Preuss said, "I get that a lot."

21

Toby was sitting up in his chair by the time Preuss got to the group home. He wasn't snoozing, but sitting comfortably, breathing softly and steadily, listening to Arlo Guthrie and Pete Seeger on one of their concert albums.

Toby had met Arlo after one of his concerts, when the performer came out on stage to sign autographs. Preuss was waiting for the crowd to thin so he could get Toby into his wheelchair, when he saw people collecting around the empty stage. Soon Arlo came out and sat on the edge and began signing programs. Preuss pushed Toby up to the stage in his wheelchair, and got his picture taken with Arlo; the framed photo hung on the wall in Toby's room.

When he heard his father, Toby smiled broadly, showing the goofy little gap between his two front teeth. Preuss leaned over the chair and wrapped the boy in a long hug.

He had spent an hour watching the Bardellini house, but nobody went in or out. He texted Rhonda Citron to ask her to go back over Meeshell's records and see if she had a car registered to her. He wished he knew Ray Tomatoes's real name—the car might be registered to him. But for now he had to confine himself to Meeshell.

His conversation with Antoinette Lee that morning was déjà vu for Martin Preuss. Like Meeshell, his older son Jason would be picked up periodically for drug offenses and petty crime as he wandered across the country. Preuss had developed a network of police contacts, primarily in the west, so he could keep track of the boy's brushes with the law.

Unlike Meeshell's mother, Preuss would not have said he didn't want to see his son again. Preuss hoped Jason would circle back into his and Toby's orbit when he was ready.

And if not . . . well, as Antoinette Lee had said, you can't make them.

But in the meantime he had Toby, sweet, beautiful Toby. Preuss didn't know anyone who loved his life, and the people in it, as much as Toby did. Whenever Preuss took his son anywhere, Toby always had the best time of anyone. As much as he could, he tried to learn Toby's joy of living from his son and practice it in his life. But it came so much easier to Toby, an old soul (as a psychic once called him).

Preuss had not eaten since lunch, and was now feeling overcome with hunger. "Hey," he said, "how'd you like to go out to dinner tonight?"

Toby didn't eat by mouth; he was fed with a G-tube directly into his belly. But he loved to go anywhere with his father, and he especially loved to go to a restaurant. The constant hubbub of voices, knives and forks clacking, and plates crashing into dishwashing tubs was music to his ears.

Toby was all dressed, so Preuss used the overhead lift to get him into his wheelchair and told the staff they were going out for a bite to eat. The night was cool but humid as they walked up the residential streets through Toby's neighborhood in Berkley to Twelve Mile Road. There they turned east and walked down the shopping district to O'Mara's, an Irish restaurant at the corner of Coolidge.

Outside was a fountain, which made Toby laugh because it sounded like his bath (his favorite thing in the world). As always whenever they returned to a restaurant where they had been before, the host remembered Toby and welcomed him with an extravagant greeting, which Toby returned.

The server, whose name badge read Karma, took one of the chairs away so Preuss could push Toby right up against the table in his wheelchair. Preuss ordered iced tea and fish and chips, and explained that Toby didn't eat anything by mouth. Karma was a young dark-haired woman with a deep, throaty voice and floral tattoos along her arms, and had never taken care of them before. She gave Toby a little moue of sympathy and bent down so her face was even with his.

"Nothing?" she said. "Not even a little taste?"

"When he eats anything, he has a tendency to aspirate his food," Preuss said. "Leads to pneumonia."

"Aww," the woman said, and rested a hand on Toby's shoulder and gave him a quick kiss on the top of his head, then looked quickly at Preuss to see if she had overstepped.

"I think you made a friend, Toby," Preuss said, to reassure her all was well.

Toby gazed up at her with a crooked, flirtatious grin.

"You sure have," said Karma, who gave Preuss a wide smile and glided away.

Toby looked around. Where did she go? his look said. Preuss was reminded that Toby's vision was getting worse. For a long time the doctors said Toby had only peripheral vision, out of the corners of his eyes. But now even this was decaying as Toby's optic nerve deteriorated steadily each year.

Karma returned with Preuss's drink and gave Toby another pat on the shoulder. When she left them alone again, Preuss leaned forward and began telling Toby about his latest cases. His son attended closely. It was impossible to tell what the boy understood, but Preuss had always believed it was best to assume he understood everything but couldn't articulate replies. Though Toby made appropriate vocalizations—"Oooh" and "Aaah" and "Mmmm"—as Preuss went deeper into the cases. It was a way to help him get his thoughts together about his days.

Karma brought Preuss's meal, along with a bowl of vanilla ice cream, which she placed in front of Toby. "I know you said he can't eat," she said, "but I thought maybe he could just get a taste? On his lips? He wouldn't have to swallow."

"That's very thoughtful of you," Preuss said. "I'll try it."

That was enough for Karma. She gave him another bright smile and left them alone.

"Oh, Toby," Preuss said. "People just don't believe me. Sorry, honey, but you can't have this."

At one time, Preuss tried giving Toby tastes of ice cream, chocolate, and other treats. But because the boy had repeated bouts of aspiration pneumonia, Toby's health providers strongly recommended that he get nothing by mouth, not even a slight taste on his lips.

When Preuss finished his fish and chips, and Karma came over to ask if they needed anything else, she noticed the melting dish of ice cream and said, "Didn't he like it?"

"It was a little too cold for him," Preuss lied, so Karma wouldn't feel bad.

"Oh, sorry." She knelt down again beside Toby. "Sorry, handsome."

Toby's flirtatious gap-toothed smile told her he harbored no hard feelings.

It was still light out when Preuss pushed Toby in his wheelchair out of the restaurant. Toby hummed all the way back to his group home, and Preuss joined him, adjusting his tone to Toby's in such a way that they performed a sort of call-and-response all the way down Twelve Mile to Toby's street, and then to his group home.

Toby's housemate Katy was getting her own bath, so Preuss pushed Toby down to his room and got him in bed with the overhead lift. Preuss took the boy's clothes off and laid a bath towel over him until the bathtub was free.

Preuss looked around the room. He had set it up for Toby when he was sixteen, so it reflected the world of a teenager, with posters from the concerts that Preuss and Toby had gone to—mostly artists that Preuss himself was interested in, and thought Toby would like based on the CDs he listened to. Judy Collins, Arlo Guthrie, Los Lobos, the Chieftains . . .

There was nothing wrong with these for a young man's room. Preuss himself had not put up any posters or decorations at all in the room he grew up in at his parents' home in Ypsilanti; he never felt at home enough there to want to personalize it, even with posters of the musical groups he loved. But as he sat looking around, Preuss felt the urge to change things, to create a new environment for Toby with different kinds of stimulation suitable for the young adult he was becoming.

The question was, how to decorate the room. It wasn't like Toby could tell him what he wanted.

Because Toby couldn't communicate verbally, Preuss never knew if Toby was happier with routines he could count on, or with changing and challenging surroundings. Preuss wasn't sure if his son could actually see the posters on the wall or not, with his profound visual impairments; he might not have even realized what was on the walls. Maybe this was all for Preuss's own benefit.

No matter. He knew nothing would be lost by assuming the best for Toby's abilities, and everything to be gained. Otherwise, Toby would wind up staring at blank walls, as Preuss himself had done growing up. Except Toby's disabilities would keep him even more isolated than Preuss had been. No, Toby needed as much stimulation as possible, not only visual but aural as well.

Katy's aide stuck her head in the doorway. "Tub's free," she said.

Preuss got bare-naked Toby back in his wheelchair and pushed him into the bathroom, where he used another overhead lift to swing Toby out of his wheelchair and into the tub.

Where he screamed, chortled, and chirped in absolute delight as his father gave him his bath and shampoo. And, after that, a good long soak with the bathtub's jets. With dreamy, half-closed eyes, Toby floated in the frothy water until his father had to hold him down on his bath chair with a gentle hand.

Back in his room, Preuss dried his son off and dressed him in an extra-large tee shirt with an image of the original album cover of "Alice's Restaurant," with an impossibly young Arlo Guthrie sitting at a table with a napkin stuck to his bare chest. Preuss played a few songs on the twenty-dollar garage-sale guitar he kept in Toby's room. After that, Preuss found an old episode of *Law and Order* on Toby's television and they watched it together, and then Preuss put Judy Collins on the CD player, kissed his drowsy son goodnight, and went home.

There he played his red Les Paul for another hour, took a shower, and got into bed.

But he couldn't stop thinking, and wound up replaying the day's events in his head.

He thought of Antoinette Lee and her own sorrow, and thought again of the ubiquity of sadness in the world. He had once heard Frank Zappa say that stupidity, like hydrogen, was one of the building blocks of the universe. But Preuss thought the real building block was sadness. Not even suffering, as the Buddhists thought, but pure sorrow. Loss was universal, and the opposite of the sadness that followed in its wake was the tiny pilot light of joy that allowed Toby to be happy and other people to carry on in the face of all the death, all the grief, all the people—the Jasons, the Meeshells, the Greg Braidens—who disappeared from our lives by the day.

And Toby, like a keeper of that small flame, transmitted it to all who came near. And while Preuss could not, by any stretch of the imagination, be called joyful, his contacts with Toby did lift his heart, and so he made as many of them as he could.

Thoughts of Toby comforted him for the rest of the night.

Friday, September 21, 2012

22

After stopping by Toby's house in the morning to help get his son (who was noisy and wide awake) ready for his school program, Preuss continued on to the office.

There he checked his emails, then sat with Manny and Rhonda in the reception area drinking the coffee that Rhonda prepared every morning to Manny's exacting standards.

Spending a half-hour like this every Friday morning had become a sort of a ritual for them. Rhonda suggested it the month before, and Manny and Preuss both embraced it. Manny commented that the time felt as if it were their reward for making it through another week.

Manny raised his white mug. He only drank his coffee from a white ceramic mug, insisting it had been scientifically proven that a white mug intensified the flavor of coffee.

He also drank it black, no cream or sweetener. "You wouldn't put ice cubes in a fine wine, would you?" he would ask, "so why adulterate a fine cup of coffee?" Preuss, who had been sober for seven years, always left that question alone.

"Nice brew today," Manny told Rhonda.

Preuss held up his own mug in agreement. Though in truth he couldn't perceive the same nuances in taste that Manny could, he agreed this was good coffee.

"Thank you," Rhonda said.

They sat in silence, savoring their drinks.

"So, Rhonda," Manny said, "how are your plans?"

"Plans?" Preuss said.

"You missed coffee time last Friday," Rhonda said. "Manny was asking about my plans for the future. Apparently, he doesn't think I'm putting my talents to good enough use here."

"I never said that," Manny pointed out. "We both value you tremendously."

"Absolutely," Preuss agreed.

"I just want to make sure you're not being stifled by the work, that's all."

The year before, she had suffered another of the breakdowns that derailed her career in law school. And while she seemed mostly recovered, Manny—her uncle—had often spoken to Preuss about his concern for her fragility.

"Going back to law school, going back to school for something else entirely, marrying a millionaire—admittedly the lowest possibility since there aren't any candidates in the frame—I'm in no hurry for any of that right now," Rhonda said. "I'm happy as a clam right here, doing exactly what I'm doing."

Manny raised his mug of coffee and toasted that sentiment.

"And we're very happy to have you here," he said. There was a "but" that all three understood would remain unspoken.

They chatted more about the cases moving through the agency, savored their coffees, and, as though at a signal, ended their impromptu break and turned back to their work. Rhonda made a call; Manny went into his office and closed his door; Preuss filled up his cup one more time and took it into his office.

He stood and gazed out the window behind his desk. This is nice, he thought. He had missed the sense of community he lost when he left the police force, but sitting with Manny and Rhonda like this helped buoy him.

He opened the file on his computer and reviewed his notes to think his way back into Braiden's life. His search for Meeshell had taken up most of the past few days; his investigation into Greg Braiden's background had receded.

Preuss had spoken with Braiden's sister, ex-wife, boss, best friend at work, and one of the two close friends outside work, Adam

Sandford. He still had not spoken with Roger Garland, but what the others told Preuss about Greg Braiden was remarkably consistent. They all described a man who seemed happy and comfortable in his life, but who had a side that was secretive and aloof. He seemed to allow no one, not even the two women who were closest to him, into his innermost thoughts—if, indeed, he had any.

And yet he had been found in dire circumstances. How did he get there? That was the question Carrie Morrison had hired him to answer, and Preuss wasn't sure he was much closer to knowing the answer. None of Braiden's friends or family had any idea that he had another life at the Journey's End.

From a certain perspective, Greg Braiden was exactly the kind of guy who might be tempted by life on the down-low . . . he seemed to be clean-living, regular in his habits, organized, maybe vulnerable because of his wife's infidelity and lonely in the aftermath of his divorce, despite having done everything else right in his life . . . maybe what Meeshell Lee offered was so foreign and so enticing that he couldn't resist it.

Preuss remembered a line he had read in a play by Oscar Wilde: "I can resist everything except temptation." Did that explain the attraction of the life Meeshell offered Greg Braiden?

And where did Ray Tomatoes fit in? Who was he? His connection was to Meeshell. Was he her boyfriend? Her pimp?

And why was Jake Aklawi so interested in him? Why did he want to speak with Ray Tomatoes? (Assuming Tomatoes was the one Aklawi wanted Press to find.) Was it really to get him out of his motel (which Preuss doubted), or was there another reason?

Were they competitors in supplying drugs and women? With Aklawi's power and reach, Preuss thought he would be able to accomplish whatever he wanted, including removing Tomatoes. So why was Aklawi asking Preuss to find him?

The thought of Aklawi reminded Preuss of Victor, Aklawi's driver. Preuss didn't believe Victor had done his worst yet; he was certain Victor would make another run at him.

For now, though, the first order of business was getting back to the mystery of Braiden's character. And the next thing he had to do was get in touch with Roger Garland for his take on Braiden. Garland's wife said he was a psychologist; maybe he would have a different insight into Braiden's character, or knew something the others didn't.

He called the cell phone number Garland's wife had given him.

Garland picked up on the second ring.

His wife had told him all about Preuss and what he wanted. "Sure," Garland said, "happy to talk with you. The thing is, though, we're going up north later today. We have a house in Ludington, up near Traverse City. We usually go for the weekend. But I can see you before we go. Say around four?"

Preuss told him that worked. It would mean he'd again have to miss helping his son off the bus, but since Garland was so hard to nail down, Preuss had to make the appointment.

He read through his notes yet again, adding details and inserting comments and questions as he went along.

He stopped when his two o'clock appointment came in. Beverly Frankel, the college student who had hired the agency to confirm rumors in their family that they were related to members of the Purple Gang.

She was a short, stout young woman in a long black skirt with a crinkled pattern and a blue cashmere sweater. She had a round face and a reddish page boy that may have been a wig, since she had dark black hair tied back into a pony tail the last time he saw her, when she came to the agency for her first visit.

He invited her into his office, and she sat down and he closed the door.

"So," she said without preliminaries, "what did you find?"

"Your family lore was correct," he said. "You are related to members of the Purple Gang."

She laughed and clapped her hands. "I knew it!"

He told her what he had done and how he had found the connections. He told her about Sarah Posner, and what the older woman had said in her Boston-Edison home.

"I've heard of her," Beverly said. "She's my grandmother's sister, I think. We lost touch with that whole side of the family before my parents died. I didn't even know she was still alive."

"It gets complicated from here," Preuss said. "Sarah's husband was named Morris. Morris's father had a sister, and the sister had a son named Isadore Adler. Izzie had a cousin on his dad's side named Leon Glick. Izzie and Leon were Purples."

She listened closely. Preuss remembered he had intended to draw a consanguinity chart for her, until he got sidetracked by the Braiden case.

"I'm not sure what that makes me to them," she said.

"I'll leave that to you to figure out. Strictly speaking, they're not blood relations. But yes, they're part of your extended family."

"Well, that's wonderful!" she said, smiling. "You've finally proved the connections!"

"I have. But," he added, "I'm not sure this is anything to be proud of. Do you know about the Purple Gang?"

"I know they were a gang of tough Jews in Detroit around Prohibition," she said with pride. "And now I know I'm related to them."

"That's true. But they weren't just tough. They were brutal, violent criminals. These two, in particular. They were the enforcers. They kidnapped and killed people. They burned down people's stores. They hired themselves out as hitmen for the Italian mob at the time. They were not nice people."

"Wow." She listened, open-mouthed. He could almost read her thoughts: *I'm related to gangsters—nerdy, frumpy me, with tough guys in my family.*

"My mother always told me it was just a family legend, that we were related to the Purple Gang. I wished she lived long enough to find this out. I'm all alone, Mr. Preuss—all the rest of my family are dead. The ones I know about, I mean."

She laughed again.

"Well, thank you *so much*," she said. "This is wonderful!"

Okay, Preuss thought. I see I'm not getting across.

"There's one more thing," he said. "When I spoke with Sarah Posner, she expressed a desire to meet you."

"I would *totally* love that!"

"I told her I'd find out your schedule and set a time up for you both."

"That's so *cool*!"

"So why don't you text me a couple of dates and times when you'd be free."

"I *will*. Oh," she said, and clapped her hands in glee. "I've got a *family*! And a *history*!"

When she left, he sat for a while, thinking about her pride in being related to tough Jews. From what he knew of the Purples, they weren't the kind of ancestors anyone should be proud of. He guessed her romanticizing of the past was more a comment on her own present than a reflection of any virtues she imagined the Purples may have had.

He hoped Sarah Posner would be able to get through to her.

From there his thoughts meandered to Jake Aklawi, whose situation might be the modern equivalent of the Purples . . . a group of immigrants turning to crime to gain the influence and power they were denied by the larger society.

And more than that, they used the outlawed vices of the day as the basis of their crimes. For the Purples it was alcohol smuggling during prohibition; for the Chaldean gangs, it was drug distribution.

Capitalism practiced at its logical extreme.

Thought Martin Preuss, Marxist.

Not that this sociological explanation excused either group. But it was an interesting parallel.

Were there others?

This is not my job, Preuss thought. Providing sociological explanations of crime in society is something better left to experts.

He straightened the files on his desk and went to meet Roger Garland.

23

A glass of iced tea sweated on a coaster on the polished wooden stump that served as the coffee table in the Garland living room. Roger Garland offered Preuss a glass, but he declined.

Garland was big and bulky but soft-looking, doughy, with a homely oval face and thinning mouse-colored hair. A fine network of wrinkles spread across a high forehead. He wore a close-cropped greying Van Dyke.

He sat on the sofa with an arm thrown casually over the back and his ankle crossed over his knee. "This is a really terrible thing," he said.

"You and Greg are close?" Preuss asked.

"We used to be." His voice was deep and earnest, and he seemed to enjoy the sound of it. "Like brothers. Lately, we've both been so busy, we haven't seen much of each other."

"I heard you play volleyball together every week."

Garland grinned. "Used to. Maybe they still do, Greg and the others. But I've just been too busy to take the time. I missed the last couple of weeks."

"The others?"

"Greg, Ryan Bennett, and Adam Sandford. Greg and Adam and I go back a long way—we went to Cranbrook together—but Ryan's a new addition. Greg met him through work and we adopted him into the pack."

Cranbrook was an exclusive boarding prep school in Bloomfield Hills. Mentioning it was intended to be akin to the effect of letting drop that you went to University of Michigan—you were supposed to yield to their elitist superiority. That's why people who went to either school told you about it within the first five minutes of meeting you.

"When was the last time you saw Greg Braiden?"

Garland looked off into the house, where noises came from upstairs, the sound of drawers opening and doors closing. Garland explained it was his wife, preparing for their trip north.

"Tell you the truth, it's been weeks."

Preuss waited.

"I think the last time was at one of our volleyball games, as a matter of fact. Back in August."

"Not since?"

"No. As I said, I've missed a few games."

"You haven't talked on the phone?"

"No."

"When you saw him, how did he seem?"

"Maybe a bit distracted."

"Distracted how?"

"As if his mind wasn't on the game. It's all for fun anyway, right? But yeah, that last time he seemed to be someplace else."

"To your knowledge, has he ever used drugs?"

Garland shifted uncomfortably on the sofa. "He did go through a period when he went a little wild."

Adam Sandford had said Greg went through a period of drug use in high school, but didn't mention it being "wild."

"Can you say more about that?"

"His parents died when we were in Cranbrook."

"I heard about that."

"We were boarding students—well, Greg and Adam boarded. I was there on a scholarship, so I lived at home. Right after his parents died is when he went a little crazy. Sex, drugs, and rock and roll—you know, the usual teen-aged stuff. Even back then, we all knew he was just trying to deal with his grief. Self-medicating by acting out. It was hard on his grandparents. That's where he lived after the accident."

"How long did his crazy period last?"

"Less than a year. He settled right down. And he's been calm ever since."

"No relapses?"

"Not to my knowledge."

"Were you using drugs along with him back then?"

"Why is that relevant?"

"Just a question."

Garland smirked. "It was Cranbrook in the eighties. We all smoked dope."

"Anything stronger?"

"Me? Never. Greg, well, Greg would try whatever you put in front of him, whether you smoked it, snorted it, or swallowed it. He never used a needle, though. And I quit entirely when I went off to U of M."

Cranbrook, U of M: check one and two.

"You heard where he was found?" Preuss asked. "And how?"

"Yes."

"In your conversations, did he ever mention that motel? The Journey's End?"

"Never. I can't fathom what he was doing there."

"Does the name Meeshell Lee mean anything to you?" Preuss asked.

Garland considered it. The fine wrinkles on his forehead deepened. "No. Should it?"

"Greg never mentioned her?"

"Not in my hearing."

"How about a guy who calls himself Ray Tomatoes?"

"Never heard of him. Who are they?"

"A couple of people Greg might have been involved with. Your wife said you're a psychologist, Mr. Garland?"

"It's Dr. Garland. Yes, I'm in private practice."

"I've been finding hints that Greg might have been leading a sort of double life. Do you have any insight into that?"

"Insight?"

"Meeshell and Ray seem to be connected with some illegal activity. I'm looking for the reason Greg got involved with people like that."

Garland shifted, uncrossed his legs, sat straighter. His professional acumen was being summoned.

He thought for a few moments, then said, in his deep, calm, shrink's voice, "Since I've never seen any indication that he even knows these people, and I don't know anything about them myself, I can't really offer an 'insight.' As for him living a double life, as you call it?" He shrugged. "Again, I haven't seen any evidence that he's anything other than what he appears to be."

"Which is?"

"A well-adjusted single man who's had heartache in his life, as we all have, but who seems to function normally, for the most part."

"And he never confided in you about anything, correct?"

"That's correct."

"Okay," Preuss said. "Anything else you can tell me that might be helpful?"

"Only that I wish you the best of luck." *Because you'll need it* went unsaid.

"We're doing our best," Preuss said, and stood.

Garland followed Preuss to the front door. Inside the house, a phone rang.

They shook hands on the front stoop, and Garland said, "We're all sort of shocked by this whole thing."

Preuss nodded, and as he turned toward the front steps, he heard Garland's wife saying, sharply, from the top of the stairs inside, "Roger. It's for you. One of your students."

Garland gave Preuss a final nod and went inside.

Before returning to his office, Preuss drove past the Tuxedo house in Highland Park. It still looked deserted, even forlorn. But then, it had looked deserted when he found Meeshell there, too.

He parked up the street and walked back. The front door was still unlocked. He paused in the living room and tried to send feelers through the building to sense if anybody was there.

He sensed nothing, so he went through the building, beginning on the second floor and ending in the basement. Nothing seemed changed since his last visit—same garbage in the living room, same temporary sleeping arrangements in the room where he had discovered Meeshell.

He knocked on the doors of surrounding homes, but no one answered.

Back at his office, he called Antoinette Lee and Ramonda Hudgens, but neither had heard anything from Meeshell.

For the moment, she was in the wind.

Preuss spent a quiet evening with Toby, going for a long walk around the neighborhood and then watching most of the first *Lord of the Rings* on a DVD until Toby drifted off to sleep.

Rather than wake him up for his bath, Preuss and Toby's aide transferred him to his bed and gently got him undressed and into his pajamas. His son was still asleep by the time Preuss pulled the cover up to Toby's neck and turned the overhead light out and drove home.

There he put Dylan's *Blood on the Tracks* on the CD in the living room and laid on the sofa. Maybe listening to the raw emotional lyrics of Dylan's comeback album from the seventies isn't the best idea in my current state, he cautioned himself. But the tangled tales of mixed connections throughout the album wound up calming him. They reminded him of what was happening now with Janey Cahill, and helped him get distance on it. He wasn't the only one going through this. Some of the lines in the songs exactly reflected his own feelings.

Until "You're Gonna Make Me Lonesome When You Go" came on. That track was too much for him, hit too close to the bone in the bubble of loneliness he lived within.

He rose, turned off the CD, and went upstairs to bed.

Saturday, September 22, 2012

24

Preuss woke in a pool of sweat in the middle of a dream where he couldn't find his way out of a vast hotel. It was a variation of a recurring dream; he would be lost in an expansive space, often an empty basement, or, like now, it was recognizable as a hotel. The common theme was being lost in a mystifying structure from which he was unable to exit.

It took a while before he was able to distinguish between the dream and his reality. Once he was reasonably sure the dream was over, he showered, dressed, and went downstairs. Saturday was his day to go to breakfast with Toby.

Their Saturday tradition was breakfast at the Big Boy on John R in Madison Heights. After a quick cup of coffee when he woke up, Preuss would pick up Toby—who was, depending on what kind of night he had, either up and raring to go, or still snoozing—and father and son would make their way to the restaurant, where all the servers knew them. Even if he was asleep when they started out, Toby would be wide-awake by the time they got to their table, and would add his own foghorn voice and high squeals of laughter to the commotion of the restaurant.

So it was today.

He called the group home to find out whether Toby was awake or not.

The nurse who answered the phone told him Toby had been up since six, talking and laughing to himself.

"Tell him I'll be over soon," Preuss said. "And then we'll do our breakfast."

"He's all ready for you," the nurse said. "He's had all his lotions and potions for the morning. He's clean and dressed and waiting for his dad."

Preuss made a cup of coffee to take with him. While the coffee brewed, he remembered this was the day that Tommy Cahill was supposed to move out. He wondered if that was still the plan, and—for the four-hundredth time—what it would mean for him and Janey. He could not have said what he hoped would happen, but he thought he might give her a call later on to see how the move went.

Meantime, he decided to take a break from the Braiden case, at least for the day. He would let it percolate in the background; it would still be there when he was ready to get back to it.

At breakfast, Toby was particularly chatty. As he babbled away, Preuss asked questions periodically as if Toby were actually saying words, and the two had a lively conversation that amused the waitresses and puzzled the patrons who surrounded them, casting Toby wondering looks for being so talkative yet incomprehensible.

Preuss let Toby talk. He loved to hear the sounds his son made, loved to interpret them as genuine communication efforts. Loved to respond.

After breakfast, he had weekend errands to run—grocery shopping, banking—and he took Toby along, lifting the boy out of the car and into his wheelchair at each stop, hanging the bags of groceries on the handles of the wheelchair, pushing Toby companionably in and out of stores.

Preuss stopped at his house in Ferndale so he could put away the groceries, and then they went to Luxury Lanes, the bowling alley on Nine Mile in Ferndale a few blocks down from the Shanahan Law Enforcement Complex, the police station where Preuss spent his career.

Bowling was not Preuss's favorite sport (was not in his top hundred favorite sports, in fact) but back when the family was still together, they all used to go bowling. Jason loved to bowl, with a wild gangly follow-through when he released the ball. Even Toby liked to bowl. The alley had a special metal ramp for use with wheelchairs; Preuss would line up the ramp in front of the chair, aim it down the alley, place the ball on top of the ramp, and then take Toby's tight fist and push the ball off the ramp. If the ramp were properly positioned, Toby could get a strike. When that happened, everybody around him cheered, and Toby cheered, too.

By the time they got to the alley, the Saturday leagues were finished and only a few lanes were in use. Preuss bowled along with Toby, and (no surprise) Toby beat him, 94 to 57. Toby got three strikes and picked up two spares, to his great delight.

They left the dark cool of the bowling alley and walked out into the milky light of a mild fall day. Preuss took Toby back to the Ferndale house, and they lounged out on the rear deck while Toby snoozed and Preuss faded into and out of a nap.

Every so often, he remembered his intention to call Janey Cahill. Somehow, that call never got made.

At four o'clock, Preuss hooked up Toby for his feeding outside, and brought a boombox onto the deck so they could listen to *Blood on the Tracks*.

He kept Toby with him until shortly before eight, when they drove back to the group home and he gave his son a bath. Then Preuss and one of the aides got Toby ready for bed and Preuss put on the DVD of the part of *Lord of the Rings* Toby had missed because he fell asleep. Toby stayed awake for the rest of the movie, then conked out as soon as it was over.

Preuss kissed his son good night and drove home.

On the way, he drove past Janey Cahill's home in the Dales neighborhood of Ferndale, south of Nine Mile. Janey's pickup truck was in the driveway but the rest of the house was dark. Probably the boys were at their father's new crib, if he actually had moved. Which meant Janey would be home alone. Asleep? On the back porch? Watching the big screen television in the basement?

He sat idling in the Explorer for another ten minutes. If there had been any sign of life in the house, he would have gone up and knocked on the door. Of course, you can always try her cell phone, he told himself, but something stopped him, a feeling that if Tommy had moved out, she might need time alone to get used to the idea.

There was no activity anywhere in the house, so he continued on toward his own place, Dylan's "Tangled Up in Blue" playing in his head.

It would be the last quiet day he would have for a while.

Sunday, September 23, 2012

25

The ring of his cell phone brought him out of a deep sleep.

"Mr. Preuss!"

A woman's voice. Loud. Frantic.

As his brain cleared, he realized it was Carrie Morrison.

"Mr. Preuss, are you there?"

"Carrie? What's wrong?"

"It's me. Oh god. I've been up all night. I'm shaking."

"What's the matter?"

"I got a phone call late last night."

"Last night?" He looked at the time on the digital alarm clock on his nightstand. 9:32 a.m. "Who from?"

"I was so scared. The man on the phone told me he knows where I live. Where my children live."

Preuss didn't even know she had children.

"Who was it? What did he want?"

"He didn't tell me his name. But he threatened me. He told me to drop the investigation into Greg, or terrible things would happen to me and my kids. Then again this morning, I got another call. He told me he knows where my children go to school, and I'd regret it if I didn't make you stop."

"Stop the investigation?"

"Yes. He never told me his name. He just said he knew all about my brother."

"But it was definitely a man."

"Yes. Mr. Preuss," she said, "I'm frightened for my children."

She met him at the agency office. At first she was too scared to leave her house, but he convinced her to come.

The building was deserted, as he knew it would be on Sunday morning. He made a pot of coffee in Rhonda's machine and stood at the window waiting for Carrie Morrison to arrive.

She roared into the lot and pulled up next to his SUV. She waited before exiting her car, looking around to satisfy herself no one was waiting for her. When she saw him wave from the window, she raced out of the car and into the building.

She was trembling with fear when she got inside the reception area. "Lock the door," she said. "Please."

He did as she asked and led her into his office.

"Have a seat," he said. "Any trouble getting here?"

She shook her head.

"All right. Let's talk about this."

In response, she laid a copy of the metro section of the *Sunday Free Press* on his desk. She pointed a finger at a story below the fold. The headline read, "Body Found on East Side."

He skimmed the piece. The body of an unidentified man was discovered on the east side of Detroit.

He looked up at her. "I don't understand."

She tapped the newspaper. "That's them!"

"Who?"

"Those people," she said. "Those people you were talking about. From that motel."

"Meeshell Lee and Ray Tomatoes?"

"Yes. He was the one who called me, I'm sure of it. They were the ones who did this." She pounded the newspaper.

"How do you know that? I thought you said you didn't know who called you."

"I did. But then I saw this in the paper. This morning he said they were going to do something that would make me know how serious they were. This must be what he was talking about. How did they know you were investigating them?"

"It wasn't a secret. I talked about it with Meeshell. She knew I was looking for answers. But we don't even know who this is. How can it have anything to do with your brother? People turning up dead in Detroit isn't exactly rare. The chances are, this is completely unconnected."

"How can it not be connected?"

He read through the newspaper story again. "Carrie," he said, "the police don't even know who this is."

"But do you hear what I'm saying? That man *threatened* me. He said if I didn't call you off, they were going to hurt my children. And I told you—he said they were going to do something to show me they weren't kidding."

"I understand you're frightened," Preuss said, "and I can see how you'd think there's a connection. But until we know who this is and what even happened to—"

"There's another thing," she broke in. "The man on the phone, he said if I didn't pay him $10,000, they're going to tell the world my brother is a drug dealer."

"If they knew about your brother and drugs," he admitted, "that's an indication it could be Ray. Has anything been in the paper about your brother? Or how he was found?"

"No. Not that I've seen, anyway."

"So how did they know to call you?" he asked, more to himself than to her. "Your brother must have mentioned you to Meeshell, and she told Ray."

"Either that or they're watching me. And my children."

"Even so," he said, "it's a long way from a phone call threatening extortion to murder. Blackmail isn't a violent crime. It doesn't attract violent people."

However they knew to call Carrie—and Meeshell and Ray seemed to be the prime suspects—their connection to the murder of a John Doe wasn't anywhere near certain.

"Did they say how you're supposed to pay?"

"In cash. He said he'd be in touch."

"There's a chance this might be a ruse. But let me know as soon as you hear anything more from him. Where are your children now?"

"I dropped them off with my ex-in-laws. I didn't want them around the house right now."

"Good. Here's what we'll do. Give me their address and we'll get someone over there to make sure your kids are okay right now. Then we'll get some security for you and your house. I'll try and find out what's going on with those two from the motel. Why don't you have a seat in the outer office and let me make a few calls. We'll get you and your kids protected. Don't worry, okay?"

She nodded her appreciation and wrote out her in-laws' address.

"Calming down a little?" he asked.

"Yes."

She stood. "I'm sorry I was so upset when I called."

"Don't worry about it. The thing we have to do now is make sure you and your family are safe. Is your kids' father around?"

"No," she said, without elaborating.

"Make yourself comfortable in the reception area. There's coffee out there if you want it."

"I'm already a bundle of nerves."

She went out to sit on the sofa in Rhonda's area. His first call was to Manny Greene.

"Hey," he said, "it's Martin. Sorry to bother you, but we have a situation."

He explained what was going on, and Manny said he would jump on arranging for operatives to watch Carrie Morrison's home and the home of her in-laws. "Leave it to me," he told Preuss.

Preuss's next call was to an old friend, Alonzo Barber, to find out about the John Doe who Carrie was so worried about. Barber was a Detroit PD homicide detective Preuss had worked with on a case a few years ago. They had gotten friendly but had lost contact after Preuss left the Ferndale force.

The call went right to voicemail, so Preuss left a message asking him to call back as soon as possible.

Manny called him back to let him know what arrangements he had made. Preuss waited for Barber to return his call, and when he had waited for another twenty minutes, he decided to close up the office and followed Carrie back to her home in Bloomfield Hills. A man was parked in an Equinox idling in front of her house when she pulled into the driveway. She stayed in her car while Preuss parked behind the man and approached the car.

The driver's side door opened and out stepped one of Manny's contract operatives, Carlos Guevara. He was big and broad, wearing a Lions cap turned backwards. They shook hands and Preuss flashed a thumb's-up to Carrie. Carrie exited her car and rushed up the front walk and let herself into her house.

"Got here fast," Preuss said.

"Soon as Manny called me. I don't live too far, so . . ."

Preuss led Guevara up to the front door and introduced him to Carrie. Guevara made a quick circuit of the house to ensure nobody else was there. He came down the stairs from the second floor and gave Preuss a nod. "I'll be outside, Mrs. Morrison," he said. He gave her a business card. "This has my cell number on it. Call me immediately if you need me. Or just give me a shout out the door. Don't worry—we're not going to let anything happen to you or your family."

She took his card and stuck it in the pocket of her jeans, and Guevara returned to his car.

"I know him," Preuss told her. "He's a good man. Ex-cop, works for a security firm my partner contracts with when he needs more help. You can trust him with your life."

Carrie Morrison said, "I'm not sure I'm in a trusting mood right now, but if you say so."

"I do."

"What do we do now?"

"Now you stay put. Call Grandma and Grandpa and tell them to bring your kids home. Another one of Manny's operatives should be there already. He'll follow them home to make sure nothing happens to them."

"What are you going to do?"

"I'll keep trying to get ahold of my contact with the Detroit Police. I'll let him know about Meeshell and Ray Tomatoes, and see if he knows anything about this John Doe. We'll try to set your mind at ease about that."

"I'm so sorry about this, I can't even begin to tell you."

"It's not on you."

She nodded, but she did not look convinced.

26

Manny stood with Carlos Guevara when Preuss came outside.

"How is she?" Manny asked.

"Scared," Preuss said. "There was a murder in Detroit last night. She's convinced it's connected with her brother."

"Whoever's behind this, we'll watch her as long as we have to," Manny said.

"I got this, Mr. Greene," Carlos Guevara said. "I won't let anything happen to her."

"Good deal."

Guevara got back into his car and Preuss walked with Manny back to Manny's Audi across the street.

"Seems like the two people I'm looking for might be the ones threatening her," Preuss said. "Also threatening to tell the world about her brother's indiscretions if she doesn't pay them $10,000."

"Are they worth ten grand?"

"Probably not. We don't even know the full extent of them yet, but an ask like this seems desperate. Meantime, I'm working a contact in Detroit, so I'll find out what the story is."

Manny looked down the empty street, then back at Carrie's house, a sprawling ranch with a wide front lawn. "Anything else you need from me?"

"Not right now."

"Keep me in the loop."

"Will do," said Preuss.

"Thanks."

Manny drove away and Preuss returned to the Explorer. He called Alonzo Barber again, and this time got through.

"My brother," Barber said. "Long time, no talk to."

"Alonzo, how you doing?"

"Never better. What's up?"

"There was an incident last night with one of my clients, a phoned-in threat of extortion and violence. I'm wondering if you can tell me anything about the people I think are behind it."

"I'm all ears."

Preuss gave Barber a quick summary of what he had done on the Braiden case. "The two are named Meeshell Lee"—he spelled both names—"and a guy I know only as Ray Tomatoes."

"Don't know either of them."

"I don't have Tomatoes's real name. I suspect he's behind the threats, trying to shake my client down for money or else he's going to spread nasty information about her brother. Who's currently in a drug-related coma, thanks, it looks like, to these two."

"Fun couple," Barber said.

"There was also a homicide in Detroit last night—"

"Just one?"

"My client thinks it's connected to this. On no good evidence, but I can't convince her otherwise."

"Let me find out what I can. ID on the dead guy?" ·

"Nothing in today's *Free Press*. That's where she saw it."

"All right. I'll let you know what I come up with. When we gonna get together? I'm anxious to see your boy again. How's he doing?"

"Doing well. I think people are always more interested in seeing Toby than me."

"Maybe if you weren't so damn cheerful all the time, people'd be gladder to see you."

"Working on it."

Barber gave him a throaty laugh. "Let's make it soon."

"I'll check Toby's calendar. He has a much busier social life than I do."

"Let me know. Meantime, I'll see about these knuckleheads."

Back at his office, Preuss emptied the pot of coffee he had left on Rhonda's machine from the morning and made a fresh pot of the Maxwell House Rhonda kept to use when Manny was out. He took a cup into his office and wrote up notes on everything that had happened in the last two days.

With the addition of what Carrie Morrison had told him that morning, it was looking more likely that Meeshell and Ray Tomatoes were behind Braiden's overdose, as well as the threat against Carrie and her children.

The only question now was, where were they?

"All quiet?"

"All quiet," Carlos Guevara said. He was still parked in front of Carrie Morrison's house. Preuss leaned into the driver's side window.

"Nobody in or out?"

"The kids came home with Grandma and Grandpa. Grandma stayed for a little while, then left. Grandpa's still in there with everybody."

Preuss patted the top of Guevara's car and walked up to the front door. He rang the bell, and an older man swung the inside door open with a large pistol in his hand.

Pointed directly at Martin Preuss.

"Who're you?" the older man barked.

Preuss held his hands up. "Easy. Martin Preuss. I'm working with Carrie."

The man gave Preuss the hairy eyeball, then stepped aside when Carrie Morrison came to the door. She patted the old guy's shoulder, said, "He's on our side," and steered him back into the house. "And put down that gun before you hurt somebody," she called after him.

"Come in," she said to Preuss.

Preuss followed her inside. She led him into the kitchen. "Sorry," she said. "He's really nervous about what's going on."

"I just hope he doesn't shoot the kids."

"He won't. Coffee?"

"Sure."

She poured him a cup. "How do you take it?"

"Black. Thanks."

"So is anything new?"

"I spoke with my guy in the Detroit Police. He's going to find out what he can about Meeshell and Ray Tomatoes."

"And the dead guy from the paper?"

"Him, too. Till we know more, we'll keep the security watch in place," Preuss said.

"That wouldn't bother me."

"You seem calmer than you were this morning."

She rubbed her hands over her cheeks, turning her skin a bright pink. "I guess I am. I was just so freaked out from those calls. And then when I saw the newspaper this morning, that really did it. With the house watched, I think I'll be okay. Can I go to work in the morning?"

"You said your gallery's in Birmingham?"

"Right. If you don't think I should, I can stay home."

"No reason not to go in," Preuss said. "You'll need a minder nearby, though. You can set that up with Carlos."

She said she would. She tasted her coffee, then said "So where are we?"

He told her what Alonzo Barber had said when they spoke earlier. "As soon as I hear back from him, I'll let you know. As far as your brother's situation is concerned," Preuss continued, "the main thing is finding Meeshell and Ray Tomatoes. We're taking the threats against you seriously."

Satisfied Carlos had arranged for round-the-clock coverage of Carrie Morrison's home, Preuss spent the rest of Sunday with Toby. After the events of the day, he basked gratefully in his son's calming aura.

They took a long walk around Berkeley, then watched the entire second *Lord of the Rings* movie. Afterwards, Preuss gave his son a bath, then sat with him at the side of Toby's bed, reading aloud a few chapters from *Harry Potter and the Goblet of Fire*.

When Toby's head began to droop, Preuss gently laid him down and covered him up with the sheet and blanket. He sat with Toby listening to Judy Collins on the CD player until his son fell asleep.

Like the boy, Preuss gave himself up to the comfort of the familiar routine, and the quiet joy of being with the person he most loved in the world.

On the way home, he called Carlos Guevara to make sure Carrie Morrison's home was secure.

It was.

Monday, September 24, 2012

27

After helping get Toby on the bus in the morning, Preuss handled a flurry of phone calls as he drove to his office.

First, he called Carrie Morrison's home and she told him everything was fine, no trouble last night or this morning. She was going to drive her two children to school and then continue on to her gallery. And yes, she assured him, she would allow the latest bodyguard that Manny Greene had hired to escort her, if he promised to be discrete and stay in the background.

Carlos Guevara had been replaced the night before by another guard, and still a third had reported for the day shift this morning. She felt a lot more comfortable than she had yesterday, and thanked Preuss for his efforts.

Next, Preuss got a call from the security firm Manny contracted with for the bodyguards. The director told Preuss they would supply three shifts a day for as long as Preuss needed them.

"I hope it won't be more than a few days," Preuss said.

"Whatever, we got you covered."

The final phone call was from Alonzo Barber, who asked Preuss if he were free for lunch.

He was. They decided to meet at a cafe in Greektown near the Wayne County Third Circuit Court in the Frank Murphy Hall of Justice on St. Antoine Street, where Barber would be waiting all morning to testify in one of the courtrooms.

"They should be off the record by one," Barber said. "If not, I'll call you."

"See you then," Preuss said.

Settled in his office, he called Reg Trombley to see what might have developed in the Greg Braiden case. The call went to voicemail and Preuss left his message, asking Trombley to call him back.

He remembered Trombley was likely in one of the meetings that Stanley Chrysler, the chief of detectives, had instituted in his efforts to manage—and control—the detectives he supervised. The latest Preuss had heard from Trombley was that Chrysler instituted two report sessions a week in addition to his one-on-one meetings with his officers. They drove Trombley crazy; he thrived on less oversight, but put up with them like a good soldier.

A good soldier.

I no longer have to worry about being a good soldier, Preuss thought. The military-style regimentation of the police was behind him forever. He easily adapted to the more free-wheeling style that Manny used to run his office.

He had more trouble adapting to the loss of the authority that a detective's shield afforded him, but he was even becoming used to that.

Alonzo Barber was waiting for him at the diner on Monroe downtown. He wore a lightweight blue serge suit with a blazing white shirt and hand-painted pastel tie in an impeccable Windsor knot. He was not a handsome man, with large ears and thick, irregular features, but he comported himself as though he were gorgeous and so he seemed to be.

Preuss slipped into the booth where Barber sat with his large hands cupped around a mug of coffee.

"My brother," Barber said with a broad grin. He extended a hand and Preuss shook it, warm from the mug.

The waitress was over before Preuss got a chance to look at the menu. "What to drink?" She was a dark young woman in a Tigers tee shirt with Maori tattoos around her arms and neck.

"Iced tea," he said. "Unsweetened."

"Know what you want?"

"Did you order?" he asked Barber.

"Yeah. Got the breakfast special. You can still order it for lunch. Eggs and potatoes. Can't be beat."

"Sounds good," Preuss told the server. "Same as his," he said, and the woman hurried away.

"I had to order soon as I got here because we're just on a lunch break," Barber said. "This is going to kill the rest of the day. The lawyers spent all morning arguing which of two contradictory medical reports should be accepted."

"How long do you have?" Preuss asked.

Barber shot his wrist out. He wore a complicated gold aviator's chronograph with a dozen functions in circles and rings and boxes in the watch face. "Half hour, maybe less."

"What did you find?"

"Couple things. First thing is the body on the east side. He's sixteen. Just a kid. Died after a verbal altercation with an eighteen-year-old male. Apparently, they knew each other. The older one wanted the younger kid's bike, and when he wouldn't give it up, the older kid shot him dead."

"Jesus."

"Jesus must have been busy someplace else."

"Doesn't sound like it's connected to my case."

"Not to me, either. Your basic knucklehead street crime. Next thing, I reached out to a friend of mine, Charles Montgomery. He's worked the Narcotics Task Force for a long time. Knows all the players. I asked him about your two."

"And?"

"Your guy, Tomatoes, Monty says he knows him."

The waitress brought their food. The eggs were sunny side up, which Preuss never ordered because they reminded him of slimy eyeballs, but these were done perfectly. Beside the eggs was a mountain of steaming crispy home fries with onions. On a side plate, two slices of wheat toast glistened yellow with butter.

Barber dug in immediately. Preuss turned his plate so the eggs were on the right side (a ridiculous habit, but the only way he could eat eggs, maybe due to his being left-handed) and began to work on his own meal.

"Good food?" Barber asked.

Preuss nodded. "What's Montgomery know? Does Tomatoes have a history of violence?"

"Listen," Barber said, his mouth full of yolk and egg white, "these guys, they all got a history of violence. Tomatoes is quite a character. Real name's Desmond Raymond Tomina."

"Ray Tomatoes is Desmond Tomina?"

"Yeah. Go figure. Probably thinks 'Ray Tomatoes' sounds more, I dunno, Sicilian. Like I always say, these chumps, they're not criminal geniuses. Anyway, Monty said it's been a long ride for Tomina. Father's been in and out of jail most of his adult life, mother ran off when Tomatoes was six. Grandma raised him the first part of his life, then the street gangs finished the job. By 14, he was a runner for the local dealers. Started dealing himself at 17. Couple times he was caught, last time got a custodial sentence. Since he's been out, Monty says he's been up to his old tricks."

"He's back to dealing?"

"Along with some pimping to diversify his portfolio."

Barber made short work of his eggs. He washed them down with his coffee and turned to the potatoes. He ate only one food group at a time. Preuss had eaten with him often after they became friendly, including bringing Toby over to Barber's house in Sherwood Forest in Detroit for cookouts, and Barber always ate his protein first, then his starch, then his veggies.

"One thing I do know about him," Preuss said, "he sometimes hangs out at the Journey's End in Ferndale."

Barber interrupted his eating to lift his fork to Preuss for an admiring salute. "That's one of his places. Monty says there's a few other skeevy motels on Woodward between Eight Mile and McNichols where he also has girls working."

"I ran into him at the Journey's End. He got away before we could talk. Anything on Meeshell Lee?"

"Couple pops for prostitution, but nothing more than that."

Preuss explained more about Greg Braiden and Meeshell Lee than he had mentioned on the phone. "My guess is," Preuss said, "Meeshell's one of Tomina's girls. She's been working Braiden. I'm not sure how they got together, but Braiden's been paying for Meeshell's room at the motel since April. And who knows what else he pays for. His sister hired me to find out how he wound up there in a coma."

"What happens you hang out in places you don't belong," Barber said. "Any progress?"

"I'm moving forward. Tomina's threats to my client put things on the fast track. If it was him."

"You want, I'll ask Monty to get in touch with you, fill you in on anything else he knows."

"Perfect."

Barber's phone on the table chimed with a text. He checked it, then put it in his pocket. "Gotta go," he said. "Judge wants to go back on the record in twenty minutes."

"What's the case?"

"Murder-suicide. Wife shot her terminally ill husband, intending to kill him and put him out of his misery, then apparently shot herself. Thing is, there's a discrepancy about who died first. She wasn't such a good shot, and her husband hung on while she was bleeding out. Lot of money at stake for the heirs."

He pulled out his wallet, but Preuss grabbed the check. "My treat," he said.

Barber nodded his thanks and stood. "This was the second marriage for each of them, and they never got around to changing their wills, so they each have different heirs. If he died first, even by one second, then she survived him and her heirs get the estate. If she died first, even by one second, then he survived her and his heirs get the estate. Jurisprudence: Gotta love it. Let's talk again soon."

They embraced and Alonzo Barber was gone.

Preuss sat for a few more moments, thinking about wills and estates, and then finished what was left of his lunch.

Which was ice cold.

On the way back to the office, Preuss stopped at Toby's to help get his son off the bus. Toby was smiling broadly and chirruping happily, which meant a good day at school. By the time he left the group home to return to the office, he had gotten Toby cleaned up, changed, and sitting in his reclining chair listening to Arlo Guthrie on the CD player.

He told his son he had to leave but would see him later on, and he left Toby vocalizing along to "Alice's Restaurant."

Driving back to the office, Preuss sang the song's chorus in the car at the top of his lungs.

Things were moving again.

28

Rhonda had gone home early, so her chair was empty. As usual, she had left her desk in a pristine state, with neat piles for work with different deadlines: immediately in the morning, important but not urgent, and whenever.

Manny sat in his office dictating a report. He wore his suit jacket, but his top shirt button was open and his tie was askew. Very unusual for the dapper older man, who was immaculately put together at all times.

"Where's Rhonda?" Preuss asked from Manny's doorway.

"I sent her home," Manny said. "She wasn't feeling well, so I told her to go home and take care of herself. Why don't you knock off, too?"

"Work to do," Preuss said. "Besides, you're working, aren't you?"

"Just puttering around till Lila gets here. She's going to pick me up and we're having an early dinner."

Lila was Manny's wife, as elegant and well-turned-out as he always was.

"Why don't you join us?" Manny asked.

"Thanks," Preuss said, "but there's still lots to do tonight."

Manny was about to say something, but a coughing fit stopped him. It started with him trying to clear his throat, then turned to polite coughing, then became a full-fledged hack attack.

Preuss stepped forward into Manny's office, but the older man held up a hand as he brought a handkerchief to his mouth.

When he caught his breath, Manny said, "Sorry."

Preuss closed the door to Manny's office and sat in the guest chair in front of the desk.

"All right," Preuss said. "What's going on?"

"What do you mean?"

"I mean what's the story with this coughing? And your hoarseness, which isn't getting better. And don't tell me it's just a cold, because you know that's bullshit."

Manny patted his lips with his handkerchief, as though finishing up after a good meal.

"I'm not leaving until you tell me," Preuss said.

"Martin," Manny began, then stopped. He took a deep, raspy breath, but before he could say anything else the outer door of the office opened. After a few moments, a knock came at Manny's door and Lila called Manny's name.

"Come in," Manny called.

She opened the door and said, "Oh, sorry! Martin, hi! I didn't know you were here."

"Not a problem," Preuss said. "Manny and I were just having a little chat."

"Do you want me to wait?"

"No," said Manny. "No, no. Come in."

Preuss glared at the older man.

Who asked him, "Have you eaten yet today?"

The same question Janie Cahill always asked.

"I had lunch."

"Have dinner, too. Join us."

"Thanks, but I'm not hungry. And I really do want an answer to my question."

Manny sighed and stood. He adjusted his collar and tie and buttoned his suit jacket. "We'll continue this another time."

Preuss stood and Lila stepped forward to give him a hug. "Come," she said. "Have dinner. You deserve a life outside this."

"I know."

"I know you *know*," she said. "But you don't *do*."

Now it was Preuss's turn to sigh. "I appreciate it. But please, this isn't a good time. Can I have a rain check?"

"Fine," Manny said. "If you change your mind, we'll be at the Stage Deli."

"I won't, but thanks."

They left and Preuss locked the door to Greene and Preuss, Investigations. He turned the reception area light off and turned on the desk lamp for his office. This was a better landing zone than his office in the Detective Bureau in the Ferndale PD—larger, even though it used to be a storage area—and better appointed. But he had still not totally made the transition to the private sector. He particularly missed the resources he used to have, Rhonda's secret sources notwithstanding.

He also missed the chances to talk with his police colleagues about cases he was on. Most cases now weren't whodunits; they were more surveillance and verifications of clients' suspicions, so there wasn't always a need for conversations as there had been on the force. And Manny was always ready—at times, like tonight, too ready—for a talk over a meal. But it wasn't the same.

He turned to his computer keyboard and typed notes from his meeting with Alonzo Barber. He printed them out and added them to his Braiden file.

He placed the file in front of him on the desk and read through it from beginning to end. He stretched out with his feet on the desk and his hands behind his head. It's either all here, he thought, or there's a piece missing and what is here will let me know what that is. I just have to put all the information in the right order.

To help him do that, he called Reg Trombley. Reg wasn't home, but Preuss talked with his wife Sandra. She reminded Preuss that Monday was the night of Reg's Men's Fellowship meeting at their church. He wouldn't be home till later, but could she give him a message?

"No, thanks," Preuss said. "I'll grab him another time."

He disconnected. He sat and debated with himself about the wisdom of making the next call, then decided to go for it.

Janey Cahill suggested meeting at a Mideastern restaurant on Woodward in Ferndale. It was after the peak dinner hour, so the covered patio was not crowded. They sat at a round metal table near the front. The sibilance of traffic on Woodward underpinned their conversation.

Preuss drank an iced tea and she had a Blue Moon. He ordered the night's special, lamb with green peas, and Janey got the vegetarian stuffed grape leaves.

"No protein?" he asked when their drinks came.

Janey said, "Didn't I tell you? I've become a vegetarian."

"Since when?"

"Been thinking about it for a while. Eating meat's getting to bother me. I'm starting to feel bad about the animals who die in fear and pain so I can have my hamburgers."

"What do the boys say about it?"

"They're totally on board. It was TJ's idea, actually. Tommy was the meat-eater. With him gone, we can do things differently."

"Healthier, too, no?"

"Yeah. I feel great."

"What about all the tobacco plants that give their lives so you can keep smoking?"

"Baby steps, Martin."

For a few moments it felt like the old days, when they could tease each other and talk like normal people.

He asked, "Boys with Tommy?"

"Yup." She glanced at her phone lying on the table. "An hour before they get home."

"How'd the move go?"

"Smooth as ice. I like this new arrangement, I have to say. About time for it. Overtime, in fact."

"Things happen in their own time."

She shrugged. "Just glad it happened."

"Thanks for meeting me," he said.

"No problem. I was glad you called."

"Yeah?"

They shared a long look, and she turned away, smirking. "Dumb shit."

He grinned, raised his iced tea by way of a toast to the observation.

"Seriously, I need somebody to bounce ideas off of," he said.

"Gee," she said, "maybe if you hadn't, I dunno, quit the force, you'd have somebody handy."

"If I hadn't quit when I did, your fearless leaders would've found an excuse to shitcan me in a hot minute."

"You don't know that."

"You might not. I do. Anyway, it's in the past."

"So what's up?"

"Can you listen to the sequence of events, and help me make some sense of it all?"

"Fire away."

Before he could say anything, the server appeared with their orders. "Anything else for now?" she asked when she got their dishes settled.

Both shook their heads and she was gone.

Janie tucked in to her grape leaves and she said, between bites, "Go from the beginning."

He outlined what he knew about the Braiden case, from Braiden in the motel room to the threat against Carrie Morrison.

She worked on her grape leaves while she processed it all.

"You met Big Jake Aklawi? The man himself?"

"In the flesh," he said.

She pulled a face. "Impressive."

"He offered to be my new best friend."

"Before he sent his thug to rough you up."

"I don't think Aklawi sent him. I'm guessing that was Victor's own idea."

"Why?"

"I made him look bad in front of the boss. He wanted to make me regret it."

"Maybe he shouldn't have killed your screen door."

"I'll deal with it."

"Be careful with him. You know about Victor, don't you?" she asked.

"Know what?"

"What I hear, he's not just Aklawi's driver. He's also his enforcer. I just saw a report from the Southeast Michigan Regional Organized Crime Drug Enforcement Task Force. It talked about Aklawi, and it mentioned Victor Kirma by name. The Strike Force is looking at him for a series of murders in the Chaldean Community."

"Related to drugs?"

"Among other things. All I'm saying is, be careful of him, Martin. He's a viper."

"I will. So look. Let's assume Braiden was taking a walk on the wild side with Meeshell."

"Okay. And what are you thinking, he got a hot shot accidentally? Or gave it to himself deliberately?"

"Everybody swears he doesn't do drugs. Nobody can imagine him killing himself."

"Wouldn't be the first time that happened," she said. "One day everybody swears he's cheerful and happy, the next day he ends it all. Everybody's shocked."

"True enough," he agreed. People were essentially unsolvable mysteries.

"And Meeshell and him what, sit around discussing great books? His friends know he keeps a room in the No-Tell Motel?"

"Everybody says it's news to them. So maybe he's also got a jones nobody knows about."

"Meeshell and this guy—what's his name?"

"Ray Tomatoes."

"Ray Tomatoes," she said. "For real? That's a name?"

"His real name's Desmond. You like that better?"

"Six of one . . . So Meeshell and Ray Tomatoes were bleeding Braiden. And now they start putting the squeeze on his sister. All the dots connect, no? Especially considering what your friend told you about Ray Tomatoes's history."

"You'd think so."

"But you don't? What's the problem?"

"I can see Ray Tomatoes being the bad guy here, but both Ray and Meeshell? I'm not feeling it."

"Why not? Everything points to it."

"Just a hunch," Preuss said.

"Ah. One of those scientific detective thingies."

"Yeah," he admitted. "Not based on much. And how do they know about his sister?"

"He must have mentioned it to Meeshell."

"That's what I thought at first, too. But you take a walk on the wild side, you talk about your sister?"

"It could just be what it looks like, Martin. These things do happen."

"Okay. I just wanted to get your take on it."

"No," she said, "if something bothers you, let's have it."

"I don't know if there is or not," he said. "I'm having trouble lining everything up. We won't know until we get ahold of the two of them."

"When was the last time you talked to Reg?"

"It's not his case. It's Bellamy's."

"Oh, right."

She chewed that over, along with a stuffed grape leaf. "I dunno what to tell you. Seems pretty cut and dried. Why do you have to make everything so complicated?"

He nodded thoughtfully. "It's what I do."

She patted his arm. "And you're damn good at it."

She left her hand on his arm, and he laid his fork down and covered her hand with his own. They gave each other a smile, and left their hands together for another few moments until she withdrew hers and reached for the Blue Moon.

They ate in silence for a few minutes, and then he said, "What do you hear about Tony?"

"Did you know he had a second heart attack?"

"No."

"Yeah. Yesterday."

"And nobody thought to call me?"

"Sorry," she said. "I assumed Reggie would tell you."

"And I'm sure he assumed you would. In the meantime, I'm in the dark."

"Martin," she said, "you know, we never hear from you. If you're going to stay out of touch, of course we're going to think you don't want us to call you."

"I called you tonight."

"Yeah, for the first time in how long?"

He had no good answer for that.

"They got Tony on the table and opened him up for a double bypass," she went on. "He's stable for now, but it doesn't look good. His heart's weak, and they still have him on life support."

"I should call Adele."

"She'd appreciate it. You got her number?"

"Reg gave it to me."

His anger at being left out again began to fade as they made small talk while they sipped strong coffee. He felt more comfortable with her than he had for a while. Maybe she was right, he thought; maybe I need to keep more involved with them.

And maybe her husband moving out would be the trigger for things shaping up between us.

They split the bill, and he walked her to her pickup in the parking lot down Troy Street from the restaurant.

"Thanks for the invite," she said.

"Anytime."

"Did it help?"

"It did."

"My money's on Ray Tomatoes and Meeshell as equal partners in this."

"Maybe."

"You still don't believe it."

"No," he said, "I'm certain they hold a lot of the answers. First order of business is finding them."

"Well," she said, "okay then."

They hugged, and when he pulled back, without thinking he aimed a kiss at her lips.

She turned her head and gave him the side of her face. She drew back at once.

"What's the matter?" he said.

"Not yet," she said. "Okay? Not yet."

He held her out at arm's length. "Janie," he said, "what's going on here?"

"It feels like once we take this step, we're going to cross a line."

"Isn't that sort of the point? You were just bawling me out about being out of touch."

"It is the point," she said. "But no . . . I've been thinking about this so much. And it feels like if we do this, we're going to ruin our friendship. I know, I know, that's an old line. We're already uncomfortable enough with each other as it is, and we haven't even done anything but talk about it."

"We said we were going to put this on hold for a while, until you felt like you were ready for it. And you settled things with Tommy."

"I know."

"And now he's moved out."

"I know that, too."

"So I repeat, what's going on here? You're still not ready?"

She pulled away from him. "I need more time, that's all."

She hugged herself, though it wasn't a cold evening. Her body language didn't say she needed more time; it said she wasn't feeling this. Now or ever.

He looked at her. She looked everywhere but at him: at the traffic, at the shops across Woodward, at the McDonald's down the street.

It felt to Preuss as if a whole conversation were passing between them, without words.

"Now you decide you're not feeling it, Janie? After Tommy's moved out and you're heading toward a final split?"

"I know. It isn't fair."

"It's not a question of fair or not fair."

"I'm so sorry, Martin. I thought this was going to——"

"It doesn't matter."

"It does."

"No. If it's not going to happen, it's better we don't spend any more time waiting for it. Or I don't, at any rate."

He felt a sudden urge to reach out and run a hand through her wild electric blonde hair, just to make physical contact with her.

Then thought: No.

This stops now.

"Okay," he said. "I think it's probably a good idea to stay away from each other. Let's take a little time and let our friendship rebound. If it's going to."

"Oh, *shit!* So we've ruined our friendship *anyway*."

"No. But we need to regroup. At least I do. Starting now."

He walked away from her, back to where his Explorer was parked in the lot next to the post office.

Toby was sound asleep, curled like a comma in his bed on his right side, his sleep side, his snoring a faint purr. Preuss sat beside him, watching him sleep, and reached over to lay a gentle hand on his son's shoulder. The boy's peaceful face seemed to glow in the light from the hallway.

Preuss rubbed his son's back, running his hand gently over the knobs of Toby's spine.

His bones are so fragile, Preuss thought. Bird bones.

He leaned over and kissed the side of Toby's head, then re-started the Judy Collins CDs. Her powerful voice rang out with the opening of "Tom Thumb's Blues" from *In My Life* and Preuss turned the volume down so it wouldn't wake his son.

He sat in the chair beside the boy's bed and listened to the rest of the album. He let himself go with the music, especially "Suzanne," the first Leonard Cohen song Preuss had ever heard.

When the CD ended and the second one began—*Judy Collins Sings Lennon and McCartney*, beginning with the gorgeous "And I Love Her"—he roused himself and went home.

There he played through his own arrangement of "And I Love Her" on his acoustic Taylor, and laid himself down on the sofa. Unusual for him, he had no music cranked up on his own CD player, but he let the echoes of the chords of the song he had just played chime in his head. He replayed the conversation with Janie, and was left with sorrow but also with a sense of relief that one way or another, things would now be settled. The possibility that had sparked between them for years was finally about to fade.

In one part of his mind, he always knew things would work out this way. He suspected she was still too emotionally involved with her husband, even though (maybe even because) he had moved out. And maybe Tommy's leaving had made her confront the feelings she had for Preuss (or didn't have, as the case may be) and she realized there weren't enough once all the impediments had been removed.

He was sad, but not destroyed.

After all he'd been through, it would take more than this to destroy him.

He closed his eyes and tried to let his mind go blank.

It didn't work. He was up for hours.

Tuesday, September 25, 2012

29

He was at his desk when his phone rang with a 313 number he didn't recognize.

"Martin Preuss," he answered.

"This is Detroit Police Detective Charles Montgomery. Alonzo Barber gave me your number."

"He said you might call."

"Okay. Howya doing?"

"Good. What's up?"

"So those two you asked about, Meeshell Lee and Desmond Tomina? Tomina's still on the loose, but we're holding Meeshell in custody. I thought you might want to see her."

Detroit Receiving Hospital was a sprawling campus in the medical center in downtown Detroit, a series of buildings that looked like concrete shoe boxes stacked on top of each other. Preuss parked in the underground lot and trotted into the Emergency Entrance on St. Antoine. He went through the metal detector and asked the admissions clerk for Detective Montgomery.

She buzzed him through the double doors into the Emergency Department. He searched through the hubbub of people with gunshot wounds and stab wounds and all the other injuries they suffered from the mayhem of everyday urban life, as well as people with ordinary illnesses but no other access to health care than the Emergency Department.

Outside a glassed-in cubicle near the central nurses' station, he saw a knot of uniformed Detroit police officers standing around an exceptionally tall black man in shirtsleeves with his tie undone. He must have been six-eight and towered over the other police.

"Martin?" the man asked. Preuss said he was, and the man introduced himself as Charles Montgomery. They shook hands and Preuss saw Alonzo Barber standing a little apart from the group of police. He was holding his cell phone to his ear, and when he spied Preuss he nodded and held up one finger.

"There's your girl in there," Montgomery said.

He indicated a young woman in one of the cubicles. The same one who had burst by him in the house in Highland Park. A pair of nurses attended to her while a man in a white coat worked on her face with gloved hands.

Through the cubicle's open doorway, Preuss saw she had been badly beaten. She was bruised and swollen around her eyes and cheeks and forehead, and her nose was swollen, stitched, and packed. Her jaw hung lopsided on her face. The doctor working on her was slowly wiring her jaw with what looked like a series of metal braces on her teeth.

"Somebody really worked her over," Preuss said.

"Yeah," Montgomery agreed. "Broken jaw, broken ribs, internal damage. When I called you, I thought you might get a chance to speak with her. But the doc's wiring her up and she's on major pain meds, so I'm not sure we'll get anything from her for a while."

"She say anything before I got here?"

"Not much. She was unconscious when the EMTs brought her in. She came to once they got her here, but she couldn't tell me much."

"Where was she found?"

"Over on the east side. Near Mt. Elliot Cemetery. Doc thinks it must have happened this morning."

"Anybody know what she was doing there?"

"Have to wait till we can ask her."

"Thoughts on who did this to her?" Preuss asked.

"First one I'm looking at is Ray Tomatoes himself."

"He's still missing?"

"Still at large," Montgomery said.

"What makes you think it was him?"

"They're a couple, these two. And he has a nasty habit of beating up women he's with. This has his name all over it."

Alonzo Barber disconnected his call and came back to where the rest of them were standing.

He shook hands with Preuss and said, "We caught one half of Bonnie and Clyde over here."

"So I see," Preuss said.

"We'll find Tomina," Montgomery said. "Just sorry I dragged you down here for nothing."

"No worries," Preuss said. "I appreciate the call. You're going to hold her?"

"We've got a couple things to hold her on. She had some drugs on her, plus she has an outstanding warrant. Meantime, the docs are evaluating her," Montgomery said. "She got a pretty bad beat-down. We'll wait to see what's what. Ray Tomatoes did this, she may give him up, she may not."

Preuss looked at the young woman being ministered to in the emergency cubicle. He remembered how her mother described her hopes for Meeshell's future. This was not what Antoinette Lee had in mind for her daughter.

"Tomatoes," Montgomery continued, "got some notoriously bad anger management skills. She did something to piss him off, he probably thought she deserved it. Plus too, it's not unusual for pimps to tune up their prosties. Especially if they think the girls are holding out on them."

Preuss said, "Could be from a john, too, I suppose."

"Could be that, too," Montgomery said. "These women live a dangerous life."

Preuss looked back at Meeshell. He had only one brief conversation with her, and didn't know Ray Tomatoes, so he wasn't in any position to argue.

"You know about Ray Tomatoes, don't you?" Montgomery asked.

"Alonzo filled me in."

"You know about his connection with Peanut Carver?"

Preuss looked at Alonzo Barber, who shrugged. "Told you about his drug connection."

"Yeah," Preuss said, "but not about Peanut."

Montgomery said, "You know Peanut Carver?"

"Sure," Preuss said. "Local rap mogul slash drug dealer. Supposed to be a major figure in Detroit's heroin trade."

"That's him," Montgomery said. "Ray Tomatoes's a member of his crew."

"Really."

"Low down, like. More like a cockroach running around the totem pole than a player."

"Any chance Peanut knows where he is?" Preuss asked. "Or he's hiding him?"

"Martin," Montgomery said, "Peanut's got a lot more important things on his mind than a low-level scumbag like Ray Tomatoes."

"Still," Barber said, "might not hurt to check it out."

"I can talk to him," Preuss said.

"To Peanut?" Montgomery said.

"Yeah."

Montgomery and Barber exchanged a look.

"What's wrong?" Preuss asked.

"Not a good idea, my brother," Barber said. "Whyn't you leave that to the police? One of which, I hasten to remind you, you no longer are."

"If Tomina's such a low-level thug, Peanut's not going to want you all up in his business about him," Preuss said. "It's to his benefit to get Tomina out of his hair. I can help him do that."

He thought about Jake Aklawi, who also wanted Ray Tomatoes gone. If Ray Tomatoes was with Peanut Carver, that might explain both why Aklawi wanted Ray Tomatoes out of his own place of business, and why Aklawi wouldn't want to risk a war by having one of his own crew get rid of him.

Montgomery and Barber shared another look. Barber said, "That may be, but don't do this, Martin."

"Seriously," Montgomery said. "Peanut, he don't play. You don't want to get involved in this without a badge."

"That's exactly why I should. He'll talk to me before he talks to either one of you."

"What makes you think you'll get anywhere near him?" Barber asked.

"Worth trying."

"So what, you're going to do this anyway?"

Preuss said nothing and Montgomery said, "We can't stop you. But it was me, I'd take along a contingent as backup."

I know just the contingent, Preuss thought . . . a batshit-crazy, paranoid contingent of one.

He stayed around the ER until the decision was made to hold Mee-shell overnight in the locked ward. When he realized he wasn't going to speak with her, Preuss returned to the office.

He made a call. The guy he wanted to speak with never answered his phone directly; Preuss would have to wait for a call-back in the man's own good time.

He stopped for a hot dog and a root beer at the A&W on Twelve Mile in Berkley, then continued to Toby's house. The door was locked because the residents were in bed, so he had to ring the doorbell.

A new aide he had not seen before answered the door and wouldn't let him in until she verified his claim that he was Toby Preuss's father with the rest of the staff.

Convinced, she let him in. The nurse and two aides at the dining room table looked up when Preuss entered. They were filling out reports and paperwork while the young men and women they cared for relaxed into sleep in their rooms.

"Sorry," one of them sang. "She's new!"

"Not a problem," he said.

He waved hello and continued down the long hallway to Toby's room. Judy Collins was singing softly on the CD and Toby was lying in his bed, curved on his sleep side. His gorgeous brown eyes were open but he breathed softly and evenly, as though he were relaxed and easing himself into sleep. He gave his father a twitchy crooked smile when he realized Preuss was there.

Preuss leaned over and kissed his son gently on the side of his face. He was fragrant with strawberry shampoo and apple soap from his bath.

"Hey," Preuss said. Toby made a short little sound, almost a hum. "Sorry I missed your bus," Preuss said. "Busy day today."

Toby made his little sound again, his own version of "No worries." Then, as though he had been holding out for his father to come, Toby smiled his crooked smile, closed his beautiful eyes, and drifted into sleep.

A pile of folded clothes lay on the chair next to Toby's bed. The aide had not had a chance to put them away yet. Preuss quietly stacked Toby's tee shirts, shorts, and little white socks in his dresser drawers, then straightened out Toby's CDs, which always got disorganized when Preuss and the other carers searched through them for disks that Toby would enjoy.

Toby enjoyed every kind of music—folk, rock, classic rock, country, classical . . . nobody ever bought him any hip-hop CDs but Preuss had no doubt Toby would enjoy those, laughing along with the beats and wordplay.

When his son's room was as neat as he could get it, Preuss sat in the reclining chair beside Toby's bed and watched his son sleep.

Preuss closed his eyes but didn't nod off. He checked that the ringer on his phone was off because he didn't want to rouse Toby in case he got his callback, and sat holding the phone in his hands.

When the three Judy Collins disks played through, Preuss sat in the silence of the room for a few minutes, then went over to put on a Sonny Terry and Brownie McGee album. When McGee's sweet baritone and guitar came on in the first song, he edged the sound up, but as soon as Sonny Terry came on with his sharp harmonica and country whoops, Preuss turned the sound back down so he wouldn't wake Toby.

He listened to the first four songs and then his phone buzzed.

"What now?" the voice on the other end demanded.

Wednesday, September 26, 2012

30

Preuss pulled the Explorer onto the apron of Vern's Minimart on Mack Avenue and Cadillac Boulevard on the east side of Detroit. Vern's was a tiny Shell station, convenience store, and snack bar. He didn't know why McShane picked this for their rendezvous, and McShane wouldn't have told him if Preuss asked.

Preuss spotted him standing inside the entrance to the store, looking out behind a neon Labatt Blue Light sign. Shortly after midnight, Franklin McShane might have been the only white man within miles (except for Preuss), but the neighborhood bad guys must have sensed how messing with him would be a very bad idea because no one was bothering him as they entered the store. Preuss watched as all the customers gave McShane the hairy eyeball as soon as they walked in the door, but then allowed him a wide berth after picking up his vibes.

Smart people.

McShane was in his seventies and lean as a nail with long grey hair tied in a pony tail under a Tigers cap. He wore his standard uniform, a beige windbreaker over green Wayne State University sweatshirt, soiled khakis, and filthy Keds.

When he saw Preuss, McShane bent down to pick something up and came out of the store quickly. He looked around before trotting over to the SUV.

He threw a tote bag into the rear seat and jumped in after it. The bag made a heavy metallic clunk. "Let's go," McShane said. He ducked down behind the front seat. "Quick."

Preuss pulled onto Mack and headed west, back toward downtown.

"Anybody see you?" McShane asked.

"Nobody I know."

"You sure?"

"Positive."

"Would you bet your life on that? More to the point, would you bet mine?"

Preuss sighed.

"Huff all you want," McShane said. "You don't think there aren't CCTV cameras around with facial recognition that can ID you before you can pull your license out of your wallet? Anybody wants to, they can track your movements to the second. Don't kid yourself, Preuss. We're always being watched."

McShane was a pain in the ass, but the ex-FBI agent's virtues—his continued contacts throughout the agency that rivaled Rhonda's for their reach, his disdain for anything having to do with the government or any organized entity, his fearlessness—outweighed the paranoia that surrounded him like the smell of tobacco lingers on a smoker. Since Manny Greene had put Preuss in touch with McShane on a previous case, Preuss couldn't count the number of times McShane had warned him that if Preuss knew what he (McShane) knew, he would be equally as paranoid.

"What's in the bag?" Preuss asked.

"What do you think?"

"Enough hardware to win a small war."

"I can't trust you to bring any weapons, can I? You and Gandhi, no guns." McShane scoffed.

"True enough," Preuss said.

"No wonder they couldn't stand you when you were on the job. Whoever heard of a policeman won't carry a firearm in this day and age?"

When he had been in the Ferndale PD Detective Bureau, Preuss refused to carry a gun—one of the many thorny issues the department had with him. He wasn't a pacifist, nor did he believe nonviolence was the answer; he thought the presence of a gun, far from being a deterrent to trouble, more often accelerated it.

"We go about this the right way," Preuss said, "we won't have any need for firepower."

"Right. And if the pope got married, he'd have kids."

Preuss continued on Mack and took the on-ramp to northbound I-75. He exited at West Grand Boulevard and drove west to Second Avenue, where he turned right.

He took Second up to a residential area and stopped in front of a two-story red brick building with a blue sign that read, "Sounds, Inc. Entertainment."

McShane sat up. "This it?"

"This is it."

McShane unzipped the tote bag and withdrew a .45 pistol, which he put in his windbreaker pocket, a .22, which he put in his khaki pocket, and a Bowie knife in a sheath that he tied to his calf under his pants leg.

"I'm ready," he said.

They stepped out of the car and McShane fell in step beside Preuss.

"Sure he's here?"

"No," Preuss said, "but it's a good place to start. Rap mogul is this guy's day job."

"Oh, I know about this guy," McShane said. "He's well-known. He's not fooling anyone with his 'I've seen the light and come to Jesus and now I produce crap music' bullshit."

They climbed the front steps of the building. Preuss tried the handle of the grey ironwork security door but found it locked. He pressed a button on the doorframe but heard nothing inside.

He pressed it again and after another minute heard a series of locks being thrown open and the door cracked a few inches on a chain. A black woman in her twenties scowled out at them.

Preuss held out his business card and said his name. "We're looking for Mr. Carver."

"What for?"

"I just want to ask him a few questions."

"About what?"

"I'd rather have this discussion with Mr. Carver, if you don't mind. Is he in?"

"He not here," the woman said.

"Do you know where we can find him?"

She looked from Preuss to McShane, and back to Preuss.

"You po-lice?" she asked.

"No ma'am. I'm a private—"

"Then why imma tell you?"

She slammed the door shut and clicked all the locks.

Preuss and McShane exchanged a look, and turned back to Preuss's car.

"How's it working so far," McShane said.

A man stepped out of the shadows along the sidewalk. He held a small rag-mop dog straining at his leash. He strolled over to them.

McShane's hands went to his windbreaker pockets. Preuss knew one of those hands gripped his pistol.

"Evening," the man said. "Did I hear you gents are looking for Peanut?"

"We are," Preuss said.

"You guys the law?"

"No. Just want to ask him about a mutual acquaintance."

The man processed that, then nodded. "Funny time to be looking for him."

"I heard this is the best time to find him," Preuss said. "We're just following up on information. Any idea where he might be?"

"I know he's not here," the man said.

"No, the woman inside made that clear."

"Tried the club?"

"Where's that?"

"Nightspot on Plymouth. Place called Jimmy's," the man said. "This time of night, that's where you'll find him. He meets his acts there. Auditions them, signs them on the spot if he likes what he hears."

"Thanks," Preuss said. He reached out a hand and the man shook it.

"Don't mind Ashley," the man said, indicating the woman in the house. "She's always like that. Girl got attitude. Get her in trouble one of these days."

"It's all good," Preuss said.

"All right," the man said. "Good luck, now."

31

Jimmy's Millionaires Bar and Grill was a neighborhood club on Plymouth Road at the corner of Marlowe, close to Hubbell in Detroit. The front and sides were concrete blocks painted black with yellow diamonds. The only sign was a garish neon blinking red and yellow above the door.

Inside, Preuss came up with a twenty for the cover charge for both himself and McShane. The place was dark and loud, with a bar along the right wall and, further in, a large room with filled tables and a bandstand at the far end. They seemed to be the only white men in the place.

A big guy in sunglasses and a black silk shirt underneath his suit coat approached them as soon as they stepped inside the dark main room. He held his hand up to halt them. "Think you guys might be in the wrong place tonight."

Casually, McShane's hand went to his windbreaker. Behind Sunglasses, Preuss saw three men maneuvering into position to back him up.

"Pretty sure this is where we want to be," Preuss said. "We're looking for Peanut Carver. He in?"

The man adjusted his jacket. "Who's asking?"

Preuss saw his own reflection in the man's dark glasses. "I have a couple questions about a mutual friend."

The guy looked from Preuss to McShane. He seemed to find the older scruffy man particularly interesting. Sunglasses gave McShane the once over and said, "Sorry, gentlemen, those shoes?" He indicated McShane's dirty Keds. "Not gonna work. Got a dress code here. Can't let you in with those. Maybe try another time, okay?"

He held out his arms to shepherd them back out the door.

Neither Preuss nor McShane moved. "We're not going to stay," Preuss said. "We're not customers. Won't take a minute."

"Can't let you in. Besides, Mr. Carver, he's busy at the moment. I'm asking you to leave."

"He's not busy at all," McShane said. "I see him right over there."

He pointed across the room to a party sitting around a table in the corner laughing it up. "Looks to me like he's having a good time. Maybe we'll join him."

"Gentlemen, I'm asking you nicely," Sunglasses said. "Don't make me—"

McShane stepped around him. Sunglasses shot out a hand to stop him. He made to grab McShane's coat sleeve and McShane turned and caught the guy's hand in his own right hand and bent it backward at the wrist, forcing Sunglasses to a knee.

The movement was so fast, it took Sunglasses's entourage by surprise.

"No touch," McShane said.

He let the big man's hand go and glared at the men standing behind Sunglasses, his hand obviously on a dangerous object in his jacket pocket.

Before Sunglasses could regain his feet, Preuss stepped around him. "Let's all just catch our breath," he told Sunglasses's posse, and backed away toward Carver's table.

McShane came up even with Preuss, saying, "Life's too short to deal with idiots."

Before Sunglasses and the others could collect themselves, Preuss and McShane crossed to the table where Peanut Carver was sitting with a half-dozen men and women. The conversation stopped dead. The three men at the table all stood, ready for action. Carver remained seated.

Sunglasses caught up to them with his hand on his holstered weapon inside his coat. His posse formed up behind him. "Mr.

Carver," he said, "Mr. Carver, I told them you were busy, but they wouldn't—"

Carver raised a hand to shut him up. He was a slender man in a blazing white jacket over a white shirt and black tie. He had dark skin the deep color of espresso and a short beard that precisely outlined his mouth and jawline.

"Are you Peanut Carver?" Preuss said. McShane stepped up behind him, at his shoulder.

"Only my friends call me Peanut," Carver said amiably. "Are you one of my friends?"

"I'm looking for one of your crew. Guy named Desmond Tomina. I don't know where that puts me on your list of friends."

Carver smiled and said, "Who do I have the pleasure of speaking with?" he asked. Honey-smooth voice, pleasant tone, nothing threatening. Just passing the time of day.

"Martin Preuss. I'm a private investigator. I understand Tomina works for you."

"What's that name again?"

"Desmond Tomina."

"No, I mean yours."

"Martin Preuss."

Carver considered him. "I don't believe we've had the pleasure, Mr. Preuss."

"Pleased to meet you."

"Likewise."

"The man I'm looking for calls himself Ray Tomatoes. Burly young guy, light-skinned, maybe white, maybe Latino. Runs drugs and women."

"And you say he works for me?"

"Detroit Police do."

"Huh," Carver said. He looked at the others in his party. They were barely suppressing smirks. "Wait. Are you saying *I* run drugs and women?"

"I wouldn't presume to surmise that," Preuss said.

Carver looked at Preuss, amused. He turned to his friends at the table. "He wouldn't presume to surmise that." He grinned and gave a deep chuckle. "Thank you, professor."

Now the smirks were turning to rolling bursts of mocking laughter.

A man in a white silk dress shirt and black vest appeared at the table, followed by two guys the size of dump trucks.

"There a problem, Mr. Carver?" the man said.

"No problem, Jimmy," Carver said.

"You sure?" Jimmy said. "These guys are creating a nuisance and I'm about to show them the door."

"Thanks, J, we got this," Carver said.

Sunglasses came up behind Preuss. "Mr. Carver," he said, "let us handle these guys."

Carver held his hand up, slowing Sunglasses down. "Take it easy, Cortez. We're just having a little talk, aren't we, Mr. Preuss?"

Carver turned to ask his table, "Anybody know—what was that name again?"

"Desmond Tomina. You might know him as Ray Tomatoes."

"Anybody know a Ray Tomatoes?"

The men at the table were still standing. Counting Jimmy and his two dump trucks and Cortez and his men, there were ten guys standing in a protective arc near Peanut Carver.

Nobody said anything, until Carver said, "I don't know anybody named Ray Tomatoes." He looked around at his audience. "I did once know a guy named Lettuce and his girlfriend Olive."

The group at the table guffawed loudly.

"Last name Salad?" one of the men standing at the table asked, causing even more laughter.

Carver turned back to Preuss beside his table. "I don't believe any of us know anybody by that name," Carver told him and straightened his tie. "Now if you don't mind, I'd like to get back to my meal and my friends. Cortez?"

Carver gave them a backhanded wave of dismissal and Cortez, the big guy in shades, was quickly backed up by the other three men who were even bigger than Cortez.

"You heard Mr. Carver," Cortez said. His voice was tight. "Time to go."

The four bouncers closed in on them and McShane's hand came half-way out of his coat pocket.

All the bouncers reached inside their coats.

Preuss put a calming hand on McShane's arm. "Let's all cool it," he said. McShane stopped but kept his hand half in and half out of his pocket and glared at Cortez.

"Time to go," Cortez said, quietly this time, impassive in his menace. "Now."

"We're going," Preuss said. He carefully laid a business card on the table beside Carver's plate. "For future reference. In case you remember Ray Tomatoes after all."

Cortez and his men herded Preuss and McShane out the front door onto the sidewalk while Jimmy and *his* men stood watching to make sure they left.

Outside, with the other three behind him, Cortez stepped to McShane. He was a head taller than McShane and three times as wide.

Cortez pulled a gun out of his pocket but McShane stepped even closer to him and wrapped a hand around Cortez's weapon, immobilizing it off to the side, at the same time pulling his own .45 out of his pocket. He stuck it in Cortez's cheek, forcing Cortez's head back.

Cortez's men pulled their guns and trained them on McShane.

"Seriously, Cortez?" McShane said. "You really want to do this?"

They stood frozen like that for a few moments. Grinning, McShane squeezed Cortez's hand around his gun so tightly that Cortez's arm trembled.

Cortez's posse closed in, but Cortez waved them back.

Then McShane let him go, but kept the gun trained on Cortez's face.

Cortez backed off, hands up, and shooed the others inside the club. At the door, he turned and said, "You mine, gramps."

He stepped back into the club.

McShane returned his .45 to his pocket and turned to Preuss. "Why'd you stop me in there?" he asked.

"You were really going to shoot them in the middle of the club? With an armed posse around you, surrounded by civilians?"

"If I had to, sure."

"You're something else."

Before McShane could answer, the door to the club opened and Preuss and McShane spun, expecting a replay with Cortez. McShane had his gun out and pointed directly at the woman who was coming through the door. She was one of those who had been sitting at the table with Peanut Carver. She was tall and elegant in a tight Chinese-style dress split at the side that showed a considerable length of leg.

McShane's gun stopped her in her tracks but didn't seem to ruffle her. Preuss almost expected to hear her say, "Seriously, McShane?"

As soon as he saw it wasn't Cortez, McShane raised the barrel and stuffed it back in his jacket pocket, where he kept his hand on it.

She came up to them. "You're looking for Ray Tomatoes?" she asked.

"You know him?" Preuss asked.

"I do. Peanut does too, but he won't admit it." She threw a glance at the door of the club. "Tomatoes is one of his street crew. He's low in the organization, so Peanut doesn't have much to do with him, but I know P knows him."

"How do you know him?"

"I remembered seeing him come to the house once for a pickup. I remember the name."

"I don't suppose you'd know where we could find him?"

"I don't," the woman said. She held her hand up and Preuss saw she was carrying a phone in a gold jeweled case. "I know somebody who might. Let me make a call."

She turned away and punched in a number. She kept glancing from Preuss to the door of the club.

Preuss heard her murmuring into the phone, then she disconnected and turned back.

"That was a mutual friend who knows him. She's not sure where he is either, but she said you could try the Embers."

"Which is what?"

"A motel. It's in Highland Park, on Hamilton. My friend said he's got girls there, thought she heard he kept a room there, too."

"Thanks," said Preuss.

She nodded to him and began to turn away. "Wait," he said. "Why are you helping us?"

"Let's just say I heard about what happened to Meeshell."

"You know her?"

"Uh-huh. People are saying it was Tomatoes did it."

"It's possible."

"I want him to get what's coming to him. I don't know if you guys are cops or what, but I'm feeling like you're going to even the score."

"We're going to try," Preuss said.

"That's why I'm doing this. But you didn't hear it from me," she added.

She held a look with Preuss a few seconds longer, then turned and was gone back inside the club.

"The hell was that all about?" McShane said.

"She knows where Ray Tomatoes might be."

"Yeah? We going after him?"

Preuss looked at the time on his phone. "Almost two in the morning."

"So? It's the shank of the evening."

"McShane—"

"If you got a lead on the man, let's go. Before he hears we're looking for him and holes up somewhere else and we'll never find him."

With McShane shaking his head, they walked around the corner and down the long side of the club on Marlowe to where they had left the car. All along the side of the building were graffitied the same kinds of gang symbols Preuss saw on the Appoline house. Here someone had tried to x them out in red paint.

They crossed the alley behind the club. Two men burst out from behind a dumpster near the club's back door. One came after Preuss and the other went for McShane.

Like most street brawls, it was over in seconds.

32

Preuss caught sight of Cortez going after McShane, but Preuss's man came at him with a two-by-four and he focused on that. His guy rushed at him, taking a big swing, but Preuss back-pedaled and heard the "whoosh!" of the wooden stud pass his head and the swing missed.

His attacker's momentum took him off balance and he stumbled.

Preuss heard the double crack of two gunshots.

His attacker came back at him with another swing, but Preuss was ready for this one and stepped inside and wrapped both arms around the arm holding the wood. In one motion, Preuss twisted his body and threw the man to the ground. Preuss felt the snap of the guy's elbow, and the guy cried out in pain.

Preuss turned the guy's wrist and flipped him onto his stomach and pulled the wood out of his hand and raised it as if to strike him with it.

"No!" the man cried. He tried to protect his head with his good arm.

Preuss let him go. The man scrambled to his feet and lurched back inside the club, holding his hurt arm close to his side.

Preuss turned with the two-by-four in his hand, but McShane was standing there looking at him with a cell phone to his ear. At his feet, Cortez lay on his back, motionless.

Preuss said, "Is he dead?"

"No," McShane said. "But he's not feeling his best."

"You shot him?"

McShane nodded. "Gutshot, but he's alive."

Preuss saw a ragged patch of fabric and a dark spot at McShane's left shoulder and realized he had been shot, too.

Two gunshots. They shot each other.

"Are you all right?" Preuss asked.

"A scratch."

He spoke into the phone. He gave the address to the 911 dispatcher and disconnected. He wiped off the phone and tucked it back into Cortez's pants pocket.

One of the other bouncers threw open the back door to the club and stood in the doorway holding a shotgun. McShane spun with his gun hand extended toward the door.

The bouncer looked at McShane and then at Cortez on the ground.

"He's alive," McShane said. "Ambulance is on the way. Cops'll be here before that. I were you, I'd come up with a story to explain all this."

Scowling in confusion, the bouncer looked at Preuss and then back at Cortez on the ground. Then he disappeared inside the club.

"Looks like the situation's under control," McShane said. "I'm guessing we don't need to stick around."

Preuss heard a siren in the distance.

"Here they come," McShane said. "That's our cue."

"We can't just go," Preuss said.

"Why not?"

"You just shot a guy. Who just shot you."

"Exactly. Self-defense. Why stick around and debate it? Let's go."

When Preuss hesitated, McShane said, "Look, you're not responsible anymore for sustaining the privileges of our fat cat capitalist overlords. You don't have to administer the political and social systems' immoral sanctions upholding the forces of greed and violence *any more*. You're a free agent, Preuss. Let's go."

He turned and walked up the street toward the Explorer.

"McShane, you just shot a guy."

McShane stopped and turned around. "He fired at me and I returned fire. It was a good shoot."

The sirens pulled up to the front of the club on Plymouth Road and abruptly went silent.

"And your former colleagues in the praetorian guard are here to enforce a corrupt society's arbitrary rules. Can we go now?"

The back door of the club burst open and guests poured out, hurrying down the alley and down the street.

McShane joined the crowd and hurried to Preuss's Explorer. Reluctantly, Preuss followed. Maybe sticking around wouldn't be the smartest idea, he thought.

They drove south on Marlowe, away from where Cortez lay in the alley.

After they had put distance between themselves and the club, Preuss pulled to the curb and stopped.

"What?" McShane said.

"Let's look at you."

"I'm fine. I told you, it's a scratch."

"Take your coat off."

"Forget it."

Preuss leaned over to pull the windbreaker off his shoulder, but McShane winced and elbowed Preuss's hand away.

"Stop!"

Preuss noticed then a ragged hole on the back of McShane's shoulder, matching the one on his front.

"A scratch? McShane, it's a through-and-through. You're bleeding all over the front seat. You have to get this looked at."

"No hospitals."

"What are you going to do, sew it up yourself with your shoe-laces?"

"No," McShane said. "But I know a guy. I'll get myself there later. First we have to find your boy."

"No, first we get you patched up. Tell me where to go for your guy."

As Preuss followed his directions, McShane shifted his position. In the dim light of oncoming cars, he looked pale.

Without looking at Preuss, McShane said, "You handled yourself okay back there."

"I'm not entirely useless."

"No," McShane agreed, "not entirely. Didn't know you had those kinds of moves."

There was something like admiration in McShane's voice. Grudging, it was true, but admiration nonetheless.

"Now you do."

"Almost makes me feel better about you not carrying a weapon."

"Almost?"

"I still think it's naive and stupid. Only gonna get you killed one of these days. And me, too, if I'm unlucky enough to be with you when it happens."

"What went on with Cortez back there?"

"He came at me, same as your guy did. Except Cortez had a weapon. He shot me, I shot him. End of story."

McShane stared at Preuss as they circled back toward the Jeffries expressway.

McShane said, "You're not still all mopey over this?"

"I'm not comfortable with it," Preuss admitted. "We left the scene of a shooting."

McShane waved it away like so much smoke. "You're still new to this. May take a while to get used to living outside the protective cocoon of the overly militarized civilian occupation force formerly known as the police."

Preuss said nothing in reply.

"Out here is where you make the real moral distinctions," McShane continued, "in the blink of an eye. None of those bullshit arbitrary directives that maintain the status quo of the privileged class. That's what you were doing on the force, you know. Hell, man, that's what *I* was doing in the Bureau."

Preuss drove in silence.

When they got to the Jeffries, McShane pulled out his .45. "Sad thing is, now I got to get rid of this little beauty," McShane said, mostly to himself. "Too bad." He ran an affectionate hand along the weapon's steel lines and angles. "Really liked this one."

McShane directed Preuss through the crowded, narrow streets in Hamtramck to a frame duplex built tight amid a row of similar houses. Preuss pulled the Explorer into a space beside a fire hydrant in front of the house.

"Wait here," McShane said, and opened the car door with his good hand.

"Forget it," Preuss said, and came around to help McShane out of the car. "I'm coming with you."

"What, you think I'm an old man?"

"No, I think you're an injured man. You need a hand."

"I'm fine," McShane said, but let Preuss help him up the walk and the front stoop. McShane rang the bell and in moments the door was opened by a squat, bald Chinese man in a formal white shirt that bulged over a huge belly.

"Come in," he said, as though he had been waiting for McShane, though McShane never contacted him.

Preuss started into the house after McShane, but McShane stopped him with a hand on his chest.

"You stay out. I won't be long."

Preuss held his hands up in surrender and sat on a rocker on the porch as the Chinese man guided McShane inside. McShane and the man spoke to each other in hasty Mandarin and McShane closed the door behind him.

In forty-five minutes, McShane came back out to the porch. He had on a different windbreaker, this one without a bullet hole, but otherwise seemed none the worse for wear.

"All set?" Preuss asked.

Without answering, McShane led the way to Preuss's SUV.

When they were inside the Explorer, Preuss said, "Do I even bother asking who that was?"

McShane paused before answering, then said, "Let's just say we go back a long way, the two of us. We have an arrangement."

He clammed up and it was clear to Preuss that he wasn't going to get any more answers.

"Want anything?" Preuss asked instead. "Coffee, something to eat?"

"What is this, a date? Let's go. Remember the motel?" McShane asked, as though Preuss were a small and not-bright child.

"How about we call it a night instead?"

"How about we finish what you got me out of bed for?" McShane said testily.

"We can do this another night," Preuss said. "You need to get some rest, Iron Man."

McShane said, "Preuss, lemme tell you something. I've been shot more times than you've had hot meals. Now shut up and let's get this show on the road."

33

They found the Embers Motel on Hamilton south of the Davison expressway, which cut east and west through the center of Detroit. The motel had two stories, with simulated flames on its attraction board. Half of the neon tubes were burned out in the name of the motel on the sign, so it read

BERS

TEL

The motel was a compact U-shaped unit around a parking lot that was packed with cars, mostly late models but a few beaters. Highland Park's version of the Journey's End, Preuss thought. Or one of them, at least.

Inside the office, a black woman who was taller and more muscular than Preuss stood in front of the reception counter. In a skimpy leopard-skin halter and short shorts of the same material, she gave both Preuss and McShane a fierce once-over, then left with a toss of her blonde wig, apparently without settling her business with the clerk behind the counter.

He was a slender young Indian man whose name tag read "Narendra."

"Help you?" Narendra said with feigned nonchalance.

"We're looking for a man who might be staying here," Preuss said through the speaking vent in the acrylic security windows that boxed in Narendra. "Ray Tomina. Know him?"

"Would he be a guest?" Heavy accent, dark good looks, not more than twenty-five.

"Possibly. Also goes by Desmond Tomina and Ray Tomatoes. Could you check your register?"

Preuss gave him the cop stare, and the young man turned toward his computer terminal. He tapped the name into the keyboard and shook his head. "No, I'm so sorry. No one registered by that name."

"Do you know anyone named Tomina? Big guy, walks around in a tee shirt and sweatpants, wears a lot of bling?"

"No sir," Narendra said. "I do not. Sorry. I know no one by that name."

Standing beside Preuss, McShane stared at the young man through slitted eyes. "Never heard of him, eh?"

"No sir."

"Uh-huh."

He looked at Preuss, then around the office, then back at Narendra. He leaned close to the speaking vent in the window. "How much you get?" he asked.

"Please?" Narendra said.

"I want to know how much you get for each prossie Ray Tomatoes runs through here. You get paid per night, or per trick, or what?"

"Very sorry, sir," Narendra said, without looking at McShane. He busied himself by straightening papers on the desk in front of him. "I don't know what you're talking about."

"Two bucks, maybe? Five? I'll bet Ray Tomatoes flips you a fiver for every john who passes through. Am I right?"

"Sorry—"

"Yeah, yeah, you're sorry. Look, son," McShane said, leaning even closer to the acrylic window. Kind and understanding. Uncle Frank.

Preuss kept a straight face at this show.

"Nobody blames you," McShane said. "It's the way of the world." He looked up at the DBA license framed on the wall beside Narendra. "Neel Kalam," he read. "That the owner?"

Narendra gave a quick nod.

"Relative, right? What, father? Brother?"

"Uncle," Narendra admitted.

"Sure," McShane said. "'Narendra' . . . What do your American friends call you?"

"Nick."

"Look, I get it, Nick," McShane continued. "Uncle Neel thinks he's doing you a favor. Gives you a job but he pays you shit, makes you work the graveyard shift in this dung heap in the middle of an American ghetto . . . You're going to school, too, during the day, am I right?"

A hesitant nod.

"Where?"

"Walsh College."

"What are you studying? I'm guessing business."

"Yes."

"Knew it. Bright kid like you."

"Good major," Preuss said.

Narendra looked like all this interest confused him.

"Bet you're doing well, too," McShane said.

The young man dipped his head modestly.

"So during these long nights, you do your studying, and maybe get a little extra when you can," McShane said. "Just to look the other way. Helps make ends meet, pays your tuition, gives you a little spending money. A fin for every trick. That's not too much to expect, is it? It's the American way."

Narendra didn't deny it.

"So look," McShane said, "just tell us where we can find Ray Tomatoes, and we'll get out of your hair. You can go back to doing whatever gets you through the hours. What is it, homework?"

Narendra gazed into the back office where a book was open on the desk. "Business law," he said.

Preuss said, "He'll never know you said anything."

Narendra looked pained.

Preuss and McShane waited.

Finally, Narendra said, "I know this man."

"Now we're getting somewhere," McShane said.

"He was here. Earlier. But he's not here now. I saw him leave."

McShane kept watching Narendra without saying anything. Narendra squirmed under his gaze. "I swear to you," Narendra said. "He's not here."

"Does he keep a room here?" Preuss asked.

"No. If he stays, he stays with one of his ladies."

"His ladies," McShane scoffed.

"What time did he leave?" Preuss asked.

"A little after midnight."

"Did you talk to him at all tonight?"

"Just for a minute. He stopped in to say hello."

"Wasn't that nice of him," McShane said. "Dropped off a little—?" He rubbed thumb and two fingers together in the universal sign for money.

Narendra shook his head.

"No?" McShane said. "When do you get it?"

"End of the week."

"He likes you, does he?"

"We talk," Narendra said.

"You like him?" Preuss asked.

Narendra shrugged.

"Believe me, son," McShane said, "it might seem like he's got the world by the short hairs. But he's no kind of role model for a guy like you. You should have much bigger hopes than to be like Ray Tomina."

"When he left, did he say where he was going?" Preuss asked. "No."

"Does he usually come back during the night?"

"He has no set schedule. But no, when he leaves, he usually does not return. Not until the next day."

"How did he seem when he talked to you?"

"Seem?"

"Was he anxious," Preuss prompted. "Did it look like he had something on his mind?"

Narendra thought about that, then said, "No. Not that I could tell."

"Okay."

Preuss laid a business card in the cash opening in the security windows. "Do me a favor? If he shows up, call me. Call anytime. Okay, Nick?"

Narendra said he would.

"I think we should check every room," McShane said.

"No!" Narendra said. "Please! You cannot do that. My uncle would kill me. I'm telling the truth!"

Preuss patted McShane's arm. "He's right. Let's go. We'll leave this young man to his work."

McShane watched the young man through squinted eyes for a few more moments.

"Remember what I said, Nick," McShane said. "Ray Tomina isn't the American dream. He's not going to come to a good end, I promise you."

He jerked a thumb over his shoulder. "And what's out there?" He pulled a face and shook his head. "Find something better for yourself. Don't let this be your horizon."

Then McShane tapped the business card that Preuss had left, and pointed a long finger at Narendra. Who took the business card and put it in his shirt pocket.

Outside they stood on the apron of the parking lot and scanned the area. Just as at the Journey's End, there was constant movement in and out of the rooms and the lot.

"You were positively avuncular with young Nick back there," Preuss said.

McShane took his baseball cap off, ran a hand over his grey head, and resettled the cap. "Look around you, Preuss. What do you see here?"

Preuss took a moment to form an answer. Before he could reply, McShane said, "It's a vision of hell, that's what it is. People buying and selling each other, wallowing in sex and violence, trying to block the pain of what they're doing with every kind of pharmaceutical. It's like a damn Hieronymus Bosch painting.

"Our boy Nick sees this every night. Lives in the middle of it. Helps make it possible. And then during the day, what does he do? Learns how to take his place in the great global capitalist threshing machine—which is just a better dressed version of what he sees here. He needs an alternative view of the world."

"Think it'll work?"

"No," McShane said, "I don't. But I tried."

McShane insisted Preuss drop him back off at the Shell station on Mack. "I'll drive you home," Preuss said, but McShane protested so strongly that Preuss jumped back on the Davison to I-75 south toward downtown. Doesn't want me to find out where he lives, Preuss thought. Thinks I'm going to call in a raid with the black helicopters.

When he pulled onto the apron of the darkened gas station, Preuss said, "Sure you don't want me to drop you somewhere? Pretty bleak around here."

McShane waved away the suggestion. "I'll be fine."

He stepped out of the car and, hauling his tote bag of arms out of the back seat, disappeared down the side street into the darkness.

Yes, Preuss thought, I'll just bet you will be.

I pity the guy who tries it on with you.

He rolled into his driveway at a little before five in the morning. Now it was the shank of the morning, he thought as he dragged himself inside his house. At least he had said goodnight to Toby before all this happened. He wouldn't be up in time to see him off to school this morning, that was certain.

His exhaustion seemed to melt away, though, as he turned the lights on in his kitchen. He stood looking out the back window, testing his body's readiness for sleep, and decided sleep wouldn't come anytime soon. Instead, he brewed a cup of instant decaf (Manny would be horrified, he thought) and took it with him into the living room. He stretched out on the sofa and thought back through what had happened since midnight.

At one time, he would never have considered leaving a crime scene, especially where there was a shooting victim. Yet tonight he hesitated only briefly when McShane said they should go.

Part of it was that McShane had already called 911. So the cops were just arriving as he and McShane left. And the ambulance would be on its way. And he was pretty sure nobody from the club would say anything, least of all Cortez or the other members of the security force. They and Peanut Carver would want as little to do with the law as possible.

Still, it seemed to Preuss that he had crossed a line, had moved a bit more away from enforcing the law.

And why shouldn't he, he thought. He was no longer a law enforcement officer. He was a private citizen.

So did that mean he could do what most private citizens did: skirt the law and lie to its representatives?

No, he thought. That's not me.

He resolved to speak with Alonzo Barber about what happened.

Then, like all guilty parties after confessing, he fell asleep.

34

"Busy night?"

Rhonda Citron gave him a sly smile.

Preuss shook his head. "Don't ask."

He continued into his office and closed the door behind him. He hadn't dozed off until around six and only slept for three hours. He showered and dragged himself into work without having had the stomach either to look at himself in the mirror for the time it would take to shave, or for breakfast. As he knew would happen, he had missed seeing Toby off for his day program.

A knock came at the door and without waiting Rhonda opened it and set a cup of Manny's special coffee in front of him. "You look like you could use this."

"You're the best," Preuss said. He took a sip. "This really is good stuff."

"Only the best for Manny."

She sat in the visitor's chair across from him. "So," she said. "Better?"

He nodded gratefully. "Much."

She watched him in silence for a moment. "You don't take very good care of yourself, do you?" she asked.

Before he could answer, she said, "Oh, shoot, sorry. I'm being impertinent. Never mind."

"No, you're right. I always seem to be the last one I think about."

"And your son Toby's the first."

"Always."

The year before, Manny and his wife had invited Preuss and Toby to dinner at their house in Birmingham. Rhonda was also there, and fell instantly in love with Toby. As who wouldn't? Toby also fell for her, as he did with any pretty woman who paid him attention.

She waited now, as though trying to decide how far to push this conversation. Finally, she seemed to opt for a strategic retreat and said, "You'll let me know if there's anything I can do?"

"I will. Thanks, Rhonda."

She nodded. Preuss knew Rhonda had her own demons to wrestle with. Last year, she had tried to kill herself in one of her sloughs of despond. Lately, though, she had seemed to be feeling better—better enough to be concerned about me, Preuss thought.

After their dinner at Manny's, when he saw how good she had been with Toby, he had briefly thought about getting to know her better. But then she had her breakdown, and Manny—who seemed to have intuited Preuss's intentions (he is a great detective, Preuss thought)—cautioned Preuss against getting involved with her. She was just too fragile, Manny said. Preuss agreed.

She laid a pair of phone message slips beside the cup of coffee. "These came in for you."

One of the calls was from Ramonda Hudgens, Meeshell Lee's cousin.

He held up her call slip. "Did Ramonda say what she wanted?" he asked.

"No. Wants to talk ASAP, though."

"Okay, thanks."

She sat for a moment longer, and he said, "I'm good, Rhonda, really."

"Excuse me for saying this, but you don't look good."

"I had an endless night. And not much sleep."

"Something fun, I hope."

He gave her a rueful smile. "Most definitely not fun. Definitely work."

"Sorry."

She watched him for another few moments, then gave him a rueful smile and left him alone.

I've let my intentions go, Preuss thought, but what about *hers?*

He shook the question out of his head and punched in Ramonda's number on his cell. She picked up immediately.

"Martin?"

"What's up?"

"I got a call this morning from Nikki Bardellini. She said the police came to her house looking for Ray Tomina."

"Why would they look there?"

"They probably have the address on file. She told them she didn't know where he was."

"And does she?"

"She told me she didn't. She asked me if I knew where Mee-shell is. I told her I didn't know that either."

"I saw her yesterday," Preuss said. Was it just yesterday? It seemed like a month ago. "Down at Receiving Hospital."

"Is she okay?"

"No, unfortunately. Somebody roughed her up. They're keeping her."

"Do they know who did it?"

"The general feeling is, it was Tomina."

"Who?"

"Oh, sorry," he said, "that's Ray Tomatoes's real name. Desmond Tomina."

"Why would he do that to her?"

"I can't answer that."

"I guess it's a silly question. There's no logic in domestic abuse."

She was silent for a few moments.

"They have a heavy thing going on, those two," she said. "Nikki said the last time she talked to Ray, he told her he and Mee-shell were planning to go off together."

"He say where? Or when?"

"Sorry, no."

"She was found on the east side, near Mt. Elliot Cemetery. Can you think of any reason she might be over that way?"

"Not that I can think of. But she doesn't confide in me anymore."

"No," he said, "sure. I just thought you might have heard something."

"How was she when you saw her?" Ramonda asked.

"Honestly, she looked bad. Whoever worked her over, he broke her jaw, gave her a couple of black eyes and facial contusions. And I don't know what other kind of damage there might have been. She was in too bad a shape to talk to."

"Oh, that poor girl. I told her this life was going to do her in."

"She was in the ER when I saw her, but they were going to admit her. You might be able to see her. Be warned, though, she was under guard."

"For what?"

"They're holding her on a couple of charges."

"What?"

He didn't feel like going into the details. It was too complicated to think about right now, and he was way too tired. "I can't go into it right now, if you don't mind."

"Okay, sure."

"If Nikki hears from Tomina, could you let me know?"

"Of course."

They disconnected. He put his phone down and it beeped with a voice message that had come in while he was talking with Ramonda.

"Mr. Preuss, this is Narendra Kalam."

His voice was low and furtive, as though he didn't want anyone to hear what he was saying.

"I just wanted to let you know, that man you were looking for, Mr. Tomina, he's here. He came back to the motel early this morning. He's in room 110. But please, Mr. Preuss, do *not* tell him you got this from me!"

The Embers Motel was even sadder in the daylight. The forecourt was half empty and littered with broken glass and empty McDonald's boxes and wrappers. In the light of day, the brick on the outside walls was a sickly yellow, and curtains hung askew on the windows of the rooms.

Preuss bypassed the office this time and went right to room 110, in the corner. He had decided to come alone, leaving McShane to do whatever he did in the morning. Although knowing that guy, Preuss thought, he could jump out from behind the chambermaid's cart, armed to the teeth.

He knocked on the door to the room. There was no response, so he knocked again, harder.

When there was still no answer, he tried the door. Locked.

He walked over to the office and saw no one behind the plexiglass at the desk. The door to the front area was ajar, and when he pushed it, he saw Narendra laid out on the floor in the office, bleeding from a gash on his head.

The front desk had been ransacked. The cash drawer had been pulled out and lay on the floor, empty. The key was still in the drawer lock. Registration papers and binders were scattered everywhere.

Preuss knelt down beside the desk clerk, who groaned.

Preuss looked around for something to use for Narendra. He found a roll of paper towels under the counter.

He bent down and gently dabbed at the side of the young man's head.

Narendra opened his eyes and tried picking his head up. He dropped his head and retched. Preuss turned the young man's head to the side so he wouldn't aspirate the vile-smelling vomit.

Narendra looked up at Preuss in confusion.

"You've been attacked," Preuss said. "You're hurt." He dabbed at Narendra's head again, then held the towel away so Narendra could see it soaked with blood. "You need help."

"No," Narendra said. "My uncle—"

"Forget your uncle, you're hurt. You need medical attention. And you've been robbed. Did Tomina do this?"

Narendra closed his eyes. He began to heave again, and again Preuss turned his head to the side. He brought up mostly bile. When he dropped his head to the floor again, Preuss called 911 and told the operator what had happened and asked for an ambulance and the police.

When Narendra caught his breath, Preuss asked him again, "Was it Tomina?"

Narendra swallowed and rasped, "Yes."

'What happened?"

"Can you help me up?"

"No," Preuss said, "you better lie still. You probably have a concussion, and who knows what else. Wait for the ambulance. It's on its way."

"No, I want," Narendra began, and tried to get himself up but didn't have the strength. He collapsed on his back.

The front door to the office opened and the woman in leopard skin who had been there the night before came in, saw Narendra on the floor with Preuss kneeling beside him, and walked right back out again.

"Is there a relief clerk due in?" Preuss asked.

"Not till tonight. I'm working a double shift."

"Not in your condition."

Preuss stood and looked through the notes pinned to a bulletin board at the side of the office.

"What are you looking for?" Narendra asked.

"Your uncle's phone number."

Narendra groaned. "No, please! Uncle Neel hates it when the police come here. I will lose my job! He will kill me!"

"Yeah, somebody's already tried that," Preuss said. "And you're done for today. Help is on the way."

As Narendra put both hands to his bloody head in despair, Preuss heard the howl of a siren racing toward the motel.

Up until now, Preuss had been unsure of Tomina's involvement in Meeshell's beating, had been thinking somebody else could have done it. Seeing Tomina's crazy anger written in blood in the motel office, it was easier for Preuss to believe Tomina not only could have hurt Meeshell, but that he actually did.

Only one person could tell him for sure.

35

The police guard outside her door at Detroit Receiving stopped him and asked his name. The cop searched through his list of approved visitors. Preuss was about to let him know he wouldn't be there, when the cop found his name. Montgomery must have put it on, he thought.

The guard flipped a thumb toward Meeshell's room, and Preuss entered.

A nurse was inside administering medicine through the IV pump that Meeshell was attached to. Meeshell looked even worse than she had the day before. Her bruises had come up in angry colors of red and purple, and she lay on her back as though she were deflated. Watching her, Preuss realized how thin she was; the sheet covering her was almost flat over her emaciated body. He wondered if she was sick.

"How is she?" Preuss asked.

"Stable," the nurse said. At the sound of his voice, Meeshell opened her eyes and turned her head with a wince toward Preuss standing beside the bed.

"Can she talk?" Preuss asked.

"She should be able to. Not clearly, and not easily. But you should be able to make out words. Five minutes, though, right?"

"Fine."

Meeshell stared at Preuss, then closed her eyes and turned away from him.

"Meeshell," Preuss said, "it's Martin Preuss. Remember?"

She ignored the question. I'm guessing the answer is yes, Preuss thought.

"Can we talk for a minute?"

Meeshell opened her eyes and glared at him. She was not happy to see him.

"Are you okay to chat for a few minutes? I know you can't move your jaw, but I need to ask you a few questions about Ray."

"Cop?"

"Private investigator. I'm trying to find out what happened to Greg Braiden."

She closed her eyes again and shook her head. That was obviously not a name she was interested in hearing.

Preuss said, "But first, can you tell me about Ray?"

She took a few deep breaths, worked her lips together. With her teeth wired in a clenched position, she said, "Dunno nobody named Ray."

"Come on, Meeshell. Don't bullshit me."

He leaned closer to her bed. "Did he do this to you?"

She hesitated, then shook her head.

"It wasn't Ray?"

No response.

"Who was it? Who did this?"

She held up a middle finger and turned her head away.

"Ray's in trouble, Meeshell. I need to talk to him. I need to know where to find him."

She closed her eyes.

"He beat up a motel clerk, and he threatened Greg's sister and her family."

"Didn't do any of those things," she got out.

"He did at least one thing, Meeshell. I talked to the motel clerk less than an hour ago and he told me who beat him up. It was Ray. There's no doubt."

When Meeshell didn't say anything further, the nurse laid a soft hand on his arm and said, "I'm going to have to ask you to go, okay? She needs to rest."

He considered asking for another few minutes, but realized Meeshell wasn't going to give anything up.

Still, he had to ask one more question. "Will you help me find him before the police do?"

As he expected, Meeshell ignored him.

He nodded to the nurse, said, "Goodbye, Meeshell" (which she also ignored), and left.

Preuss started up Woodward, intending to drive to his office.

He had just about come to believe that Ray Tomina was the one who beat Meeshell, but now she denied that. Was she denying it to throw Preuss off her boyfriend's trail? Would she do that if he really had beaten her?

Of course, he thought. Women protected their abusers every day of the week, often for more brutal attacks.

So that wasn't necessarily the truth. What about all the other denials? Denying that Tomina beat the motel clerk, that he tried to blackmail and threaten Carrie Morrison . . . it was all of a piece, he decided. She was too unreliable to believe about anything.

Without any substantive information from Meeshell, Preuss was left with the conclusions he had already thought his way through to: Tomina must have beaten up Meeshell, Tomina attacked Narendra, Tomina tried to blackmail Carrie and threatened her family, and Tomina (with the help of Meeshell) was responsible for Greg Braiden's condition.

What did all that have in common?

Tomina's penchant for violence.

Especially to get money. He beat up Narendra to steal the money from the motel; maybe he beat up Meeshell to get her earnings from her, and she wouldn't give them up.

He also threatened Carrie Morrison and her children if she didn't pay him.

And Greg? Where did he fit into this formula? Was Tomina trying to get more money from him than what Braiden was already giving Meeshell? And when Greg didn't give it over, Tomina shot him up?

Before he could consider that, his phone rang with a number he didn't for the moment recognize.

He tapped the hands-free answer button on the steering wheel.

And immediately regretted it.

36

"Hey guy."

The silken, malevolent voice of Jake Aklawi's driver filled the cabin of the Explorer.

"Victor," Preuss said. "Long time no talk to. How you been?"

"Mr. Aklawi wants to see you."

"Yeah, Victor, tell him I'm busy, okay?"

Victor paused for a long moment before saying, "I guess you didn't hear what I said."

"No, I heard you fine. I guess you didn't hear me."

Preuss disconnected and continued on to his office.

He had just pulled into a parking space outside his building when his phone rang again. Same number.

He punched the connect button on his steering wheel and heard Jake Aklawi say, "Mr. Preuss. Victor tells me you hung up on him."

"I did."

"Any particular reason?"

"I didn't want to talk to him."

Aklawi gave a soft chuckle. "He didn't like that."

"I don't care."

"You seem angry, my friend."

"Tell Victor the next time he sends someone after me at my own house, I won't be so gentle."

Aklawi said nothing. Then he said, "He did that?"

"He did."

"What happened?"

"Last week, a punk was waiting outside my house. In the dark. He came at me from behind. I fought him off and Victor rolled up to pick him up and get away. Brave, right?"

Preuss listened to Aklawi's steady breathing for a full half-minute.

"I'll speak with him," Aklawi finally said.

"You do that."

"I apologize. He'll be dealt with. How are you coming on that favor you're going to do for me?"

That was it. Preuss snapped.

"Look, let's get a few things straight, Jake. I don't work for you. We're not friends. I don't do you favors. And I don't appreciate your boy going on the muscle with me."

"That was unfortunate, and out of my control. I told you I'd deal with it."

"You need to get it back under your control. And why are you so interested in finding Tomina? Just unleash your bulldog on him."

"Let's discuss this in person," Aklawi said quickly. "Will you meet me for coffee?"

Aklawi was waiting for him at a Coney Island at the corner of Seven Mile and Charleston in Chaldean Town, east of Woodward in Detroit. He sat at a table near the rear of the restaurant, sipping from a bowl of soup. Victor sat at a table nearby, wolfing down a Coney dog and scowling at Preuss as he walked in.

Preuss scowled back.

Preuss sat down with Aklawi, and a waiter hurried over.

"Are you hungry?" Aklawi asked. "I recommend the bean soup. Thick and tasty." He lifted his spoon to show Preuss.

"Just coffee."

The waiter rushed away and Aklawi raised his own cup of coffee to his lips as if he had all the time in the world.

"What couldn't you tell me over the phone?" Preuss said.

"The less business I do over the phone, the better for everyone. I assume all my lines are tapped."

The waiter brought Preuss's coffee. Preuss tasted it. Manny's
coffee was superior, but this wasn't bad for Coney Island coffee.

"You sure you won't try the soup? You won't regret it."

Preuss shook his head and waited.

Aklawi shrugged, sipped more soup. "We seem to have a misunderstanding," he said.

Preuss remained silent.

"As I told you, it's important I speak with the boy I asked you
to look for. You were going to tell me if you found him."

"I haven't found him," Preuss said.

"Have you looked?" Aklawi asked, this time with an edge.

"Did you know he works for one of your competitors?" Preuss
asked.

Aklawi ate his soup in silence for a few moments, as if he
hadn't heard what Preuss had asked him.

"Of course you did," Preuss said.

Aklawi smacked his lips. "Sure you won't try some?" He held
up the spoon again. "Best in town."

"You already know he works for Peanut Carver," Preuss said.
"You don't want me to find him because he's giving your motel a bad
name. You want me to find him because he's on Carver's payroll."

Aklawi concentrated on his soup.

"I would have thought a guy like him would be too low in
Carver's organization for either one of you to bother with."

Aklawi wiped his mustache carefully, the paper scraping over
his wiry brush. He raised a hand and the waiter fairly ran over to take
the empty soup bowl away.

"So there must be another reason you want him," Preuss said.
"I'm interested in what that might be."

"You're no fool," Aklawi said. "I underestimated you."

"Many do. What else is going on here?"

"There's something else you should know about him."

Preuss waited.

"He's Chaldean."

"Tomina?"

Aklawi nodded solemnly.

"Tomina is a Chaldean name?"

"You thought he was Italian? Especially with the whole 'Ray Tomatoes' business? He's a stupid young man." Aklawi shook his head at Tomina's failings.

Tomina was swarthy, but Preuss had known many Italians with swarthier complexions.

"So Peanut poached one of your tribe? And you're looking for what, revenge?"

"I want to talk to him. Sit down and ask him why he's turning his back on his own people. On his family." Aklawi shrugged. "He's also my godson."

Preuss glanced at Victor, who was returning his look with daggers.

"And your boy over here can't find him?"

"I've had him looking. But you're a detective. Victor has other useful skills."

This earned Preuss a particularly foul leer from Victor.

"This is where our friendship comes in," Aklawi said.

"We're not friends, Jake. We're on opposite sides."

"Sides." Aklawi waved away the concept. "You may think there are sides. Good. Bad. There are no sides. There's only loyalty to family and friends, or not. Sides mean nothing. If my life has taught me anything, it's that."

Loyalty to the tribe, or not . . . A single, and old, formulation, the personal and emotional link of blood to blood. Which too often results in the spilling of others' blood.

"Remember what I said about being a good friend, Preuss? For those who return my friendship. And I'm a bad enemy to those who don't."

"Got it the first time," Preuss said.

"People who do favors for me, I do favors for them."

"What favors could you do for me?"

"Everyone needs a favor. Everyone has enemies. Everyone has family that needs protecting," Aklawi added ominously. He stared at Preuss with dead eyes.

Preuss felt as though a hole had opened in the center of his chest.

"Are you threatening my family?"

"From what I hear, you don't have much of one left. Just that one young man." He turned to Victor. "What's his name?"

"Toby," Victor spat.

"Toby," Aklawi said. "He's not quite right, I hear. That's a shame."

Preuss rose to his feet as though inflated by his sudden surge of anger.

"Don't go," Aklawi said. "We're not finished."

"Oh, we're finished."

"I think you misunderstand me," Aklawi said.

"No," Preuss said, "I get you just fine."

"In that case, my hand of friendship." Aklawi extended his rough hand.

Preuss left it hanging in the air.

Preuss leaned down and said, through gritted teeth, "I find out you or your flunky go anywhere near my son, you're going to find out what I do to *my* enemies."

Aklawi held both hands up in a gesture of shocked and confused innocence.

"Stay away from my son."

On his way out, Preuss stopped and leaned his hands on the table where Victor sat. He put his face into Victor's. "I find out you went near my boy, I'll kill you. You hear me, *guy?*"

He stood straight and swept Victor's glass of Coke into his lap.

Victor was on his feet in an instant, but Aklawi barked an order to him and Victor sat back down with reluctance.

Good idea, Preuss thought.

I'm in a very bad mood tonight.

37

He called the group home and asked them if Toby had gotten his bath yet. They said he was just about to go into the tub, and Preuss asked if they could wait until he got there.

It felt like a month since he had seen Toby, but it had just been one day—one long, tension-filled day. He missed his son terribly and needed to spend time with him while the boy was still awake. His beloved child had always been Preuss's island of sanity and innocence in the middle of the ocean of lies and deceit and violence in which he passed his days.

If anything happened to Toby because of Jake Aklawi or Victor, no power would keep either one safe from Preuss's wrath.

When he got to Toby's house, Toby was lying on his bed in just his diaper and a bathrobe covering him.

"The water was already in the tub," his aide Melissa said, "but as soon as you called, we let it all out. Now you're here, we'll fill it up again with nice warm water. Right, Tobe?"

But Toby's attention was on his father's face, looming over the bed, taking in the beauty of his son—his oval face, his almond-shaped and almost sightless eyes, his smooth waxen skin, and the Brando-esque bump at the bridge of Toby's nose.

"Well," Preuss said, "finally. I get to see you while your eyes are open."

Toby gave him a crooked smile.

Preuss bent down and wrapped his arms around his son's shoulders and gave him a hug that lasted so long Toby began to squirm.

Preuss ended it with a kiss on Toby's sweaty head and released him. He removed the robe and undid the straps on Toby's diaper and rolled him off of it. Blue lines of pee striped the front. Preuss rolled up the diaper and tossed it in the trash can, then took a handful of baby wipes and cleaned off Toby's crotch and rolled his son onto the lift pad. Preuss hooked him up to the overhead lift and hoisted the boy up and into his wheelchair.

He covered Toby with the bathrobe and pushed him into the bathroom where the tub was filling up. As soon as Toby heard water splashing, he squealed in joy. The only thing he loved more than his bath was the full-body stimulation of swimming.

Preuss used the lift in the bathroom to get Toby into the bath chair inside the tub and unhooked the bath sling connected to the lift. When the tub was filled up, Preuss turned on the whirlpool jets and Toby was in heaven.

Preuss let him soak for a long time, replenishing the hot water as the tub cooled. The actions of bathing his son allowed him to transform the anger he felt toward Aklawi into love for this beautiful, vulnerable child.

He gave Toby his shampoo and took a washcloth and soaped the boy up, paying special attention to lifting his stiff arms to soap his pits. He rinsed Toby off and let him soak for a few more minutes. Then he let the water out of the tub and reconnected the lift to the sling and lifted the dripping wet boy up and into the chair. Toby vocalized loudly, complaining either because his bath was over or because he was cold. Or both.

Preuss wrapped the bathrobe around his son and wheeled him back into his room to get him up on the bed and dried off and into his pajamas.

He told Toby about the latest development in his cases— about what he had learned about Greg Braiden and the sad turn in the life of Meeshell Lee. Toby attended closely to what his father was saying.

"And that's what I've been doing, sweetheart," Preuss told his son. "That's why I haven't been over to visit you since last night. But you understand, don't you?"

Lying on his right side—his sleep side—Toby gave his father the merest hint of a smile. Goofy and blissful.

"Knock knock," the nurse said. She entered Toby's room with a small tray of syringes filled with Toby's nighttime meds and a feeding bag filled with Toby's formula.

"Come in," Preuss said. "We're just sitting here chatting."

"Glad to see your dad?" the nurse asked.

Toby made a small noise, not quite a grunt and not quite an articulated word, but clearly an assent.

"All right," the nurse said, "I'll just get you set up here, and I'll get out of your way."

"Not a problem," Preuss said.

The nurse squirted Toby's meds directly into his G-tube button with a plastic syringe, followed it with a rinse of water in a large bolus tube, and then connected the tube from the feeding pump and hooked him up for his dinner. She turned the pump on, and it made its characteristic whirring sound. When Toby was much younger and still lived at home with the intact family, Preuss would turn on Toby's portable pump and then sing along with the whirring, which sounded like Rolling Stones lyrics:

> *Some kind of ventilator*
> *Some kind of ventilator*

He would hold Toby in his arms and rock him to the repetitive rhythm, all the while feeling the boy's substantiality—his weight, his smells both pleasant and unpleasant, the sounds he would make in his high, childish voice as he tried to sing along with his father.

Now, with his love for the boy even more encompassing than it was then, he turned on the Judy Collins CDs, and Toby drifted off to sleep to the ethereal calls of the whales in "Farewell to Tarwathie."

Preuss remained in the chair beside his son's bed while the CD player ran through the Judy Collins CDs he had queued up. When they were finished, he pulled himself to his feet, gave his son a soft goodnight kiss on the side of his temple, and left.

He drove past his house and went twice around the block, checking the street for strangers and strange cars, especially a Camaro.

When he saw nothing out of the ordinary, he pulled into his driveway and turned on the spotlight on the driver's side. He shone it into his front bushes and the bushes of his neighbor, then decided all was quiet.

And it was; no sign of Victor or anyone else outside or inside the house.

He made a cup of decaf and took it out to the back deck. He stood breathing in the remnants of the day's fall warmth, still radiating off the deck wood. The sky was a cloudy dark blue. Rain, possibly heavy at times, was forecast for the next day; he could already smell it coming.

He set his cup on the deck and lay back on the chaise. I'm not going to fall asleep, he told himself. I'm just going to relax out here for a little while, and then I'll go inside and take myself up to bed. Where I'll sleep like a normal person. Instead of chasing around the City of Detroit with a maniac in the middle of the night.

He was still on the chaise in the early morning when rain woke him, cold and stiff.

Thursday, September 27, 2012

38

Along with the rain had come cooler temperatures. In the damp air of the group home, his son was still asleep.

Preuss got Toby's clothes ready as his morning aide gently woke the boy, and the nurse came in with his morning medicine and his first feeding of the day. Toby woke up but slid back into sleep as his pump dripped formula into his G-tube.

By the time Preuss got him dressed and held the umbrella over him as his aides walked him out to the waiting van in his wheel-chair, Toby was wide awake and humming happily.

Preuss watched the bus take his son away. Toby looked around, enjoying his morning, his ride, his life.

Preuss trotted back inside the house to retrieve his raincoat. Toby's morning aide, Maria, was making Toby's bed while another of the aides, Issa, was bringing a basketful of his clean clothes to put away in the drawers. The two women were chatting, but stopped when Preuss entered the room.

"He got off okay?" Maria asked.

"He did. He finally woke up and was smiling and happy."

"Such a sweet boy," she said. She had been Toby's aide since he moved into the house. She was an older Greek woman with a gentle way with her charges.

"Sorry," Preuss said, "don't mean to interrupt. Just want to get my coat and I'll be out of your way."

"That's okay," Maria said. "We're just talking. Issa was telling me she's going back to school."

"That's great," Preuss said. "Where?"

"Oakland University," Issa said.

"What are you going to study?"

"Nursing. I want to get my BA."

"Wonderful," Preuss said. "Good luck."

"Thanks."

He retrieved his coat from Toby's chair and nodded to the two women and left.

Manny's door was closed. "Is he in?" Preuss asked Rhonda.

She shook her head, making the confection of her hairdo wobble. "He called in. He won't be in till later."

"He say why?"

"Nope."

Preuss filled his mug with coffee from Rhonda's machine and sat on the sofa in her outer office.

"Do you know what's going on with him?" Preuss asked.

"In terms of what?"

"His health. He's had that cough for weeks, and his voice seems to be getting worse by the day."

"Worse how?"

"You haven't noticed how hoarse he is?"

"Sure. But he says it's just a cold."

"How long does a cold last? He's had this for months. The other thing is, he's hardly ever around anymore."

"So ask him."

"I did."

"And?"

"He wouldn't say anything."

"Well, there you have it," she said.

"Have what?"

"I'm sure if he had a problem, he'd tell us."

"I'm not so sure. He hasn't said anything to you?" Preuss asked.

"Nope."

"Next time he comes in, will you pay attention to how you think he is?"

She said she would, and he went into his office. He would have to ask Manny about it again. And refuse to be put off.

He pulled up the file for Greg Braiden on his computer and noted the events of the past days—his conversations with Ramonda, Meeshell, and Carrie Morrison, and the attack on Narendra at the motel.

He also added a note about his meeting with Aklawi.

As he entered the information, Preuss circled back to the question of who hurt Meeshell. He still wasn't totally convinced Tomina had done it, despite the evidence of Tomina's violent temper in his treatment of Narendra.

He sat thinking about Narendra, wondering how the studious clerk was doing.

And why Ray Tomina would have beaten him so badly, or caused such destruction in the motel office. Was it anger, or something else . . . maybe something he was looking for, besides the money? And wasn't finding?

Then he wondered if the Embers Motel had security footage of the office, and what it might reveal.

It was still early in the day, and the residents of the Embers hadn't yet begun to stir. Preuss left the Explorer in a parking space next to the office and went inside.

Narendra was not behind the thick acrylic partition. Instead, a young woman, dark-complected and slender in a sari, sat behind the desk. She might have been in her twenties, he guessed. The registration area had been tidied up, with all the binders back in place on the shelves.

The young woman, whose name badge said Harshi, looked up at Preuss warily.

Preuss passed a business card through the cash slot in the plexiglass window.

"I'm looking for Narendra," he said.

"He's not in today."

"Is he feeling better?"

Harshi looked curiously at Preuss, who said, "I'm the guy who found him yesterday. He was in bad shape."

"He's still in the hospital, under observation. He might come home today."

"Good. Are you a member of the family?"

Now Preuss really had the young woman confused. Who was this guy? How did he know so much?

"Yes."

"Neel is your uncle, too?"

"No, my father."

He looked behind her. "The office was pretty messed up. Are you the one who straightened it?"

"I am. It was bad," she agreed. "I had to scrub Narendra's blood off the floor. Very unpleasant."

"I saw it. The man who did it—were you able to figure out what he was looking for?"

"No."

"Nothing was missing?"

"Just the money in the cash drawer. He took it all."

Preuss wondered if Tomina had wrecked the office just to cause destruction. Maybe he wasn't trying to find anything. Did he blunder in on Narendra's call to Preuss?

"Do you have security cameras here?"

Harshi looked around and pointed to the winking red eye of a closed-circuit camera aimed at the front desk. "Up there. We have them all over the property."

"Do they work?"

"Of course," she said, her eyes flashing darker that he would insult her by asking.

"Have the police asked to look at the CCTV tapes?"

"No," she said. "There was no need. Narendra was very clear about what happened."

"Can I take a look at them?"

Here she gave Preuss a long, searching look.

"I'm a private investigator," Preuss said. "If we can look at those disks, we can see what happened yesterday."

"But we already know what happened."

"We know who caused all the damage. What we don't know is what else the man who hurt Narendra might have wanted. The security footage will tell us."

"That will not be possible," she said. "These are not for viewing by the public."

"Look," he said, "the man who did all this might have been involved in other serious crimes. Including murder," he added, to get her attention. "The tapes might give us information about those. Could you call your father and ask him if it's okay if I look at them? Narendra knows me. Call him, too, if you want."

She shook her head firmly.

Okay, he thought.

This is not going to happen.

"How about if you call Narendra and ask him about me? He'll tell you I'm okay. Would you do that? I'll leave, so you won't have to worry about me even being here."

"I'll think about it."

"Thanks. If you talk to him, please ask him to call me when he can. Would you do that? I want to know how he's feeling."

"I guess."

"Great, thanks."

He turned to leave the office, then remembered another question.

"Do you work here a lot?"

"I usually do the day shift. I was off yesterday."

"The man who did this thing yesterday is Ray Tomina. Do you know him? He stays here sometimes."

Again, that made the poor young woman stop and consider where that question was coming from.

"Yes," Harshi admitted. "I know who that is."

"Is he here now?"

"I haven't seen him since I was here two days ago."

"If you do see him, my advice is to call the Highland Park police. They're looking for him for what he did to Narendra. Among many other things," he added.

39

At the Southfield office, Manny was still out.

Rhonda handed Preuss a phone message.

Beverly Frankel, the Purple Gang client.

"Mr. Preuss," she said when he called her back, "thanks so much for returning my call."

"How are you, Beverly?"

"I'm *great*! So, I'm wondering if you had a chance to set anything up with Mrs. Posner?"

"No, I haven't," he said. "Sorry. I've been tied up on another case."

"No problem. Just checking."

"I'll set up a meeting as soon as I have a few minutes. You were going to email me your schedule?"

"I can just tell you," she said. "Afternoons are best. I have classes in the mornings. But if that's the only time she can see me, I'll work around them. Weekends are good, too."

"Okay," he said, "that's helpful. I'll be in touch."

"And of course I'd like you there, too. Will you come?"

"That's really not necessary. What you have to talk about is between you and Mrs. Posner."

"I know. But if it hadn't been for you, I'd never have known about this side of my family. Please! I want you there. You *have* to!"

He said he would let her know when he arranged something and promised to be in touch.

He called Sarah Posner, but the call went unanswered.

As soon as he hung up, his phone rang.

Harshi Kalam, from the Embers Motel.

"I talked to Narendra," she said. "And my father. And they both said it was okay to let you see the security recordings."

"Wonderful," he said. "Can I come now?"

She set him up on a computer in the room behind the office. She gave him a stack of CDs. "We usually only save them for two weeks before we record over them. But we haven't gotten around to rewriting these, so there's over a month here. I also gave you the one from this past week, including yesterday."

"Perfect," Preuss said. He settled in with a cup of coffee from the vending machine in the office and started through the disks, working backwards from the most recent ones. There were six security cameras, each trained on a different view: one on the inside of the office, one on the outside of the office, two on each side of the parking lot, and one each on the inside corners of the buildings.

The image onscreen had six panels, each recording in real time. To begin with, he concentrated on the camera inside the office. He backed up the disk to the previous morning and sent it forward at triple speed. He watched Narendra going through his daily routines, with people comically toddling up to the counter and haggling with him, and equally as comically toddling away in various states of annoyance.

When he got to the point where Ray Tomina came into the office, Preuss slowed the playback speed to normal. There goes one theory, he thought: Narendra was not on the phone with Preuss when Tomina appeared. In fact, Tomina came into the office a good fifteen minutes after Narendra hung up from his call with Preuss.

He watched as Tomina came up to the counter, across the security window, and began talking with Narendra. For his part, Narendra looked guiltily nervous (having just called Preuss about the man standing in front of him?). Tomina asked him questions, which Preuss couldn't hear, though he saw Narendra shaking his head several times.

Then Tomina went crazy.

He drove the flat of his hand into the security glass, which drove Narendra back away from the desk.

Tomina ran around to pull at the door leading into the front desk area. He pulled and jiggled and kicked it, and the door opened as if by magic and Tomina ran inside and leapt onto Narendra, who immediately fell into a fetal position as Tomina began pummeling him.

Tomina kept asking Narendra questions, and Narendra kept shaking his head. Finally Tomina rained blows down on Narendra's head and body until Narendra stopped protecting himself and lost consciousness.

Tomina flipped him over and went through his pockets. He withdrew a set of keys and opened the cash drawer—so that was the first thing he went for after all. He pulled the drawer open and up-ended it on the floor. Cash and coins flew everywhere.

But the interesting thing was, Tomina looked around on the floor, then returned to the opening where the drawer was and felt around inside. He was looking for something other than cash, Preuss realized.

When he didn't find what he was looking for inside the cash drawer opening, Tomina swept through the rest of the office, knocking books off the shelves and pulling papers and staplers and pens and pencils and other office supplies from the other drawers.

Now he seemed to be in a frenzy, his face twisted in fury. He tried to get into the back office, but the door was locked with a push-button combination lock. He pushed and pulled and kicked it, but the door wouldn't budge.

He scooped up the cash from the floor, landed one more punch on poor Narendra's head, and fled.

Preuss watched his progress on the other camera screens: out-side the office, across the parking lot to a room, in and out of the room in two minutes, then jumping into his Monte Carlo and speed-ing out of the lot.

Preuss watched as a few men and women from the motel came into the office, saw the scene inside, and turned and fled.

Then he saw himself, entering and taking in the mess.

He hit pause and went into the outer front office.

"Find what you need?" Harshi asked.

"Maybe," he said. "It seemed like Tomina was looking for something inside the cash drawer. Do you keep anything in there besides money?"

"Not anymore."

"What used to be there?"

"We used to keep our security camera disks there. Last week, Narendra moved them."

"Where are they now?"

"In the safe. In the back room," she added.

"So nobody could have gotten to them yesterday?"

"No. As you can see, they're all here now. And we keep this door locked at all times. Nobody has the combination except Uncle, Narendra, and me."

He thanked her and returned to the computer screen in the back office.

Going at triple speed, Preuss watched the rest of the security disks. He breezed through hours of cars and men and women and fights and the parking lot that went from empty to full, filthy to clean, day to night, in the blink of an eye.

In the late afternoon, he found what Tomina might have been anxious to get his hands on.

On a misty morning in late August, on one panel of the security cameras that showed the east end of the parking lot, Preuss saw a black Crown Vic pull up in front of room 110. He watched a large black man exit the car, knock on the door that Ray Tomina opened, and go into the room. Forty-five minutes later, he came out and got back into his car and drove off.

The man was Charles Montgomery.

As in, Detroit Police Detective Charles Montgomery.

Friend of Alonzo Barber.

40

Preuss bought two coffees from the stand in Campus Martius Park in downtown Detroit and took them to a table under a canopy beside the fountain. Ochre leaves fallen from the honey locust trees around the park littered the chairs and formed a spotty carpet on the ground.

Alonzo Barber took his coffee. "Much obliged," he said.

At this hour of the balmy fall evening, activity was all around them. The Tigers were playing the Kansas City Royals at the ballpark nearby, so a constant stream of cars flowed around the park on Woodward Avenue toward parking lots. Couples sat under the canopies sipping drinks. A raucous group of young men and women passed on the sidewalk. Singles sat either on their phones or else simply staring out at the activity. Twenty- and thirty-somethings zipped around the sidewalk on old-fashioned kids' scooters, the newest downtown fad.

"What's so urgent?" Barber asked.

"I spent an inordinate amount of time today reviewing security footage from the Embers Motel in Highland Park."

"I can only imagine how uplifting that must have been."

"Not so much uplifting," Preuss said, "as eye-opening."

Suddenly serious, but maintaining his cool, Barber said, "Okay."

"I was trying to find out why Ray Tomina might have wanted to steal the security disks."

"How do you know he did?"

"The office was torn up, and the cash drawer was opened and emptied. And that's where the security disks used to be kept."

"Used to be?"

"Now they're in the safe."

"If the drawer's also where the money was . . ."

"But that wasn't what he was looking for. He opened the drawer and the money fell out. And yeah, he took the money, but he kept looking for something else."

"And you think it was the disks?"

"I think he was looking for them, and the clerk wouldn't tell him where they were, and that's why he beat the poor guy up."

"How would he know that's where they used to be?"

"Evidently, he comes into the office quite a bit. He must have known that's where they were kept."

Barber opened the lid of the coffee cup and took a loud slurp of his coffee. "What's all this have to do with me?"

"Not you," Preuss said. "Your buddy Montgomery."

Preuss watched Barber, but the other man didn't reveal anything.

"Keep going," Barber said.

"I saw him on the security footage. He went into a room with Ray Tomina."

Barber said nothing. He blew across the mouth of his cup.

"And not once, either," Preuss continued. "I went back a month, and I saw him there four times. Once a week. Stopping off to see Tomina. Each time, they met for thirty or forty-five minutes."

Barber was silent.

"Do you know anything about this?" Preuss asked.

"You're sure it was Tomina?"

"Positive."

"And Monty? You're sure it was him?"

"Montgomery's a hard man to miss. Unless you confuse him with a construction crane."

When Barber still didn't say anything, Preuss asked, "What do you know about him, Alonzo?"

"Montgomery?"

Preuss nodded.

"What are you *saying* about him?" Barber threw it back at Preuss. "Are you saying he's dirty?"

"I'm not saying anything. I'm asking."

Barber shook his paper cup to stir up his drink. When he didn't say anything, Preuss said, "You know him better than I do. I'm looking for a reason for him to meet with Tomina every week for a month. And who knows how much longer before that?"

"This have a bearing on your case?"

"It might," Preuss said. "It might also have a bearing on your friend. I know you guys're—"

Barber held up a large hand, cutting Preuss off. "Stop. Right there. You don't know anything about our friendship, his and mine."

Barber stood up, adjusting the sharp crease in his suit pants, and walked over to a trash bin, where he dumped his cup.

"I'm not trying to cause trouble, Alonzo," Preuss said. "I just want to know what's going on here."

"I'll speak with him," Barber said. "I'll be in touch. Meantime, don't mention this to anybody. Right?"

Preuss stayed in the park for a while after Alonzo left. He stretched out on the chair and let his head hang over the back. It was a cloudless evening after a rainy day. Perfect for a baseball game, he thought. He remembered he had wanted to take Toby to a game before the season ended; they would have to go soon.

He replayed his conversation with Barber. If anybody's friendship is at risk here, Preuss thought, it's ours. He felt as though he had crossed a line with Barber that he didn't even know was there, had cast aspersions on a fellow officer. Preuss had never seen this grim side to Barber, and it saddened him to think that this might change things between them.

As he let his head hang over the back of the chair, he watched the sky. The silhouette of a peregrine falcon, its wings outstretched, passed across his field of vision, gliding on the thermals above the downtown. The falcon population was rebounding in Detroit thanks in part to the city's high buildings that the birds used for their nests.

He imagined this one was looking to snatch its dinner, a squirrel or chipmunk, or even a city rat, as it made its lazy sail.

Death descending from the sky, he thought. The lethal inevitability of it.

Death the general order of things. Sooner or later, the world wasted everything. And everyone. Lighting the way to dusty death . . . he had read that once. Death is the end for us all, he thought; everything else is just biding time.

He drove past the group home. Lights were on in the house, but that was because the night staff was awake; all the residents, including his son, would be asleep.

Ordinarily, he wouldn't think twice about going in to see Toby. In his current frame of mind, however, he didn't want to look at his son and think about the boy not existing any more for all eternity.

So he decided to let Toby sleep in peace, and drove down Woodward toward his house in Ferndale.

He had no unwelcome visitors waiting in the bushes. He didn't even have the energy to climb the stairs to his room. Instead, he dragged himself to the sofa in his living room and collapsed.

He stayed like that, his thoughts spiraling like the falcon he had seen earlier over Campus Martius, until he drifted into welcome sleep.

Friday, September 28, 2012

41

By the time Preuss reached his office in the morning, Montgomery had already left a message.

Preuss called him back.

"We need to meet," Montgomery told him.

"When and where?"

It made Preuss miss Friday coffee time.

Back downtown.

Montgomery was waiting for him on one of the concrete rows of seats in the Main Amphitheater at Hart Plaza at the foot of Woodward Avenue. The big man sat with his elbows on his knees and his hands clasped in front of him. He stared without expression down at the empty stage.

Preuss sat next to him. Montgomery turned his big head to acknowledge Preuss, then looked back at the stage.

"I saw the Sun Ra Arkestra here last year," Montgomery said, without looking at Preuss. "During the Jazz Fest. They some wild cats, man."

"I've seen them."

That got Montgomery's attention. "Seriously?"

"Sure."

"Here?"

"No. This was years ago, in New York. Sun Ra was still alive. I was there with my wife on vacation. He was playing someplace in the Village, I wanted to see what he was like."

Montgomery looked at Preuss with a new interest. "You heard Sun Ra in person." More a statement of disbelief than a question.

"I did."

"You a fan?"

"I'd heard his albums. I wanted to see the man himself."

"And?"

"I'd never heard or seen anything like it."

Montgomery turned away, nodding. "Got that right. Isn't to everybody's taste. Brother from another planet for real."

Preuss nodded agreement.

"Claimed to be from Jupiter, or some shit."

"Sounded like it, too," Preuss said.

That made Montgomery laugh. "Sun Ra. Preuss, you surprise me," he said.

Then Montgomery grew serious. "Alonzo called me last night," he said.

"I figured he would."

"Told me what you saw on the Embers' CCTV."

Preuss said nothing.

"Said you had questions about what you saw."

"I do."

"Don't blame you," Montgomery said. "I would, too."

"So what were you doing there, Charles? What was that all about?"

"Only one ever called me Charles was my mother. Everybody else calls me Monty."

"Okay, Monty. Why were you and Tomina on that surveillance tape?"

"You think I'm dirty?"

"I don't think anything. That's why I'm asking."

Montgomery grunted. He leaned his chin on a big fist.

"Alonzo speaks well of you," he said. "Said you were a good cop. Honest, too."

"I tried to be. Wasn't always easy."

"Never is. He said you got railroaded out of the job."

"Ancient history."

"Also said I can trust you." He gave Preuss a sidelong glance. "That true?"

"It's true. You don't have anything to worry about from me."

"What I'm going to tell you can't go any further. You okay with that?"

"Sure," Preuss said.

"Tomina?" Montgomery said. "He's a CI."

It took Preuss a few moments to process that.

"Ray Tomatoes is a police informant?"

Montgomery nodded. "When I met him those times, he was passing me information."

"About Peanut Carver?"

Montgomery nodded. "And other lowlifes. Including Jake Ak-lawi, who he used to run with. That's why I didn't want you talking to Carver. Didn't want you sticking your nose in, giving him ideas, getting him to think too much about Tomina."

"So Tomina was looking for the security disks after all," Preuss said. "He wanted to make sure nobody saw you together, blow his cover."

"And possibly end his life."

Now it made sense why Aklawi was so hot to find him, Preuss thought. He must have found out Tomina was an informant. But how? Who would have told him?

"Why now?" Preuss wondered. "Why's he so worried about what's on the security disks now? Because he knows I'm after him?"

"That'd be my guess. I suspect he's getting ready to run and he doesn't want to leave anything behind."

"Could be," Preuss said. He remembered Ramonda telling him that Meeshell and Ray were getting ready to bolt.

Neither man spoke until Montgomery said, "This stays between us."

"Absolutely. Does Alonzo know?"

"He does now. But you don't need to talk to him about this. Nobody else knows, except the people in the department who need to. I'm only telling you because Alonzo said I could trust you."

"I appreciate that."

Montgomery was quiet for a few seconds, then said, "You went to see Carver after all?"

"I did."

"I hear you left a bit of a mess behind, too."

Preuss said nothing.

"In the alley behind the club?"

"How do you know about that?" Preuss asked.

"Jimmy's Millionaires is under surveillance."

"So you know what happened?"

Montgomery gave him a curt nod. "Don't worry about it. It's taken care of."

He sat staring down at the empty stage for another minute. Then he unfolded himself from the concrete row and stretched to his full height. "I hear anybody finds out what I told you about Tomina," Montgomery said, "I'll know where it came from."

"Depend on me," Preuss said. "Monty, where can I find him?"

"You can't."

"I need to talk to him about my case."

"Not gonna happen," Montgomery said. "Stay out of this, Preuss. I don't care what your musical tastes are. This ain't your business."

Montgomery took a giant stride over the row of seats behind them and trotted up to Hart Plaza and was gone.

No, Preuss thought, this is exactly my business. Now it was more important than ever to find Tomina.

While he was still alive.

42

Preuss caught them just in time.

Meeshell Lee sat in a wheelchair in the hallway outside her room. She was handcuffed to the chair, and a big Detroit uniformed officer stood beside her as another one spoke with the discharge nurse at the desk. An orderly waited behind the chair.

She glared at Preuss as he came up to her.

"Are you leaving?" he asked her.

When she didn't answer, the cop beside her said, "We're taking her to the video arraignment downstairs. Doc said she's well enough."

Meeshell looked at Preuss sourly. She bared her teeth and showed him her wired-up mouth, a startlingly savage gesture.

He knelt down beside her. "Meeshell," he said, "I know you don't want to talk to me, but we don't have much time and you need to listen. Ray's in trouble."

"Tell me something I don't know," she said between clenched teeth.

"No, he's in more trouble than you know about. There are people out there trying to kill him. And they're going to do it, unless I find him first."

She scoffed, turned her head. The uniformed officer at the desk gave Preuss a hard look.

"Meeshell, listen to me. The people looking for him, they're not playing. If you care for him at all, you'll tell me where I can find him. If I don't get to him before they do, they'll kill him."

Meeshell watched him, looking for a sign she was being played. But the seriousness of what he was saying penetrated.

"For real?" she asked.

"For real."

The uniformed cop turned from the desk and said, "That's it. Let's roll."

"Step back, sir," the cop beside the wheelchair said to Preuss.

"Meeshell?"

"I said, step back," the cop said, harder now. He motioned Preuss away from the wheelchair.

Preuss stood and stepped away from them.

"Wait," Meeshell said to him. She beckoned Preuss back and he knelt beside her.

She grabbed his lapel. "You telling me the truth?"

"I'm not lying. He's in danger. Tell me where he is."

"You know Nikki Bardellini?"

"In Southfield? That's where he is?"

She shook her head.

"Let's go," the big cop in charge said. "Move back."

"No," Meeshell said, but the orderly began to push her toward the elevators. Preuss followed along.

"Nikki has a boyfriend," she told him. "Lives up in Pontiac. Dwayne Dubicki. That's where Ray is."

The address Rhonda found for Dwayne Dubicki was on a street of identical tiny white framed bungalows three blocks from the GM stamping plant in Pontiac. A weathered wooden wheelchair ramp zigzagged across the front of the house.

A hand-lettered sign on the door frame read, "Bell don't work." Preuss knocked, and the door swung open.

He stood looking at a painfully thin man in a wheelchair. Preuss recognized him as the man who had lurked in the doorway to Nikki Bardellini's home the first time he went there looking for Meeshell. Unlike Toby's custom-designed wheelchair, this one was worn and plain, with scratched aluminum tubes and a cracked leather seat.

"Yeah?" the man said. He had thinning limp hair and seemed to be missing every other tooth.

"Dwayne?"

"Yeah. Who's asking?"

Before Preuss could say what he wanted, he saw Ray Tomina pass by a doorway at the rear of the tiny home.

At the same time, Tomina looked in his direction.

When they made eye contact, Tomina took off toward the back of the house, and Preuss shouted, "Ray!"

He tried to get past Dubicki into the house, but Dubicki blocked his way with the wheelchair.

Preuss leapt off the porch onto the driveway and rounded the corner into the backyard just as Tomina burst from the side door. Tomina ran into the backyard toward the garage and the stockade fence separating Dubicki's property from the one behind it.

Preuss threw himself at Tomina just as Tomina tried to scramble over the fence. The two men fell heavily to the ground. Preuss was on top of him bending Tomina's arms behind him before Tomina could gather his feet under him.

"Easy," Preuss said. "I just want to talk."

"I got nothing to say."

"What'd you do to Meeshell?"

Preuss's question made Tomina stop struggling. "What happened to Meeshell?"

"You don't know?"

"No. I don't know what you're talking about."

"She's in the hospital."

"The *hospital*! What for?"

"She got the shit beat out of her."

The look Tomina gave him over his shoulder convinced Preuss that whoever beat Meeshell, it wasn't this guy.

"Who did it?" Tomina asked.

"Let's go inside and talk," Preuss said.

He pulled Tomina to his feet and began walking him back toward the house, but Tomina dug his heels in the grass. "Who did it?" he demanded again.

Preuss pushed him forward with an effort.

Gunfire erupted from the driveway. Tomina cried out as a bullet to his shoulder drove him back against Preuss.

Aklawi's thug Victor stood in the driveway with a handgun aimed at Tomina and, behind him, holding him up, Martin Preuss.

Backpedaling, Preuss dragged his captive further into the backyard as Victor advanced on them, firing wildly.

Preuss thought: Victor may be a good man with a knife in a fight with a screen door, but he can't hit shit with a gun.

More firing. Bullets slammed into the stockade fence, the garage door, and the grass.

There was a lull, then the sound of metal hitting the concrete of the driveway. Victor ejecting the spent magazine.

Preuss pulled Tomina behind the garage until they were jammed into the corner. They could go no further. Nothing to hide behind. Nothing to use as a weapon. No way to clamber over the high stockade fence, no rear door to the garage.

Victor appeared at the corner of the garage and slammed another magazine into his pistol. He grinned at the scene.

Preuss covered Tomina with his body, whatever protection that would afford him.

"Mr. Aklawi only sent me to cash in Tomatoes," Victor said. "Yeah, but Preuss, maybe you're gonna be, what do they call it? A twofer? What do you think, *guy*?"

"Victor," Preuss said, "you don't want to do this."

"Oh yeah, I do."

"It's not going to end well."

"You right about that, guy," Victor said, and, still grinning, raised his pistol. "Which one goes first?" He moved his pistol from one to the other. "Eenie, meenie . . ."

It's not going to matter which one goes first, Preuss knew. Victor couldn't miss at this range. It didn't matter what kind of crap shot he was. What mattered was the cold glee he was bringing to this job.

All Preuss could think about was Toby, who would be left alone if Preuss died. Toby's gorgeous round face with his crooked smile and Jeanette's brown eyes. Alone in the world.

Yesterday I worried about him going extinct, he thought, and really it's going to be me.

Who will take care of my Toby?

Will this be my last thought on earth? Preuss wondered.

Will the last sound be Victor's moronic chuckle as he came closer, moving the pistol from one man to the other, taunting them?

Victor fired again, and the bullet caught Tomina in his thigh.

No, Preuss thought. Not without a fight.

"Victor," he said, "listen to me. I'm not talking about us. I'm talking about ending badly for you."

"You don't worry about me."

"You're going to explain to Aklawi why you killed us both in cold blood?"

"That's the plan."

"Did he tell you to do it? Kill us both?"

That made Victor's smile falter, and he stopped. Preuss pressed on.

"Big Jake didn't tell you to kill me," Preuss said, "did he?"

"He don't care if I do," Victor said.

"Oh, really? I think that's not part of what he told you to do. You're in enough trouble with him, Victor. What's he going to do when you disobey him again?"

"You think he gives a shit about you, guy? He don't. He told me if you get in the way, it's no great loss."

"Maybe so. But I don't think he wanted you to just blast away in broad daylight. Am I right, Victor?"

"That's my own idea," he said with stupid pride. "Besides, I don't see nobody watching."

"You don't know who's watching. You don't know who's in these houses, maybe recording you right now. Calling the police about seeing somebody getting shot and recording the whole thing on their phone."

While he talked, Preuss edged up to his feet. Behind him, Tomina, shot twice, lay motionless.

"Maybe they're on their way right now," Preuss said. "Hear any sirens?" He pointed to the sky, inviting Victor to listen.

He was getting through. Preuss saw Victor's hesitation. If he could talk him out of this, they had a chance.

"Maybe you should just take us back to Aklawi," Preuss went on. "You'll get us out from prying eyes, and he can find out what Tomina told the cops. And you can see how he feels about me. Remember the last time you made a decision about what to do with me? He wasn't happy."

That did it.

Victor lowered the gun. Preuss felt a sudden flush of happiness; he had just gotten the rest of his life back.

"Now," Preuss said, "how about you put that gun away and we'll—"

A shout came from the driveway.

Victor turned his head toward the sound, and Preuss heard another explosion and in the next instant Victor flew off his feet into the stockage fence.

He crumpled into a heap in the scrub weeds.

Preuss shouted, "No!"

He rushed toward where Victor lay and knelt beside him. Blood blossomed on the right side of Victor's chest. No breath sounds. No pulse.

Preuss looked out into the driveway and saw Dwayne Dubicki sitting in his wheelchair, holding a shotgun pointed at him.

"What did you do?" Preuss yelled. "He was giving up!"

"Didn't look like it to me," Dubicki said.

"Call a goddamn ambulance," Preuss shouted to him.

When the man in the wheelchair didn't move, Preuss shouted to him again and Dubicki did a wheelie on his two rear tires and pushed himself around to the front of the house.

Preuss went back to see how Tomina was doing. He was bleeding from the wounds to his shoulder and leg, and he was panting.

Preuss knelt beside him. "Ray," he said, "an ambulance is on the way. Hang on."

Tomina writhed in pain.

Then his eyes rolled back in his head and he passed out.

43

The Oakland County Coroner pronounced Victor Kirma dead at the scene.

A crew from the County medical examiner's office brought him out in a red body bag. An ambulance crew tended to Ray Tomina.

The Oakland County Sheriff's Office provided police services for the City of Pontiac. Preuss gave his statement to a deputy, who told him to wait to speak with Inspector Emma Blalock of the Special Investigations Unit. She was in transit to the scene.

Preuss waited in his Explorer. Dwayne Dubicki's rifle was legally registered. He told the deputies he brought it outside when he heard gunfire, and saw Victor pointing a gun behind his garage. When he shouted and Victor turned, Dwayne thought the gunman was aiming at him and his life was in danger. He fired at Victor, and the shot killed him instantly.

When Emma Blalock showed up, the deputies filled her in on what they found. She nodded her understanding and approval. She came over to Preuss, who stepped out of the car to shake hands with her.

"How are you doing?" she asked.

"Better now. Little while ago, not so good."

"You're a lucky man. Again. Want to tell me what you're doing up here?"

He explained how he came looking for Ray Tomina, who was a witness on a case he was working on. He told her how Jake Aklawi sent Victor after him on Tomina's trail, and what happened leading up to Dubicki's discharge of his weapon.

"Speak with Charles Montgomery on the Detroit PD about Tomina," Preuss said. "I've been coordinating with him."

"Uh-huh."

"He'll confirm my story."

"Uh-huh."

She held his gaze. They had a history, Preuss and Emma. It wasn't so long ago that they went out together a few times, and she had wanted to pursue a more serious relationship with him than he was comfortable with. Things had been touchy between them ever since.

"Did you give your statement?" she asked.

"One of the deputies took it."

She nodded.

"Am I free to go?" he asked.

"We're not charging you with anything, if that's what you're asking."

"That's what I'm asking."

"I'm not wild about you bringing your problems up here, Martin," she said. "Again."

Rather than argue with her, he said, "Understood." He just wanted to get away.

"How's your boy?" she asked.

"Good," Preuss said. "Toby's doing well."

"He was lucky today, too."

"Don't I know it."

She watched him with cold eyes, then said, "Yeah, get out of here."

Rhonda Citron brought Preuss a cup of Manny's coffee and sat in the visitor's chair across from Preuss's desk. His hands shook as he brought the mug to his lips.

"Quite the day," she said after he explained what he had been through.

His cell rang. "And it's not over yet," he said.

He recognized the number for Jake Aklawi.

"Need anything else?" Rhonda asked.

He shook his head. "I'm good. Thanks."

"You'll let me know if there's anything I can do?"

"I will. Thanks, Rhonda."

"I'll leave you to it, then," she said, and went back to her desk.

Exactly who he didn't want to talk with right now.

Or ever.

He let the call go to voicemail.

There was only one remedy for all this day's toxic testosterone.

On his way to Toby's, he remembered a passage in *The Maltese Falcon*, a story Sam Spade told about a man who had a peaceful, non-eventful life until he was walking down the street and a beam fell from a building under construction overhead and barely missed him. He had a sudden epiphany about the fragility of the structures we build our lives on, about the randomness of life, about the role of blind chance in our world.

And he determined then and there to change his life to accommodate his new insight. So he left his wife and his children and his steady boring job and his old life, and began to travel.

Eventually, he wound up creating the same boring, peaceful life someplace else, with another boring wife and boring children . . . he had just changed one boring, risk-free life for another. His destiny was to live a boring life.

Likewise, Preuss told himself, I walked away from a life of deceit and danger on the police force, but recreated the same thing, only in a different setting, at Manny's agency. He thought he was changing his life, but not much changed except the view.

And to top it off, today he almost left his beloved son an orphan.

He got to Toby's after nine. His son was already in bed but wasn't asleep yet. The nurse was in his room, giving Toby his night meds for seizures and for relief of the gastric upset the seizure meds caused.

"He's been waiting for you," the nurse said. "Toby, look who's here!"

She squirted the meds into his G-tube button from separate syringes and followed them with a flush of water through a bolus tube. She withdrew the tube, closed his button, and stepped out of Preuss's way so he could get next to the side of Toby's bed.

"All yours," she said.

Toby was resting quietly, and when his father loomed into his line of sight he looked up and gave Preuss a sweet, beatific smile. Sometimes, Preuss thought, I love this kid so much I think my heart is going to explode.

Earlier today, it almost did. The thought of leaving his child alone left him with a physical ache in the pit of his stomach.

"I'm sorry, honey," Preuss told his son. As usual, Preuss assumed Toby intuited what he was talking about—his near-death experience, how close Toby came to losing what little was left of his family.

And if Toby couldn't intuit specifically what his father was apologizing for, Preuss knew Toby was remarkably emotionally sensitive—perhaps as one of the compensations for his cognitive impairments—so the boy would sense Preuss's remorse.

And possibly he would even know, with some mysterious telepathic power he might possess, the reason for the remorse.

"Man," Preuss said, "am I glad to see you."

Because his son was still awake, Preuss drew the sheet and thin blanket off the boy's shoulder and sat him up on the side of the bed. A smile from Toby was a good start, but he really needed a Toby hug.

Toby leaned into his father. Preuss put an arm around him to prop him up. Everything about the boy—the love for his father that he radiated, the low hum he made, the solidity of his torso and the corresponding fragility of his bones and limbs—helped to calm Martin Preuss.

They sat like that for a long time, rocking back and forth.

When he could feel Toby's tight muscle tone slacken as the boy slid into sleep, Preuss gently laid his son back down on his side and covered him up. Toby's eyes were shut, and his mouth gaped open as he slept.

Preuss adjusted his son's head on the pillow so Toby wouldn't get a kink in his neck, then sat down in the chair beside the bed and watched Toby sleep. His Judy Collins CDs had ended, so the only sound was Toby's soft, regular breathing and the quiet purr that was his snore.

When the nurse came back to hook up Toby's pump for his night feeding, Preuss kissed his son goodnight and left the group home.

He followed his son's street down to Eleven Mile Road, and turned toward Woodward. He drove south on Woodward through Royal Oak and Huntington Woods into Ferndale.

At home he made himself a cup of decaf and took it out onto the deck.

The night was still warm, but as always at this time of year he felt a hint of the chill that was to come in the next few months. He shuddered, whether from the weather or the day's events, he couldn't say.

As he stood there, a surge of emotion overwhelmed him. He felt as if his proximity to death that day, staring into the dead eye of Victor's gun not six feet away, had somehow dissolved the barriers he had erected against his terrible feelings of sadness and guilt following the death of his wife.

Now, as then, without the protection of that barrier, he felt bereft and isolated, unable to muster any hope for change in the future, any mitigation of his terrible unhappiness.

He put his hands over his face and tried to will it all away. But it was impossible. All he could do was give in to it and ride it to the dark places where it took him.

He regained control by thinking about Toby.

His beautiful Toby. Toby would understand how he felt, he was certain; but he had to keep things together because Toby depended on him. And he depended on Toby.

The boy had saved him once before, in the aftermath of Jeanette's death. Now he would have to do it again.

With those thoughts to push against the darkness, he closed up the house and trudged up the steps to his bedroom.

Saturday, September 29, 2012

44

Lightning woke him.

He had been sleeping soundly until a flash of blue-white light and the crack of a lightning bolt brought him upright. It sounded as though something nearby had been struck.

He discovered he was trembling.

He peered out the window that fronted his street but saw nothing out of the ordinary. Just rain teeming down.

He went around to the back window and saw a large pine tree had been struck on the other side of the wooden stake fence that separated his house from the one behind. The top third of the tree had been sheared off. It was still smoking.

By the time he threw on his raincoat and went outside, the older couple who lived behind him were also out examining the damage. Unlike Preuss, they had thought to bring umbrellas. The tree was on their property, and the struck section had fallen into their yard without hitting either of their houses or the back fence. The three of them decided to deal with it in the morning, and they went back inside their homes.

It was half past two. Preuss stood in his kitchen, his coat still draped over his shoulders, sopping wet. Through the window over the sink, he watched the rain pour down in his backyard and saw the raw wood of the pine tree's new wound. He could still smell the scorched resin.

Alone in the house, he remembered coming downstairs in years past while the rest of his family slept upstairs, Jeanette in their bed, Jason in his room, Toby in his. During those nights, Preuss would stand in this exact spot, looking out the window as he did now, and he would wonder if he really deserved the happiness of the family that had somehow formed around him.

Later he would ask himself whether he had deliberately set out to sabotage his life by drinking to excess because he felt he didn't deserve such happiness. And so he did what he could to ruin it.

If that had been my plan, he now told himself, you did a good job. He now had a dead wife, a lost son who hated him, and another son whom he couldn't take care of by himself and who had to live apart from him, in a group home where strangers took care of his most intimate needs.

He rested his hands on the counter and hung his head. Yeah, right. Good job indeed.

His sense of isolation from the evening before persisted in this early hour. Would he ever break through it? Would anyone ever penetrate it? Or was this it—increasing isolation interrupted by visits with his son? With his hope of any other kind of relationship dimming, like a candle guttering in its base?

He filled a glass with water and downed it. He hardly ever felt like drinking alcohol anymore, and even now had no desire for it. When he got sober, he had tried AA but found the reliance on a higher power to be ridiculous. If he had a sponsor, though, Preuss might be able to call him right now and know that he could find a sympathetic ear, someone who understood what he was going through.

But who did Preuss have? He could call Toby, but this morning he needed something besides his son's unconditional nonverbal love. Reg Trombley would listen to him, but Preuss would feel terrible about waking him up. Tony Tullio was in Florida on life support, so he was out. (Preuss would have to remember to ask Reg or Janey about him).

Janey.

What about her?

As he thought about her, she seemed to be the person he could call right now, at—what was it, quarter to three in the morning?—and get the most sympathetic listening-to.

At least he could in the old days, before their long friendship kept threatening to turn into something more. Yet where they were now, the current state of their relationship, argued against his calling her for succor.

No, that time had passed, he thought, as their last encounter had made clear to him.

He saw his reflection in the kitchen window. He didn't recognize the face that looked back at him—drawn, dripping wet, and unbearably sad.

He shouldn't call Janey. He knew that.

Except he picked up his phone and dialed her cell.

He woke her. Her groggy voice said, "Hello?"

"Hey," Preuss said. "It's Martin."

It took another moment for her head to clear enough to say, "What's the matter? Is Toby okay?"

With everything that was going on between them, she still thought to ask first about Toby.

Before he could say anything, he heard a man's voice say, "Who is it?"

He recognized Tommy's baritone, growly and sleep-befogged.

Tommy, sleeping next to Janey?

"Martin?" Janey said. "What's wrong?"

"Nothing," he said, at once regretting what he had done. "Look, I'm sorry. I'll talk to you tomorrow."

He disconnected and set the phone on the counter as if it were burning hot.

Well, he thought, that was a bad idea.

A minute later, the phone rang.

Janey.

He picked it up. He thought about not answering, but knew he had to connect the call.

"Martin—what's the matter? Is everything okay? Is Toby all right?"

Her voice was low but clear now, all vestiges of sleep gone. He imagined her having taken the phone out into the hallway of her second floor so she wouldn't disturb Tommy. Sitting on the top step, maybe, shaking her wild electric curls of hair from around her face to help wake herself up.

"What is it?" she asked.

He said, "No, Toby's fine."

"Then what's the matter?"

How to even broach the subject of what the matter was?

Did he even know?

"Sorry I called so early." Or at all. "Sorry to wake you."

"Don't worry about it," she said. "I just wish you'd tell me what's going on."

"Was that Tommy I heard?"

She took a few moments before responding. "Yeah."

"You're back together? Now that he's moved out?"

"I don't know. He said he wants to try again. Wants to try a fresh start."

Another fresh start, Preuss thought. As if that were ever possible.

"Look," he said, "I'm sorry I called. We'll talk tomorrow."

Without waiting for her reply, he disconnected. All at once exhaustion overtook him and, the little light of hope flickering even lower and colder, he went back up the stairs.

But sleep didn't come.

Instead, he lay thinking about how close he came to dying the day before. And about fresh starts.

He wished Janey well. He wasn't convinced it would work out for her and Tommy—would have bet against it, in fact—but that wasn't his problem. And he certainly wouldn't have told her. In a way, this would be a chance for a fresh start for Preuss, too—for a life where the possibility of Janey and all she represented was now finished.

For good, he hoped.

His thoughts turned to Ray Tomina—what he had done, how he had ended up. How he helped Charles Montgomery. How he had wanted to outrun his life, make his own fresh start with Meeshell Lee. Until his life caught up to him.

That got him thinking about Meeshell.

Remembering what else Ramonda had said, how Meeshell and Tomina were planning to get away to a new life.

That reminded him of something else Ramonda had told him. How Meeshell had already tried—at one point, at least—to put a plan together for a new start. A plan to go to school, to begin a new life through education. Certainly an intention many people shared, whether or not they were in a life like Meeshell's. Even the aide at Toby's house the other morning was planning to do this.

The aide at Toby's house.

Issa, her name was.

She talked about going back to school.

Just like Meeshell, even though Meeshell never went very far with her plan.

And then, just like that, cutting through his maundering early-morning thoughts, it came to him.

45

He stayed awake for what remained of the night and got up for good after five. He made himself the first coffee of the day and took it out to the back deck to watch the night blend into the first caramel light of day.

He wanted to spend the entire day with his son, especially after his near-death experience the day before. But he knew it would be too dangerous to take Toby along with him on his travels. So they went to Big Boy for their traditional Saturday morning outing, and then he took the boy back to the group home after breakfast with the promise that he would return later in the day and they'd spend the evening together—maybe even going to a movie, which Toby loved.

He got his son stretched out in bed for an after-breakfast nap, and lingered at the doorway, watching Toby relax into sleep. Preuss silently apologized again for the risks he took the day before, and reluctantly made himself leave the sleeping boy.

Ramonda Hudgens lived in a condo in Auburn Hills, midway between Rochester and Pontiac.

She met him at the front door and stood aside as he entered the hallway. He followed her as she led the way past a room set up as an office and through her living room into the kitchen.

"I appreciate this," Preuss said. "Sorry to bother you on the weekend."

"It's no bother," she said. "I was glad to hear from you. Sounds like you're making progress?"

"I might be."

She showed him the tote bag on the kitchen island. It was the bag Meeshell left at the house on Tuxedo when she escaped from him. "That's what you asked about?"

"That's it. May I?"

"Be my guest."

He unzipped the bag and spread the sides apart.

"Have you seen her lately?" she asked.

"I talked to her yesterday," he said.

"How was she?"

"Helpful, actually. She told me where Ray Tomina was."

"And you found him?"

"Oh yeah. I found him."

"That doesn't sound good."

"No. But he's in a safe place. For the time being."

He sorted through the tote.

"I just piled everything into it when I left the house," she said. "Even the money and the drugs. I thought Meeshell might need it. Not the drugs, of course . . . but I didn't want to leave them in that house. So I just kept it all together."

"I'm glad you did."

"What are you looking for?"

"Tell you in a second."

He withdrew two items and held them up to show her.

"Are those important?" she asked.

"Yes," he said. "I believe they are."

He sat in his car outside her condo and examined what he had taken out of Meeshell's bag: A used textbook, *Introduction to Psychology*, and a wire-bound Wayne County Community College notebook.

The notebook seemed new. He thumbed through it and found a few pages of scrawled handwritten lecture notes—there couldn't have been more than three pages of notes here, all dated in January, he noticed; Meeshell must have dropped out early in the semester. He also found a photocopied syllabus for a course, PSY 101, Introductory

Psychology, which met Wednesday evenings, 7:00-9:55, during the January semester.

Taught by Dr. Roger Garland.

Who claimed he didn't know Meeshell Lee.

He rang the buzzer at Garland's home, and when there was no answer he pounded on the door. Still no response. No cars in the driveway or parked around the front of the house. A Guardian shield on the door made him look up and see a security camera trained on the front stoop.

The next-door neighbor out raking his lawn said they usually went away on the weekends, but he didn't know where their destination was. Preuss thanked him and returned to the Explorer.

He remembered Garland telling him they went up north every Friday to their cottage. In Ludington, Preuss thought he had said. Is that where they had gone?

If Meeshell had taken Garland's class, then Garland lied when he told Preuss he had never heard of her. True, if she didn't attend his class for very long, it's possible he never got to know her, or may have forgotten her. And if it was a big course, she might have been one name among a hundred.

He rifled the pages of the college notebook and discovered a sheet folded between blank pages in the middle. It was a Xeroxed page with seventeen alphabetized names and phone numbers—perhaps the class list Garland had given his students so they would have the names of everybody else in the class, in case they needed to call one of their classmates for information about the course.

So it was a small class. Meeshell Lee's name fell between Jamal Harrison and LaTonya Leonard. Garland would have known Meeshell, or at least would have recognized her name when Preuss asked him about it. And the course was only last January, so it wasn't as though it had been years ago.

Giving him the benefit of the doubt, Preuss thought, it was entirely possible that Garland genuinely forgot that Meeshell was in his class.

But the coincidence was simply too great. Without the benefit of the doubt, Garland lied about knowing her.

But why? Why didn't he want Preuss to know about their connection?

He waited for another hour. When the Garlands still didn't come home, he went to his office, where he spent a half-hour searching the web, then, when he found what he was looking for, he printed out a page and drove to Ferndale.

46

A ranker fug than usual surrounded him as he entered the stairwell to the second floor of the Journey's End. A dense gumbo of sour old clothes, marijuana, urine, ammonia, and stale sex. Must have been a busy night last night, he thought.

When he came out onto the second-floor walkway, he took a deep breath of what passed for fresh air.

He walked past the room where Greg Braiden was found and stopped at the next room.

The emaciated woman he had spoken with before answered his knock.

"Hey, Angela. Remember me?"

"Sure do. You the one tell me you ain't no cop no more."

"It's the truth."

"What you want now?"

"I want to show you a picture. Do you have a second?"

"I got all the time in the world, honey. But you can't come inside, so don't even think about it."

"Not a problem."

"I know you told me you not po-lice, but ain't so sure I believe it. You still look like po-lice."

"That might never go away," he said. "Here." From a manila file folder he pulled the page he had printed at the office and handed it to her. "I want you to look at something. Recognize this guy?"

She peered down at the printout of a *Grosse Pointe News* article about a City Council meeting on high water bills.

She looked up at him slyly and shook her head. "Yeah, you know, that memory of mine . . ."

He was ready for her. He handed her a twenty.

She snatched it from him.

"Now I'm looking at him," she said, "I believe I have seen him."

"Where?"

"Around here."

"Meeshell's room?"

"Yeah. He been steady coming round to see her."

"One of her regulars?"

She nodded.

"When was the last time you saw him?"

"Been maybe a month or so."

"Remember when he started coming around?"

"Oh," Angela said, "really? I don't know . . . this memory of mine . . . play tricks on me."

Another twenty clarified her remembrance.

"Can't be sure," she said, "but I think it was around the beginning of the year. In the wintertime."

"Winter of this year?"

"Uh-huh."

The winter of 2012 . . . that would have been during the semester when Meeshell started her course at the community college.

Was that how they met? Or did they know each other before that? Did she take the course because she knew him already?

Preuss doubted it, if he first appeared at the same time as the semester began.

"Good enough for me, Angela. Thanks."

He passed her another twenty and she retreated behind her door. He went back to the Explorer in the parking lot.

Where he returned to the file folder the printout with the photo of Roger Garland standing at a podium complaining about his water bills at a City Council meeting.

If Garland was one of Meeshell's regulars—which Angela had just confirmed—did he also know Ray Tomina?

Would Garland have spent time with Tomina at the Journey's End?

Or at the Embers?

Why would he have done that? What could Tomina do for him? Provide drugs? Women?

One way to find out.

47

After the previous day's shooting, the ambulance had taken Ray Tomina to St. Joseph Mercy Oakland Hospital on north Woodward Avenue in Pontiac. One of the bullets from Victor's gun shattered the top of his humerus, and the injury was severe enough to require surgery. He was being held under armed guard until that could happen.

The Sheriff's deputy outside Tomina's room refused him entry, so Preuss asked him to call Emma Blalock. After a brief consultation with her by phone, the deputy said Preuss could go in, but only for ten minutes.

Tomina lay in bed with a brace on his shoulder.

When he saw Preuss, he turned his head away—exactly the same movement that Meeshell Lee had made.

Martin Preuss, bringer of sunshine where ever he goes.

"Ray," Preuss said. He pulled the chair over to the bed. "How you feeling?"

"Who followed you this time?" Tomina asked bitterly.

"Close call yesterday."

"Ya think?"

"Did you know the shooter?"

A noncommittal shrug. "I got people after me all over the place."

"Yeah," Preuss said, "you're a real tough guy. I'm guessing you did know him. He worked for Jake Aklawi. Just like you used to."

Tomina ignored that. "Where's he now?" he asked.

"The morgue."

Tomina processed that.

"You put him there?" he asked.

Preuss shook his head. "Your buddy Dwayne."

"Didn't think he had it in him."

"Ray," Preuss said, "Meeshell's in custody down in Detroit. Remember I told you she's in the hospital?"

Tomina said nothing.

"So you didn't beat her?" Preuss asked.

"No."

"That's what Meeshell said, too."

"Because it wasn't me."

"Who was it?"

"No idea."

"It was you who tried to blackmail Braiden's sister, though. The bank dried up when Braiden OD'd. So you needed a new source of income."

Tomina replied with a tense silence.

"If you tell me what you know, I can help you. I can help Meeshell."

"You can't do nothing for me," Tomina said. "You're the reason I'm in this shithole."

That, at least, was hard to argue with.

That night, Preuss took Toby to see *Finding Nemo* in 3D. They sat in the first row so Toby might be able to see the action looking through the 3D glasses out of the corner of his eyes. During the loudest moments of the action onscreen, nobody could hear Toby screaming in joy.

Or if they did, they didn't care.

For his part, Preuss was more interested in Toby's reactions than he was in the movie itself. He loved the shifting expressions on his son's face in the white light reflected from the screen—looks of wonder, enjoyment, concern, above all pure happiness.

Sunday, September 30, 2012

48

Preuss spent the first part of the day with Toby on a long walk around Toby's neighborhood. Preuss was amazed at how many people not only said hello to Toby, but also knew his name.

Afterwards, Preuss lifted his son into the car and put the wheelchair in the back and they went grocery shopping. Preuss hung reusable net bags from the handles of the wheelchair, and filled the bags up as he pushed Toby around the store.

As usual, they ran into someone who knew Toby, and they stood talking, including his son in the conversation. Toby carefully attended.

In the afternoon, Preuss kissed his son goodbye and went to the Garland home.

If they were coming back from the cottage, they might be coming in during in the day.

He parked down the street and around the corner, where he could keep an eye on their home.

At eight, his patience paid off. A silver Volvo turned onto their block and rolled into their driveway. It pulled all the way up into the backyard.

Preuss rolled the Explorer around to the front of the Garland home, then turned his motor off. He saw Garland and his wife exit their car and haul their weekend bags and cooler into the house. He heard Garland chatting and laughing. His wife was stonily silent. Watching them, Preuss remembered what Garland's wife had said to her husband when Preuss first spoke with him.

Remembered the harsh tone of her voice. That wasn't just a message from a student she was delivering. She was giving him her own message, too.

For his part, Garland didn't seem stressed or concerned about anything. He walked around with his nose in the air, smirking as if he didn't have a care in the world.

Inside the house, the lights went on as they walked from room to room.

Preuss waited another two hours, until he saw all the lights in the front of the house go out. When he was satisfied the place was shut down for the night, he waited another hour, then started the Explorer and returned to Ferndale. Now that he knew they were back, he would deal with Garland in the morning.

Monday, October 1, 2012

49

The Rivertown district in downtown Detroit was another effort to remake and rename an older area of the city, just as the venerable and more than slightly seedy Cass Corridor was now called "Midtown" and "Cass Village." In Rivertown's case, the old warehouse district near the Detroit River had been completely done over with new buildings housing new businesses, new restaurants, and especially new lofts and condos.

Roger Garland kept his private practice office in one of the River Place buildings, a red brick fortress with a spectacular view of the river and, across the water, the green banks of Windsor.

Garland's office was also, Preuss realized when he mapped River Place on his phone, two blocks from the Mt. Elliot Cemetery, where Meeshell Lee was found beaten nearly to death.

Another piece dropped into place. Preuss didn't believe in coincidences; they were just events that connected in ways he might not understand yet.

Preuss parked beside Garland's silver Volvo. There was a guard at a station inside the building, and Preuss told him he had an appointment with Dr. Garland. The guard made a show of checking an online list and said, "Don't see your name on his calendar."

"It was a last-minute-type thing," Preuss said. "An emergency. It came up late last night. Dr. Garland said to just come in this morning and he'd see me. He must've forgotten to add my name."

That was good enough for the guard, who nodded with disinterest and had Preuss sign in. The guard directed him to an elevator that would take him to the second floor.

Very secure, Preuss thought.

He stopped outside a door that read, "River Place Psycho-therapy Associates." He tried the door and found it unlocked. He stepped into a small anteroom that smelled strongly of wicker and a sweet incense. On a table were a plate of mints and a literature holder containing brochures for a detox program and suicide prevention.

Another door led out of the anteroom, but that was locked. Preuss sat in one of the plush wicker seats and waited.

Earlier that morning, after stopping off to help get Toby ready for school, he drove to the Garland home in Grosse Pointe Park. Garland's wife, CeeCee, told Preuss that her husband had already left for his office to see his private patients.

At ten before the hour, the outside door opened and an older man stepped into the anteroom. He stopped in the doorway when he saw Preuss sitting there, looking back at him. It wasn't Garland. Must be a patient.

The man checked his watch, looked like he was going to say something, and then decided against it.

He left.

The good doctor's ten o'clock appointment, perhaps, Preuss thought.

Just as well.

The doctor is fully booked this morning.

Exactly ten minutes later, the inside door opened and a woman came out dabbing at tears streaming down her face. She ignored Preuss and rushed out the door to the outer hallway.

Preuss grabbed the inside door before it closed, and stepped into a loft that was so spacious, it momentarily left him as disoriented as the man who had just poked his head inside the anteroom. This was not simply an office, it was a residence, with a galley kitchen, living area with sofas and chairs around a low glass table, and, toward the back of the place, a pair of closed doors.

In a moment, Preuss heard the sound of a toilet flushing and shortly Roger Garland opened one of the closed doors and shut it behind him. Rubbing his hands together, he completely missed Preuss standing in the living area.

Garland went through to the galley kitchen and poured a cup of hot water from the kettle. He withdrew a tea bag from a ceramic jar and dipped the bag a few times.

He turned and noticed Preuss.

A look of surprise crossed his face, then he got himself under control at once and assumed the smirk that seemed to be his standard expression.

"Well," he said. "Mr. Preuss, isn't it?"

"It is."

"And how did you?" He vaguely pointed the mug of tea toward the door.

"Just walked in."

"Ah," Garland said. "You were waiting out there when Ms. Anderson left."

"Correct."

"I'm sorry, but I'm not going to be able to speak with you right now. I'm seeing patients."

He made a show of pointing his mug at the clock on the wall above the refrigerator.

"In fact, I'm due for one right now," Garland said. "If you want to see me, you need to make an appointment. So if you don't mind?"

He held out a hand to shepherd Preuss out the door, but Preuss took a seat in the conversation pit instead.

"Oh, look," Garland said, "I don't know what game you think you're playing, but this isn't funny. I have patients to see."

'I don't think you'll be seeing your ten o'clock," Preuss said. "He came, but then he left."

"Did you scare him off?" Now Garland seemed genuinely annoyed. "How dare you!"

"He's not here, Roger. So how about you drop the faux indignation and have a seat. We need to talk."

"We'll see about that."

Garland put his mug of tea on a coaster on the glass coffee table and said, "I'm just going to make a call to the police and tell them about the intruder in my loft. We'll sort this out when they get here." He crossed to the kitchen counter and took up his cell phone.

"Great idea," Preuss said. "Why don't you start with Detective Charles Montgomery? I have his number."

"Who's that?"

"The Detroit police detective in charge of the assault on Meeshell Lee. I think he'll be interested in talking with you."

Garland shook his head as though in regret at Preuss's stupidity. "I told you before, I never heard of anyone by that name." He punched in 911.

"You did say that," Preuss said. "Which I found odd, since she was a student in your psychology class at Wayne County Community College last year."

Preuss heard the whisper of the 911, but Garland disconnected the call and set the phone down.

"How can you possibly know that?" he asked.

"It's like I'm a detective or something."

Preuss waited.

"All right," Garland said at last. "I did know her."

"Roger, have a seat and let's talk about this."

Garland sat across the low table from Preuss.

"She wasn't a student for very long," he said, "and I'd forgotten her when you asked about her. Do you have any idea how many people I meet in a year? Students, patients, professional and social contacts? I simply can't remember them all."

"Did you know her before she was in your class?"

"Certainly not," Garland said, with the same supercilious defiance.

"Did you ever see her outside of class?"

"Of course not." Garland shook his head as though Preuss were the most pathetic specimen he had ever come across. Behind his eyeglasses, though, Preuss saw doubt forming.

"You were seen at the Journey's End," Preuss said. "Any comment about that?"

"It must be a mistake. I've never been there."

"My witness was positive."

"Your witness was wrong."

"No. It was a positive identification. Here's what I think happened, Roger. I think you met Meeshell in your class, and it's true, she wasn't there long. But she stayed long enough for you to get talking with her, and you realized who she was and what she did. Just parenthetically, do you do that with all your female students?"

"I have no idea what you mean."

"You meet them all in private conferences, get to know them, find out how vulnerable they are, how open to your charms. Then give them your home phone number?"

"I resent that."

"Resent it all you want. You went to that motel to have trysts with Meeshell."

Garland only shook his head, but the network of fine wrinkles on his forehead deepened and Preuss knew he was right.

"What was it you said about Greg Braiden? He went a little crazy with sex, drugs, and rock and roll after his parents died? I'm guessing the same thing happened with you once you met Meeshell. She took you to a world you could only dream about before. And you loved it."

Garland was silent. He stared at his mug of tea on the table.

"And then what happened?" Preuss continued. "You had to share this stroke of good fortune, had to show somebody else what you found? Maybe show one of those golden boys you hung around with you had something they didn't? Get them jealous of you for a change?"

Garland mustered a look of petulant indignation.

"So you took Greg down there," Preuss said. "Then something happened between Greg and Meeshell, and he started coming down there, too."

Garland threw him another look, this one of raw hatred.

"Wait," Preuss said, "you didn't know that, did you? Not at first. You didn't know Greg was seeing Meeshell, too."

Garland stayed silent, and Preuss pressed it.

"Is that what happened, Roger? You found her. You told Greg about her because you wanted to rub his nose in it. And he took her from you. And neither one of them told you anything about it."

Garland said nothing.

Preuss took his phone from his pocket. "You know what? I think we should call Detective Montgomery after all."

"No!"

Preuss punched in numbers and listened to his phone for a few moments. He said, "He's here," into the mouthpiece and disconnected, his eyes on Garland the whole time.

"Why did you do that?" Garland demanded. His voice was now strained and high, no longer the smug baritone he seemed so in love with. He jumped to his feet.

"Why did you beat up Meeshell Lee?" Preuss countered.

"I didn't touch her."

"You're lying. She was found two blocks away. Were you trying to punish her for taking up with Greg?"

"No."

"I think it was."

"I said no!"

"Then why?"

"Because—"

He stopped himself.

"Because why?"

Garland sat again.

"Why did you beat her, Roger?"

Garland looked at Preuss, trembling now, as though an emotion had begun to boil up inside him with no outlet.

"Because she told me she was leaving."

"But you already knew she was seeing Greg."

"No," Garland said impatiently. "Not just leaving me. Leaving town. Permanently."

"With Tomina?"

"I don't know."

"But you didn't want her to go?"

"Of course I didn't want her to go."

"You thought beating the shit out of her was a good way to persuade her to stay?"

Another shake of his head.

"Then why did you do it?"

Garland scoffed. "She asked me to meet her at the cemetery. Then the little bitch tells me she's leaving and has the nerve to ask me for money. Can you believe that? Can I give her a 'going away present'? For everything we'd been through together?"

"So you thought you'd teach her a lesson?"

"No," Garland said. "I wanted to remind her of what she would be losing if she left me."

"So you beat her senseless? How does that make any sense?"

Garland leaned forward.

"You don't understand," he said. "She liked it rough. She *liked* being hurt. It was part of our . . . our game."

"Roger, you broke her jaw. You broke her ribs. You can't possibly think she liked that. No," Preuss said, "I think when she asked you for money, all your resentments came out and you couldn't stop yourself from taking them all out on her."

"She liked it," Garland protested weakly. "That's why I knew Greg could never satisfy her."

"Why? Because he never hurt her?"

"Yes. Exactly."

Getting to the heart of the matter now.

"Tell me about Greg, Roger. What happened to him?"

"Very sad," Garland said.

No kidding, Preuss thought.

"I brought him to the Journey's End the first time, you were right," Garland said. "I wanted to show her off to him. I asked Meeshell to get a friend so we could party. And she did. And this happened a few times. I didn't know it then, but Greg came back. On his own. But he wanted to see Meeshell, not her friend."

Garland gave a pained little laugh. "It's a whole other world down there, Preuss. A whole other world, the likes of which you've never seen."

Preuss didn't tell Garland how many times he had actually been in the Journey's End to make arrests, or what he'd seen there. He didn't want to interrupt this monologue.

"When Greg was there with me, we saw and did things he only read about or saw in the movies. He couldn't get enough of it."

"Neither could you."

"No."

"You partied with drugs, too."

"We did."

"Where'd you get them?"

"Ray Tomatoes."

"So Greg really did do drugs?" Another lie from Garland, who swore Greg was clean.

"Sure," Garland said. "Pills and cocaine. He was a fiend. You should have seen him. The first time he tried, it was like a dam burst. Heroin, too, but he only snorted that. He never touched the needle. Neither one of us did."

"So how'd he wind up on the floor with a spike in his arm?"

Garland stared at Preuss through eyes that seemed to grow deep and haunted as he thought back to that night at the motel.

"It was you," Preuss said.

Garland turned away, couldn't meet Preuss's eye.

"I didn't know, you see," Garland said. "Before that night, I didn't know Greg was coming on his own to see Meeshell. I thought he only went there with me to party with her and her friend. But that night, I showed up at her room without telling Meeshell I was coming, and I found her and Greg together."

"That must have been a shock."

"Meeshell was *mine*," Garland cried. "I saw him there and lost it. I saw red. All my life, I had to work hard to get what those guys had handed to them. I was the scholarship boy at Cranbrook, while they sailed through on Daddy's money. I had to study and they barely cracked a book. Then here was another thing I earned on my own that Greg just waltzed in on and took over.

"I saw them together and I went nuts," Garland went on. "I wrecked the place. I hit Meeshell. I beat on Greg. I was so furious, I don't even remember what all I did. Afterwards, Meeshell told me what happened. She said I knocked him out, and while he was lying there, I shot him up with a needle she had and some of Ray Tomatoes's dope. She said she tried to stop me, but I wouldn't let her. I went insane."

Garland shifted his position. "My whole life," he said, "I'd always done the right thing. I was the 'good boy.' Always got good grades, always worked hard for them—went straight through graduate school, got married to the right person, drove the right cars, lived in the right place. It was all the way it was supposed to be."

He looked up at Preuss. "But where was *I*? Where was *I* during all that?"

He reached out and picked up his tea with shaking hands. "I'd played my little games with the co-eds in my classes at WC3. But I *found* myself with Meeshell. I *found* where I wanted to be, doing what I wanted to be doing. It was like I met myself for the first time with her down there."

"Sex, drugs, and rock and roll," Preuss said.

"Yes. Yes!" Garland cried, as if Preuss finally understood. "Until I saw Greg there, and it was like he took it all away from me."

"But who tried to blackmail Greg's sister? It wasn't you, was it?"

"I don't know anything about that. It might have been Tomina. When I met her at the cemetery, Meeshell told me he'd been bleeding Greg for money all along. He'd tell him, 'What's your family going to say, they find out about your secret life?'"

Garland made a gesture of dealing out money. "So Greg paid and played."

"When Greg OD'd," Preuss said, more to himself than to Garland, "that's when they decided to split. Tomina tried to blackmail Carrie Braiden to get the money to leave, and when that wasn't working fast enough, Meeshell asked you for money."

"I'd found myself, you see," Garland said again, ignoring Preuss. "In that stinking little room, I found myself. And my friend took it all away from me. He showed me that woman was just a common whore who would do what she did with me with anybody. With *anybody*!"

With that, as though the fuse that had been lit finally made it to the bomb, Garland exploded. He jumped up and threw his mug against a wall of books. It burst into a hundred shards that rained ceramic and tea across the spines and over the floor.

All the resentments that had been seething in him for years broke through. He bent over and screamed. He brought it up from the tips of his toes, and it raised the hair on the back of Preuss's neck.

Then, as abruptly, Garland grew quiet, the echoes of his meltdown still ringing off the brick walls. He took a few deep breaths, worked his lips together, stood looking at the mess he had made.

"I need to clean this up," he murmured. Without looking at Preuss, he said, "There's a mop and pail in the hall."

As if sleepwalking, Garland shuffled past Preuss toward the entrance to the loft. He opened the door and stepped through—"Just down this way," he told Preuss over his shoulder.

Preuss sat watching the shattered psychologist's slow-motion escape.

50

Charles Montgomery was waiting for Garland outside the building, along with two big Detroit uniformed cops. They nabbed him as soon as he exited. He put up no fight.

The charge of the attempted murder of Greg Braiden at the Journey's End in Ferndale trumped Montgomery's charges of aggravated assault for the beating of Meeshell. Once Garland was arraigned in Detroit, Montgomery would get in touch with the Ferndale police and sort matters out for Garland's transfer to them.

Preuss and Montgomery stood in the middle of River Place Drive watching the Detroit PD cruiser leaving with Garland in the back seat. On the river, a lake freighter sailed past, slow and stately as a cloud.

"Pretty sure we'll dig up a few Controlled Substance violations on him," Montgomery said. "And who knows what else they'll find in Ferndale."

"What's going to happen with Ray Tomatoes?" Preuss asked.

"He's gonna have some things to answer for, even if he is an informant," Montgomery said. "He'll face justice."

"All we can hope for," said Martin Preuss.

Back at his office in Southfield, Rhonda balanced the great complicated concoction of her platinum blonde hair on a neck bent over her desktop of papers.

"Anything going on I should know about?" he asked.

"Manny's in court, but he'll be back later today. Otherwise all's quiet. No messages for you, I don't think. Hang on."

He waited while she checked her pile of salmon-colored "While You Were Out" slips.

"Yup. Message here for you after all."

He took the slip. It was from Beverly Frankel.

He thanked Rhonda and took a mug with Manny's special coffee into his office.

He had not spoken with Carrie Morrison for a few days, so first he called her cell.

"Mr. Preuss," she said. "I was just about to call you."

"Sorry I haven't been in touch," he said. "Things have been moving pretty fast. I have news for you."

"So do I. I'm at the hospital. With my brother."

"Is everything all right?"

"No," she said. "Greg died a little while ago."

"Oh Carrie, I'm so sorry."

"He started to fail early this morning, and they called me to come in. He never regained consciousness. The doctor told me even if he had, he might not even be able to recognize us. That's how far gone his brain was."

Preuss said nothing.

"I can't say this is unexpected," she said. "So in a way, it's a blessing."

"That's one way to look at it," Preuss said.

"You said you've been finding things out?"

"I have. They can wait, though."

"No, I want to know. I want you to keep going with this more than ever now."

"A lot's happened in the last few days. I found some answers to our questions."

"Well," she said, "that's something. It won't bring my brother back, but . . ."

"No," he agreed. "But it may help you find closure."

"Maybe," she murmured. It didn't sound like she thought that was likely, and Preuss didn't push it. He wasn't sure, either. "I appreciate what you've done," she said. "I know Greg would too. If he could have known."

"Let me know if I can do anything for now."

"Thank you," she said. "I'll be home later on. I have arrangements to make, but maybe you can stop by and fill me in?"

"How about I come in the morning? I'll let you be with your family tonight."

"That's kind of you, thanks."

They disconnected and Preuss sat back at his desk, turned the desk lamp on, and called Reg Trombley. When the call went to voicemail, he left a message.

"Reg, I just got off the phone with Carrie Morrison. Greg Braiden's sister. She told me her brother died this afternoon. Could you pass that along to whomever?"

Next he called Charles Montgomery. Again, there was no answer on the cell phone so he left a message.

"Monty, it's Martin Preuss. I just spoke with Greg Braiden's sister. She told me her brother died a little while ago. That changes the picture, so I just wanted to let you know. Talk soon."

He disconnected and placed the phone on the desk. He could no longer bring himself to offer the usual platitudes at a death. At least now they're at peace. At least now they're in a better place. He never believed they were in a better place—he didn't believe there was a better place—and he had seen too many stupid, pointless deaths to believe they were at peace.

Dead was just dead.

Next he called Beverly Frankel.

"Mr. Preuss, hi!" she said. "I hope you're not upset, but I got too impatient with waiting, so I made an appointment with Sarah Posner, just like you said."

"That's great."

"And I'm going to see her on Saturday."

"Terrific. I hope it works out for you."

"Can you come? I'd love for you to be there!"

"When is it?"

She told him, and he said, "I'll put it on my calendar."

"Oh, Mr. Preuss—thank you *so* much!"

Her youthful enthusiasm was tiring, Preuss thought when they said goodbye.

He turned his attention back to the Braiden case. With Ray Tomina out of commission, and Meeshell Lee and Roger Garland in custody, the security detail was no longer needed in front of Carrie Morrison's house in Bloomfield Hills. He called Carlos Guevara to pull it. He would tell Carrie when he saw her.

He sat for another few minutes, then, unable to focus, left the office.

He stopped for a hot dog at the A&W in Berkley and got to Toby's after the bus dropped his son off. Toby was dozing in bed when he got there.

He sat in the chair beside his son's bed and watched the boy sleep. He marveled at how big Toby was getting. Even though Toby was still small for his age, soon enough Preuss wouldn't be able to carry him anymore. And he was dead weight, too; with his disabilities, Toby couldn't wrap his arms around Preuss's shoulders to help out.

The boy must have been knackered because he stayed asleep for a long time. Preuss sat there, grateful for the quiet time. He was knackered himself after this day.

He closed his eyes and was just drifting off when his cell phone rang.

Janey Cahill's name on the calling screen.

One more person I don't want to talk to, Preuss thought. He let it go to voicemail.

The ringing stopped and after a minute the message chime went off. He listened.

"Hey," she said, "it's Janey." Her voice hesitant, tentative. "I just want to let you know, Reg just called me. Tony got moved to the cardiac step-down unit. They're thinking he's out of the woods for now."

She was silent for a few moments, then said, "Just wanted to tell you. Hope you're doing okay."

He sat, knowing he wasn't going to call her back but relieved at the news about Tony Tullio.

Then he roused himself and returned to his office to work on the final Braiden report.

Tuesday, October 2, 2012

51

Carrie Morrison's home was quiet when she let him in.

"My minders are gone?" she asked.

"They are. You won't need them anymore."

"Can't say I'm sorry to see them go."

He followed her into the living room.

"Sorry again for your loss," Preuss said.

She accepted with a dip of her head. "Thanks. Maybe it's for the best, as I said."

"How are your kids doing?"

"As well as they can do, I guess. They loved their Uncle Greg. This isn't their first brush with death, unfortunately. Their father died a few years ago. Can I get you anything?"

"No, thanks. And you? How are you?"

She grimaced and pulled her hair back in a gesture of frustration. "Holding it together. I expected this, like I told you. At first the doctors said he was going to come out of it, but then as the days passed and he wasn't getting better, they began getting me ready for the worst. But it's still hard."

"Sure."

"I'm keeping the gallery closed for a few days to make the arrangements. There isn't much family so we're going to have a small private ceremony."

"Have you talked with Heidi?"

She sighed. "Oh yes."

"Doesn't sound like it went well."

She waved it away. "It never does. Still, I had to let her know. She asked me to tell her when the service is. And I will, of course. Sure you don't want anything? Coffee?"

"I'm good."

"My friends all want to come over and do something for me, but I have to tell them no. All I want right now is time to process this. I don't want their cakes and pies and all the food they bring over. You should see it. Want a pan of lasagna? I have about eight."

He smiled, shook his head.

"From what you said, things are coming to an end?" she asked.

"They are."

"I'd like to know what you found out."

"Carrie, we can do this another time. There's no rush. I figured we could do it when I give you the final report."

"No. I want it over with. If there are any more shocks, I want to know what they are."

"Parts of it might not be easy to listen to."

"Mr. Preuss, none of this has been easy. Just give me the highlights."

Or the lowlights, as the case may be, he thought.

He gave her a summary of what he had found. How Roger Garland had originally gotten involved with Meeshell Lee at the Journey's End, and then brought her brother there, to show off his good fortune; how Greg began seeing Meeshell on his own without Roger knowing, and then wound up being conned into paying for the room (Carrie hung her head while he related that part); how Ray Tomina was blackmailing Greg and then, later, after Greg went into the hospital, Tomina tried to go after Carrie herself; how Roger Garland walked in on her brother and Meeshell that night at the motel, and how he confessed to giving Greg the injection of heroin he got from Tomina; and what had happened to Meeshell, Tomina, and Roger Garland—two in the hospital, all in custody.

She listened in silence, hugging herself when he talked about Roger Garland's role in all this.

By the time Preuss finished, she was weeping into a handful of tissues. He waited till she stopped and blew her nose.

"And I thought he was Greg's friend," she said.

"Greg thought so, too. Until the end."

"My brother had this whole secret life none of us knew any-thing about," she said. "Except Roger, of course. He fed all those de-mons Greg was dealing with, that I had no idea of."

Preuss said nothing.

"I thought he was so happy in his life," she said. "But it was all false." She began to cry again.

She dabbed at her eyes, blew her nose again. "He had every-thing, didn't he? Everything a man could want. Oh, Greg, my poor brother. You thought you found something you needed, but really you lost so much at that awful place."

She gave her head a sad shake. "I guess he kept his real hid-den from everybody. And maybe even from himself, too. Isn't that sad? To go through your life without sharing who you really are with anybody, even the ones who loved you the most. I'm not only sad for what we've all lost, but mostly for Greg. He never had anybody he could trust with what he knew about himself. Nobody really knew him. It breaks my heart to think about it."

Preuss agreed; it was terribly sad.

There was nothing else he could have said that would have lifted her sorrow, no wisdom to impart, no feel-better bromides, no platitudes about how we never really know anybody, how we're all mysteries to each other. And ourselves.

So he said nothing.

As he watched her expressing her sorrow, Preuss realized she could also have been talking about him. Not that she would know this, of course. But the isolation she described her brother living in—with no one to share his true self with, no one to trust, battling his demons alone in ways that destroyed him—it all applies to me, too, he thought.

He had his Toby, but as much as he loved the boy—and he loved him fiercely—Preuss had to admit that ultimately he needed something else, too, just as Greg Braiden had. Preuss had been trying to pretend he didn't. But in the end, he did.

Just as Toby deserved his own rich life, deserved his "equivalent center of self," as Jeanette used to say, using a phrase she had read in a nineteenth century British author in college, so did Preuss. He had often thought about it in relation to Toby. And intellectually, he knew it about himself, too. But watching Carrie Morrison grieve for her brother, he saw himself as being like Greg Braiden. Preuss had just found different ways to keep his demons of guilt, sorrow, and remorse at bay.

Not as destructive as Greg's, but just as isolating.

As though his silent realization had also allowed her to break through a barrier of her own, she gave him a weak smile and said, "Thank you. Not only for what you've done here, but for sticking with this."

"You're quite welcome."

"I'm sorry I gave you such a hard time at the beginning."

"Don't mention it."

"That seems so long ago."

He agreed; the beginning of a case always seemed to be a lifetime away from the ending. You were always a different person at the end of an investigation than you were at the beginning.

"I'll send you the final report as soon as I get it together," he said.

"Okay."

"You're sure you'll be all right?"

"No," she admitted. "This is all pretty overwhelming."

"It is."

"I lost my brother. But the man you found in his place—I don't even know who that was."

No, Preuss thought. That was always the danger, as he had told her in the very beginning—learning more than you wanted to know.

You have to be careful what you ask for, he thought. You might get it.

But he kept that bit of wisdom to himself.

Instead, he stood to go. She stood with him and without a word stepped forward and put her arms around him and held him close. It happened so fast, he couldn't act on his impulse to back off. As she held him, he felt the curves of her body, as well as a deep trembling inside her, as though she were on the verge of breaking apart and only his embrace kept her together.

He smelled the floral scent of her hair, so different from the stale tobacco smell of Janie's wild curls.

"Thank you," she murmured. "For everything."

He returned her embrace, and as they stood together he felt something begin to stir deep inside him, an unfamiliar sensation like a rupture in the ice packed tight around his heart.

52

Rhonda was at her desk.

Sniffling into a tissue.

"Hey," Preuss said, "what's the matter?"

A dozen possibilities crossed his mind, including the thought that she might be having a relapse in her fragile emotional stability.

She gave her nose a wipe and said, "It's Manny."

Manny's door was open. Manny sat behind his desk, as straight and natty as ever. His wife Lila sat in one of the visitor's chairs. She patted the arm of the other chair, to indicate Preuss should sit.

Preuss lowered himself into the seat and waited.

"Rhonda tells me you got the Braiden case wrapped up," Manny said.

"Yes." Then something made him say, "Almost."

As though they were having a friendly office meeting, Manny raised his white cup to his lips and took a sip. He savored the taste of his coffee and asked, "What's left to do?"

Preuss looked at Lila, who rolled her eyes. That's my Manny, her expression said. All business all the time.

"I'll tell you after somebody tells me what's going on," Preuss said. "Why is Rhonda out there crying?"

Manny and Lila exchanged a look, and Lila nodded toward Preuss. *Tell him,* her gesture said.

"I have news," Manny said.

"Okay."

"As you've noticed, things haven't been quite right with me lately."

Preuss said nothing.

"I haven't been entirely forthcoming. I've been consulting specialists, getting biopsies and so forth. That's where I've been when I've been out of the office. That's where I was when Carrie Morrison came in, and why I asked you to take the meeting."

Say it, Preuss thought.

"And it turns out I have a problem. It's cancer. Of the throat."

There it is, Preuss thought.

"What stage?" he asked.

"Three. But it's not as bad as it sounds," he added.

"No?"

"No. The cancer hasn't spread, not to the lymph nodes or, as far as they can tell, anyplace else."

"What's the plan?"

"They want to start with surgery," Manny said. "With radiation and maybe chemo as adjuvant therapies."

"And the outlook?" Preuss asked.

"He's going to be fine," Lila said.

"Everything's going to be all right," Manny said. "There's nothing to worry about."

Sure, Preuss thought, because cancer's just a minor ailment. What could possibly go wrong?

Preuss heard Rhonda sniffling in the doorway to Manny's office. She stood gazing at Manny with a tragic frown.

"The doctors' outlook is very positive," Manny said. "And so is mine. And look, I'm eighty-five years old. I've had a good life."

"Don't *talk* like that," Lila said.

"The docs want to start treatment in a couple of weeks," Manny said. "I'm planning to be in the office as much as I can, but of course, I'm going to have to be out a lot."

"He's going to take a *lot* of time off," Lila said. "Let's be honest, Manny."

"Martin," Manny continued, "you and Rhonda are going to have to step up a bit more than usual."

"Of course," Preuss said.

"You and I can talk about what cases I have going. I should be finished with a couple of them, but Martin, you're going to have to take over the open ones."

"This place is the last thing you should be thinking about right now," Preuss said.

"Thank you," Lila said. "That's just what I told him. But you know my husband."

"Yeah," Preuss said, "I do."

"We might need to take on one or two temporary associates," Manny said. "Plenty of time to talk about that."

"We'll get by just fine," Preuss said. "You concentrate on your health."

"You were right all along," Manny told him. "You knew all along there was a problem."

"I should be a detective," Preuss said.

"Oh, Uncle Manny," Rhonda said, even though Preuss knew she wasn't supposed to call him Uncle in the office. She rushed in and put her arms around the older man as a new fit of crying overtook her.

Manny accepted it with grace. "It's going to be fine," he said. "Everything's going to be fine."

53

Preuss stopped at Toby's house to kiss Toby goodnight and listen to music with him, then continued back to Ferndale after his son fell asleep.

He went out on the back deck. The night had turned humid and the sky was still overcast with a thick blanket of violet clouds. He gazed into the back yard. Leathery tan oak leaves had begun to fall from the trees on his property. They lay scattered in spots over the grass; in another few weeks, he would be knee-deep in them.

After that, the long Michigan winter would move in.

He had known something wasn't right with Manny, it was true, no matter how many times Manny denied it. But he was glad Manny was secretly getting medical attention, even as he had rejected any hint of a problem.

His thoughts drifted to Carrie Morrison, and his meeting with her. Especially the sensation of her being in his arms. When was the last time he had felt that? Not even with Janey, whose hugs, he had to admit, were always—what? More friendly than the sudden embrace at Carrie's earlier in the day.

Or maybe Carrie just had a momentary need for human contact, and my reaction was a measure of what's missing from my life as well, he thought.

His cell rang inside the house.

He went into the kitchen. Without picking it up off the counter, he looked at the incoming number. He expected this, and he was partly relieved that it was happening and he didn't have to guess when it might be coming.

He considered letting it go to voicemail, but at the last second he connected the call. All he heard was steady breathing on the other end of the line.

"Preuss," the raspy voice said at last.

"Jake. You heard about Victor?"

"Of course."

A long sigh from Aklawi's end of the call.

"You disappointed me," Aklawi said.

Preuss said nothing.

"He was a good boy, Victor. He had his faults. But he was learning. He was useful. He had a good future. You took that away."

"No," Preuss said. "He did that himself."

"You were there. You should have stopped it."

"I tried. He was two seconds away from killing me, and I talked him down. We were getting ready to come back to see you, but somebody else shot him first. It wasn't me."

Aklawi went on as if Preuss hadn't spoken. "You never did tell me where Tomina was. Victor had to follow you to find him. The one request I made of you. Out of friendship."

Now it was Preuss's turn to sigh. "Jake," he began, "you talk friendship, but you weren't honest with me from the start. If—"

Aklawi cut him off. "You're what got him killed!"

"What got him killed was another maniac with a gun."

"No," Aklawi said, "what killed him was you. Not telling me you found Ray, that's what killed him. Along with that rat bastard Peanut Carver."

"What does Carver have to do with it?"

"You really think Dwayne Rubicki would think to shoot Victor by himself unless he was paid to do it? Why would Rubicki care if you and Tomina died?"

"Rubicki was working for Carver, too?"

"Of course."

"So Carver—"

"Had Tomina and his whore girlfriend under his protection all along. Rubicki killed Victor to protect Tomina."

Then Carver didn't know Tomina was an informant, Preuss thought. If Carver had known, he would have let Victor kill Tomina when he had the chance.

"Rubicki will be dealt with," Aklawi said.

"Jake," Preuss said, "why did you want Tomina dead? And don't tell me you only wanted to talk with him because he's your god-son and he betrayed the tribe, because we both know that's bullshit. Don't insult my intelligence."

Preuss heard only Aklawi's heavy breathing.

There was only one answer, Preuss realized.

"Of course," he said. "You knew he was talking to the police."

Aklawi said nothing.

"Who told you?" Preuss asked.

"The word came down."

"Who from?"

"A little birdie."

"In the police?"

Aklawi ignored the question.

"Remember what I said about my friends and enemies?" he asked instead. His voice was calm, almost regretful. "Don't forget that, Preuss. One day, maybe tomorrow, maybe in ten years, I'll make sure you understand the truth of what I say when I tell you I'm a terrible man to have as an enemy."

"You try whatever you want with me. But you remember what I told you: You touch my son and you're a dead man. I don't care how many Victor replacements you find."

"I won't hurt your son," Aklawi said. "You have my word."

"Really? How much is that worth?"

"It's *you* you need to worry about."

Aklawi was silent for a few moments. Then said, "You have my word on that, too," in a voice that was low and heavy with menace and sadness.

He disconnected.

Preuss set the phone on the deck railing.

"I'll see you when that day comes," he told the backyard.

Just what the world needs, he thought. More revenge. Because there just isn't enough of it.

That's when the missing piece—the piece that had been bothering him—fell into place.

Wednesday, October 3, 2012

54

Meeshell Lee was back in Detroit Receiving Hospital. Denied a personal bond, she had been remanded to the Wayne County Jail after her arraignment. There she had gotten in a fight with another inmate, and her jaw needed rewiring.

The police guard outside her room searched through the list of approved names and found Preuss's. He nodded, and Preuss entered Meeshell's room.

She was alone. She sat in a chair beside the bed with her eyes closed. Her chest rose and fell, but not evenly. Preuss didn't think she was asleep.

"Meeshell," Preuss said.

She opened her eyes. It took her a few moments to focus before she recognized him.

"Remember me? Martin Preuss."

She closed her eyes.

"Doing okay?"

She turned her head away from him.

He moved a chair next to hers.

Still looking away, she said, "What do you want?" Her voice was dull. Pain meds, he thought.

"You heard what happened to Ray?"

No response.

"He's in custody," Preuss said.

"He okay?" she said after a moment.

"He took a bullet, but he's okay."

"You shoot him?"

"No."

"Who did?"

"Victor Kirma."

Her eyebrows drew together in a look of confusion. Preuss didn't bother explaining; he had other things on his mind.

"He's alive?" she asked.

"He's alive."

She sighed.

"I talked with Roger Garland," Preuss said. "Who's also in custody."

The name made her clench her jaw, then wince from the pain that cut through her meds.

"He told me everything," Preuss said.

Now she turned toward him and blinked a few times, trying to focus on him.

"Almost everything," he corrected himself. "He told me he was the one who gave Greg Braiden the injection that killed him."

"Greg's dead?"

"Yeah. Nobody told you?"

"No."

"He died the day before yesterday. He was too far gone by the time the EMTs got there. He never came back."

She looked away again, into the blank eye of the television set hanging from the wall across from her. At the board with the names of her nurse and PCA. At the list of restrictions. Looked anyplace but at Preuss. Braiden's death jumped her into a whole other level of trouble, and Preuss could tell she knew it, even as out of it as she seemed to be.

"Roger told me he got so upset and was so juiced with anger at seeing you and Greg together, he couldn't remember what happened that night," Preuss said. "He said you told him he gave Greg the shot."

She kept looking away from him. She raised a shoulder under her hospital gown. *So?*

He leaned forward. "The thing is, Meeshell, I don't think it was Roger who did that. I'm pretty sure it was you."

She rolled her head on her pillow. It was more a gesture of "I don't want to hear this" than a denial.

"Roger told me he gave it to Greg with dope from Ray," Preuss went on. "With a needle he got from you."

She said nothing.

"But how would a guy who never used a needle know what to do? How to cook it, where to stick it? He wouldn't. It must have been from you," Preuss said. "Only thing I don't understand is why. I can understand why you told Roger that *he* did it—so you could jam him up for it. Because you knew that's what would happen. But why give Greg that shot?"

She didn't say anything for a long time.

Then, face still impassive, she raised her chin and pulled the hospital gown down, away from her collarbone.

Preuss saw a chain of faint bruises all around her neck in a pattern that could have come only from fingers. Then she pulled the gown off her shoulder to reveal a bruise that was a few days old and already turning yellow.

"Roger did those when he beat you at the cemetery?"

She shook her head.

"When you were playing sex games with him?"

She sneered and shook her head again.

"Those are from Greg?"

She nodded, pulled her gown back up to cover the injuries.

"When?"

"That night," she said.

"At the motel? The night this all happened?"

She nodded.

He remembered Garland telling him that she took up with Greg Braiden because Greg never hurt her. Apparently, that had changed.

"Was that the first time he hurt you?"

Another nod.

"Why would he do that?" Preuss asked.

Her blurry red eyes turned hard. Through clenched teeth and her wired jaw, she said, "Because he could."

The way of her world.

"And you were tired of being treated like that," Preuss said.

"I was sick of it. I was sick of all of it."

"You shot Greg up because he was beginning to hurt you. Just like all the rest?"

When she didn't answer, he said, "Roger used to hurt you, too, didn't he? He told me you liked it rough."

"Man, nobody likes it rough," she said.

He sat watching her. This was a different person than the hard-nose who refused to talk to him before. Everything about her was different—her manner, her voice, even her language. This was what was left of the respectable girl whose loss her mother had mourned.

"What happened, Meeshell?"

"Roger went nuts when he found Greg in my room," she said. "Usually, he tells me when he's coming over, but that night he just showed up. He started throwing things, knocking us both around. He pushed Greg into the mirror over the dresser and knocked him out cold. I hit him over the head with a lamp, and then everything went quiet. They were both lying there. They were at my mercy. At *my* mercy, for once. I knew what I had to do. I got out the works Ray left at my place, and shot Greg up. 'First and last time you ever hurt me,' I told him.

"I was getting ready do the same with Roger when he came around before I could get the spike out of Greg's arm and into his. So I told him he was the one who put the needle in Greg when he was raving around. Told him he had to get out of there before someone found him. He believed me and split."

"Then you did the next best thing to killing him. You put him in the frame for what you did to Greg. So you got your revenge on the two men who hurt you."

"More than two men," she said.

At first, he thought she was referring to all the other men who used her badly. Then he realized she was talking about Ray Tomina.

"Ray, too?"

"Yeah."

"You were the one who told Jake Aklawi that Ray was a police informant," he said.

No response.

"You never had any intention of leaving with him, did you?" he asked. "You always intended to get away on your own."

"That's right."

"You were going to leave it all behind—Ray, Roger, Greg, the life, all of it."

She closed her eyes and turned her head away.

She would leave it all now, it was true. Just not the way she'd planned.

Preuss said nothing for a minute. Then he said, "I can't sit on this, you know that, right? The cops have to know what you did."

"Do what you gotta do," she said. "I did what I had to."

Then she went quiet.

And in truth, there was nothing more to say.

Saturday, October 6, 2012

55

Sarah Posner brought out a tray with a bone china tea set and three matching cups with creamer and sugar bowl. Preuss had offered to help her, but she declined with an impatient wave of her hand. She placed the tray on the small wooden table with three curving legs that stood between Preuss's chair and her winged-back chair in the large house in the Boston-Edison Historic District. She fell into her seat with a grunt of relief and poured tea into the cups, then passed them around to her guests.

Beverly Frankel accepted her cup with thanks, then returned to silently paging through an old album of newspaper clippings.

"You see?" Sarah said.

"Wow," was all Beverly could manage.

Sarah had given her the album. It contained newspaper clippings from the defunct *Detroit Times* going all the way back to the second decade of the twentieth century in Detroit. Yellowed and as fragile as Sarah Posner herself, the clippings were articles accompanied by lurid photos of dead men lying in pools of blood in apartments, in hotel rooms, in barber shops, in Detroit restaurants, and sprawled across curbs on city streets. Clippings also showed the ruins of buildings that had been bombed in the vendettas that tore through Detroit in the 1920s and 1930s—dry cleaning shops, gambling dens, and blind pigs.

The articles showed Beverly the brutality of the Purple Gang in a way she hadn't realized before. In particular, the articles featured the two Purples that Beverly had been so pleased to be related to, Izzie Adler and Leon Glick, and their roles in the murders, extortions, bombings, and massacres that roiled the city.

"I had no idea," she said.

"Most people don't," Sarah said. "Not anymore. Most people today have no idea what those times were like. It's all lost to history. But we knew."

Beverly turned over the pages in the album and read about assassinations of policemen, radio personalities, and other gangsters. About the Purples' connections to Al Capone and mobsters of the time.

"This," Sarah said, "is what you were so anxious to find out about. Your connection to this history of murder and crime."

Beverly sat, chastened. The bravado and pride in her family connection to the famous gangsters were gone, wiped out in the face of the evidence from the clippings.

"My husband Morrie knew them," Sarah continued. "Knew what they had done. He told me that's why he became a pianist and a piano teacher. He wanted to help make up for the ugliness of what his family had done by creating beauty in the world. To prove to people—and I think to himself—there was more to us, more to life, than what those terrible boys did."

Beverly looked at Preuss, who had sat silently ever since Sarah welcomed them into her house. She gave him a small, embarrassed smile, as if apologizing for being so oblivious.

Sarah Posner held her teacup out, indicating the album in Beverly's lap. "I'd like you to have that," Sarah said. "Hang onto it. Keep alive the memory of what those terrible men did."

"Thank you, I will," Beverly murmured, as she turned over a yellowed page showing the ruins of a bombed-out dry-cleaning factory, another casualty of the Purples' protection racket in the Cleaners and Dyers War in Detroit in the 1920s.

56

The tall man in the spotlight wore a leather vest over a white shirt with his sleeves rolled up. He twisted his mouth in a soundless howl as he bent the high E string on his black Les Paul up, up, up, almost to the breaking point.

He arched his back and bent his knees and kept his attack on the string going. The high distorted whine cut through the Blue Goose Inn in St. Clair Shores all the way to the back of the small venue, where Martin Preuss sat at a table with his arm around Toby.

Who rocked from side to side in his wheelchair with his own mouth gaping open in perfect happiness, even though there was no possible way he could see through the crowd to the tiny stage where the guitarist resolved his solo on the shiny guitar and launched into the turnaround to loud applause from the room. The tall man stepped back up to the microphone and began to wail the next verse of the song, a cover of "Key to the Highway" that this band made their own.

Toby yelled in glee, his falsetto shout lost in the screaming blues of the band—Jim O'Brien on lead, Emmanuel Garcia on rhythm guitar, O'Brien's son Dylan on drums, and a guy Preuss didn't know on bass—and the whistles and clapping from the audience.

None of the band was young, except for the drummer; O'Brien himself had long grey hair and stubble like iron filings. Because they had been around so long, they had a massive local following. O'Brien had played with all the big names who emerged from the Michigan rock and roll scene since the sixties, as well as many of those who toured through, including Bob Seger, Mitch Ryder, and Jimi Hendrix. One of O'Brien's songs was recorded by the great Les Paul, who won a Grammy for it and created a special edition guitar for O'Brien in appreciation. It was the one he was playing now.

Preuss had been promising his son he would take him to a live concert, and tonight was the night. A succession of singers and other musicians sat in with the band, wailing on guitar, harmonica, trumpet, and sax, and from the stage O'Brien had called Preuss up to play in the first set after Preuss said hello to the band during their set-up.

Preuss demurred. He didn't want to leave Toby alone without anyone watching him; he hadn't brought any of the aides from the house with him, so it was just the two of them.

If he had brought an aide for Toby, he would have loved to sit in. O'Brien was a legendary musician, and Preuss had played with him and other members of the group on other gigs. O'Brien had been a big influence on Preuss in his early playing days, back when he thought music and not law enforcement was going to be his life's work.

As it was, however, he was just as happy to sit with his son and enjoy the music together.

During the second set, O'Brien asked Preuss again to play. "Help me get this guy up here," O'Brien implored the crowd. They whistled and hollered, but Preuss shook his head. Staying close to his son was more important.

And Toby was in his glory.

He loved music, and he especially loved live raucous music played at great volume, like tonight. The music was so loud that Preuss had put soft ear plugs in Toby's ears so his hearing (one of the boy's few functions that worked perfectly) wouldn't be damaged by the noise.

The plugs didn't diminish Toby's pleasure. Whenever O'Brien stepped into one of his extended solos, Toby would throw his head back and waggle it as if he entered the same kind of ecstatic pocket that O'Brien was in. When Toby enjoyed situations this much, Preuss felt as though his heart would explode with love for the boy. Nothing was better than seeing Toby so happy.

Unfortunately, by the time the second set ended, Toby was so overstimulated that he had a seizure. Preuss put his arms around his son and held on, comforting the boy until his trembling and whimpering and stiffness passed. As always, the seizure left him dazed and wrung out. The people sitting around them asked if they could do anything, but there was nothing to be done. The seizure had to run its course.

But when it happened, Preuss knew it was time to take Toby home, no matter how much he was loving the show.

So when O'Brien said they were going to take another short break, Preuss stood and pushed Toby's wheelchair between the tables. He couldn't get near the stage to say goodbye to O'Brien, who was surrounded by other musicians setting up to jam in the third set. He caught O'Brien's eye and lifted a hand in farewell.

O'Brien brought his hand with thumb and little finger extended to his mouth to mime "Call me."

Preuss threw him a thumbs up and pushed Toby in his wheelchair toward the door. The crowd parted for them with smiles for Toby and pats on the back for Preuss.

Outside the roadhouse, the night air was cooler than it had been earlier in the day, and sweet from the day's rain. His own ears ringing from the show, Preuss got Toby buckled into the back seat of the Explorer and stowed the wheelchair in the rear. Preuss turned the car on and let down all the windows. He sat breathing deeply for a few moments.

He turned and looked at Toby, who was now beginning to fade from the effects of his seizure and the afterglow of the show.

"Doing okay?" Preuss asked him.

Toby turned his face toward his father's voice. He was still out of it, with sleepy eyes, but Preuss knew he could tell where his dad was; Toby was watching him out of the corners of his eyes.

"Okay," Preuss said. He reached back and patted Toby's knee through his jogging pants. "Time to go home. We'll come back another time."

But Preuss didn't turn to face the front. He kept watching Toby. He reached back and took Toby's hand, bent at the wrist, into his own. Because of the contractures of Toby's cerebral palsy, the boy kept his hands balled into fists, so Preuss gently pried Toby's fingers open and held his hand, warm and damp with sweat.

He watched his son, and thought as he did that Toby, too—like Greg Braiden and Roger Garland—had a secret life. If I'm a visual shadow to you, Preuss thought, then you're a comprehension shadow to me. It would be impossible ever to know what Toby was thinking. Preuss knew he could speculate all he wanted, and through careful attention to the boy's body language and the tones of his vocal expressions he could discern his son's moods. But his actual thoughts and memories would have to remain part of Toby's eternal secret.

What hopes and wishes Toby might have entertained would forever remain mysterious and inaccessible.

Like the mystery of Greg Braiden's identity. Speculate all we want, Preuss thought, but what drove Braiden to seek the wild life, and his turn toward violence, would forever be a mystery. On the face of it, he seemed to have, as his sister said, all the gifts a man could have in the early years of the twenty-first century: an adoring daughter, a satisfying job, enough wealth to be comfortable, physical health and well-being, a loving sister—the good life.

Yet they weren't enough. He needed more, or different, kinds of stimulation. He needed to feed his wild side, his dark side.

For his part, Roger Garland was seething with resentments, and those caused havoc to everybody in his world. The calm, serene shrink was a mask, a performance; his real life, his secret life, was as dark and damaged as Greg Braiden's.

Meeshell and Ray also had their secrets . . . Meeshell's was her need to escape the life she had made for herself, and what she was prepared to do for that. It collided fatally with Braiden's darkest urges and, ultimately, led to his death.

Tomina's secret almost brought about his end, too.

And in the end, the cold dark lies they all told to preserve their secrets couldn't save any of them.

Preuss continued to hold his son's hand. Slowly, Toby came around; his nearly-sightless eyes took on more focus, and he leaned his head back and looked at the Explorer's headliner, as though watching images from the blues bar spread out on the dark material.

"Welcome back," Preuss said.

He gave Toby's hand a gentle squeeze. He felt the infinitesimally small pressure of Toby's fingers returning it. Toby gave him a goofy, crooked grin.

They sat that way for a while longer, each one holding on to the person he loved best in the world, until Toby shivered from the chill air. Preuss let go of his son's hand and closed the SUV's windows, then started on the trip back to the group home.

Acknowledgements

The two Purple Gang members mentioned in these pages are, like all the characters and situations in this novel, entirely fictional. The Purple Gang itself was not; for information on them, I am indebted to *The Purple Gang: Organized Crime in Detroit 1910-1945*, by Paul Kavieff.

Warm thanks for their assistance and support in the preparation of this book go to Jerry van Rossum, Diana Kathryn Wolfe-Plopa, Wendy Thomson, and Andrew Lark; the Royal Oak and Berkley Public Libraries, two wonderful establishments where much of this book was written; Rich Carnahan of Publish Pros for his continuing cover design artistry; and Linda Bigger for her editorial expertise.

As always, I must thank Jamie Kril, not only for providing the model for Toby, but for the abiding spirit that infuses these pages; and my wife Suzanne Allen, whose love and support continue to sustain me.

Finally, my warm thanks to my readers who have been following me over the course of this series. Your encouragement means more than you can know.

If you enjoy reading the Martin Preuss Mystery Series, please consider posting a review on Amazon, Goodreads, or my website, www.donaldlevin.com.

Also by Donald Levin

CRIMES OF LOVE | BOOK 1

One cold November night, police detective Martin Preuss joins a frantic search for a seven-year-old girl with epilepsy who has disappeared from the streets of his suburban Detroit community. Unwilling to let go after the Oakland County Sheriff's Office takes the case from his city agency, he strikes out on his own, following leads across the entire metropolitan region. Probing deep into the anguished lives of all those who came into contact with the missing girl, Preuss must summon all his skills and resources to solve the many crimes of love he uncovers.

THE BAKER'S MEN | BOOK 2

Easter, 2009. The nation is still reeling from the previous year's financial crisis. Ferndale Police detective Martin Preuss is spending a quiet evening with his son Toby when he's called out to investigate a savage after-hours shooting at a bakery in his suburban Detroit community. Was it a random burglary gone wrong? A cold-blooded execution linked to Detroit's drug trade? Most frightening of all, is there a terrorist connection with the Iraqi War vets who work at the store? Struggling with these questions, frustrated by the dizzying uncertainties of the case and hindered by the treachery of his own colleagues who scheme against him Preuss is drawn into a whirlwind of greed, violence, and revenge that spans generations across metropolitan Detroit.

GUILT IN HIDING | BOOK 3

The third entry in the Martin Preuss mystery series finds Preuss called out to search for a van that has disappeared along with the woman who was driving and her passenger, a handicapped young man. Working through layer upon layer of secrets, Preuss exposes a multitude of contemporary crimes with roots in the twentieth century's darkest period. Complex, chilling, and compulsively readable, *Guilt in Hiding* finds Preuss investigating the most disturbing and unforgettable crimes of his career.

THE FORGOTTEN CHILD | BOOK 4

Newly retired Martin Preuss passes his days quietly with his beloved son Toby. When a friend asks him to look for a boy who disappeared forty years ago, the former investigator gradually becomes consumed with finding the forgotten child. Meanwhile, ex-colleague Janey Cahill persuades him to help her locate the missing father of a troubled young girl. Juggling both cases, Preuss revisits the countercultural fervor of Detroit in the 1970s-and plunges into hidden worlds of guilty secrets and dark crimes that won't stay buried.

AN UNCERTAIN ACCOMPLICE | BOOK 5

Twenty years have passed since Raymond Douglas went to prison for the kidnapping and murder of a local businessman's wife. Now Douglas's daughter has hired private investigator Martin Preuss to track down a previously-unknown accomplice to the crime—who may or may not even exist. But no sooner does Preuss get involved than he finds himself entangled in two murders, a family whose wealth has bought them nothing but trouble, a body discarded in a dumpster, and a web of deceit stretching across metropolitan Detroit from the mega-rich suburbs to a hardscrabble trailer park.

www.ingramcontent.com/pod-product-compliance
Lightning Source LLC
Chambersburg PA
CBHW050536260626
47157CB00002B/316